JIMIJIX
SPECIAL BREW

A crime thriller

TOM DOTS DOHERTY

First published, September 2015. This edition, April 2024.

ISBN: 979-218-36206-5

Other books by Tom Dots Doherty

ShamrockSnake

TummiTurtle

For Aileen

MONDAY — ONE

You've changed since Claire and Sarah were murdered," Peter said.

"In what way?" I asked my business partner.

The advertising agency's shaven-headed creative director had obviously thought about our encounter prior to coming into my office yet still seemed unsure of what to say.

"In all sorts of ways," he replied. "The biggest issue being that you've become what you used to hate. Someone who licks up to clients, no matter how stupid they are. The way that you look has changed too."

"The way that I look?" I asked.

Peter spread his hands, which trembled slightly as he spoke.

"Yes, it's like you have adopted some kind of uniform. The navy blazer, the grey slacks, the button-down blue shirt, and the dark necktie that's always pulled down from your open collar. Your hair is a lot shorter than it used to be too, plus you've bulked up."

"So that's it, is it," I asked. "You've decided to sell your shares and leave the company because, in your opinion, I've changed since losing my wife and daughter?"

"Yes, that's exactly it," my partner replied. "I want to leave because everything is different here now and I've had enough."

I let Peter calm down for a moment and then leant forward and spoke in a lower tone. "I presume that you've discussed all this with Rachel?" I asked him.

Peter nodded. "We've talked about little else for the past two years," he told me.

"Does she also feel that it would be a good idea for you to leave?" I asked.

"Yes, she does," Peter said. "When I first broached the subject, Rachel was dead set against me leaving here," he said. "She said that I was being disloyal to you after all that you've been through, and was convinced that it would only be a matter of time before you returned to your old self and got a new woman in your life." Peter paused. "When that didn't happen, Rachel began to see things differently and changed her mind. She doesn't see much of me lately and seems to have finally realized how unhappy I am here. And then there's the whole weekend thing." Peter pulled a troubled expression to let me know that he hadn't intended to discuss what he had just referred to.

"The whole weekend thing?" I asked him.

"Every weekend, you call me on either Saturday or Sunday morning," Peter said. "Even my young son knows that if my mobile phone rings early on a weekend morning, it's going to be you. It's always the same. You've just heard something, or read something, that changes the work we've prepared for a client or a pitch. Some new development that we'd be mad not to take account of. Don't get me wrong, Killian, you're never nasty, just concerned that we're doing the right thing and I always capitulate and arrange to meet you in here later that day. Well, I'm sorry, Killian, but that won't be happening anymore."

Peter's words faded out, and he looked exhausted. "I'm really sorry about this," he said. "But I just can't take it anymore. I have to leave. You used to fight for good work and argue with clients when they wanted us to do something that we didn't like, but these days you just agree that we will deliver whatever crap that they ask us for."

Every word that Peter had said was accurate. The way that I worked and dressed had changed, so had my hair and physique, and even my behavior. It had all changed since I lost Claire and Sarah. And yet it felt to me like I was the one who was being treated unfairly, as if I was the victim.

"Would you change if Rachel and Andrew were murdered?" I asked Peter.

Both surprised and offended by my question, my partner pulled his head back.

"Of course I would change," he said. "But I wouldn't expect everyone else around me to change too."

What is said can never be unsaid, and from the regret on Peter's face, I saw that he hadn't intended to hurt me as much as he just had.

"So that's what I've done," I stated to him. "I got everyone in here to share my grief and then expected them to change too?"

Peter shook his head. "I'm sorry, Killian, I didn't mean to put it like that, but yes, that's what you've done. Three years ago, you'd go mad, lose your temper about something stupid, and fire half the agency. Everyone accepted that and knew that we'd hire them again the next morning. They put up with your weird behavior because of who you were and because they loved you. People used to joke that they had to walk around here with their resignation in their pockets. But that's all changed. Now, you look like the one who is about to be fired. You've changed, Killian, and yet it seems like you expect us all to change too."

"I'm sorry about that, Peter, I really am," I said and shook my head.

In response, Peter leant towards me with his hands spread in front of him. "I'm sorry, Killian, but for the past three years, we've been walking around here on eggshells. We've had to be polite, and careful about what we said in front of you, even when you made ridiculous promises to clients," he said. "We've helped you to carry your emotional baggage but it's been three years now, and we want our old friend back. You've become too…too…nice."

"Too nice," I repeated. "Have you discussed this with anyone else in here?"

Peter waved away my question. "That you've changed? Yes. It's been a constant topic of conversation in the advertising agency for at least two years now. Did I tell anyone else that I'm leaving? No. You know that I wouldn't do that without talking to you first."

"No, of course you wouldn't," I said and sat back. "I'm sorry, Peter, I really am. And I'm not going to argue with you about anything that you've said today. If you want to leave and set up your own advertising agency then I'm not going to stand in your way. Although there are a number of things that we will need to sort out before you do that," I said. "But please just understand one thing," I said. "That the last three years haven't been easy for me either, and I just wish that you had talked to me before now and told me where I was going wrong. In that regard, can I please have some time to think things over?"

MONDAY — TWO

An anxious but relieved-looking Peter nodded and looked like he was about to provide a positive answer to my question when there was a loud knock on the glass door into my office and Linda, my personal assistant, opened it before I had replied to her.

I had inherited Linda when Peter and I had bought out the advertising agency from its previous owner, Ted O'Shea, five years earlier.

Back then, I was reluctant to employ someone to perform what I considered to be an obsolete position, but Linda had soon demonstrated the importance of her role as a personal assistant to me and had displayed an unequalled knowledge of the advertising agency's employees and clients.

"Dave is on the phone," Linda told me. "He said that he tried to reach you on your mobile and needs to talk to you urgently," she added, and then nodded a greeting to Peter.

"Thanks Linda, please tell Dave that I'll call him back in a few minutes," I instructed her and then turned back to Peter.

"Okay," Linda replied and then threw her eyes up as she left my office.

Before I spoke to Peter again, I flipped my muted mobile phone over on the desk and checked its display. I had missed two incoming calls, one from Dave, my younger brother, and one from his wife, Louise.

I had missed two calls from Dave the night before as well. Obviously, my brother was anxious to reach me, which usually meant that he needed to borrow money in a hurry.

I looked back across the desk at Peter, who looked anxious to leave my office. There were a lot of pledges that I could make to him, but I knew that they would all sound hollow. Instead, I pulled a weak smile and told him that I appreciated what he had just shared with me.

"Thanks for that, Peter," I told him. "I know how hard it must have been for you to say those things but I really needed to hear them."

"Thanks, Killian," Peter replied as he got to his feet and left me alone in my office.

When he was gone, I sat back, closed my eyes, and began to think over what Peter had just said. Less than a minute later, I was disturbed by another loud knock on my glass office door as Linda returned.

"I'm really sorry about this, Killian," she said when she had opened the door and edged into my office. "But Louise is on the phone. She demands to speak with you and has also claimed that she has tried but couldn't reach you on your mobile phone."

I nodded my acceptance and pointed at the telephone on my desk. "Thanks, Linda," I said. "Please put Louise through."

It wasn't the first time my sister-in-law had called the advertising agency and insisted on speaking to me when she had an issue with her husband. Which was something that I hadn't foreseen when, four years earlier, I had used the power of nepotism to employ Dave as a JimiJix on the Jasper's Chicken Restaurants account.

By then, Dave's ambition to become an entertainer had run its course, and he needed a job to earn some of the money required to raise his new-born son.

What I didn't predict back then, was that by hiring Dave, I was also putting in place an arrangement that Louise felt gave her permission to call me whenever she wasn't happy with her husband.

Monday — Three

"I'm sorry to annoy you about this, Killian," Louise said when I took her call. "But I feel that something is up with Dave."

"You feel that something is up with Dave?" I replied, pushed my chair back, and looked out through my large office window as late summer sunshine tickled the surface of the river Liffey as it flowed past the north quays.

"Yes," Louise said. "Dave was acting strange when he got home last night," she said. "He stayed up half-the-night but, when I went down and pleaded with him to go to bed, he wouldn't tell me what was going on, or even what had made him so miserable. This morning, he didn't even say good-bye when he left here. And now," she added and repressed a wail, "I can't get him on his mobile phone."

When Louise began to cry, I turned back to my desk and spoke to her. "Was Dave acting like that all day yesterday?" I asked, picked up my mobile phone again, and turned it over. I saw that I now had three missed calls, one from Louise, and two from Dave, the latest of which had come in from him just a minute earlier. So, Dave had called me again since I'd refused to take his call to my office.

Louise sniffed twice before she answered my question. "No," she said. "Dave called me when he got back to the car park at Jasper's last night. He was in great form, and said that he was really looking forward to coming home and having dinner with me.

7

"And yet, he was acting real moody when he got there?" I asked.

"Yes," Louise said. "Dave appeared preoccupied when he got home, wouldn't eat anything, and wouldn't tell me why he was like that either," Louise said.

"Really? And what time did he get home at?" I asked.

"He called at about eight, and then spent about another thirty-minutes driving home, so he would have gotten home here at about eight-thirty last night," Louise replied.

When Louise had answered my question, I checked my mobile phone again and saw that the time of the two missed calls from Dave the previous night had both been logged after eight-thirty.

So, my brother had wanted to discuss something with me rather than with Louise when he got home. I deducted that whatever had upset Dave, must have been job-related rather than something to do with his personal life.

"Don't worry, Louise," I promised my sister-in-law. "I'll get in touch with Dave and see what's up with him. It's probably something to do with his job. Will I get him to call you when I've talked to him?"

"Yes, please do," Louise said. "And I'm sorry about this, Killian."

When my call with Louise had ended, I thought back over some of the comments that Peter had made and then picked up my mobile phone and called Dave's number.

When my call went straight through to his voice mail, I left a message for Dave to call me back and then used my desk phone to summon Kate Fallon into my office.

"Please bring the JimiJix schedule with you," I added before hanging up. The thirty-year-old account director on Jasper's Chicken Restaurants sauntered into my office seconds later.

Tall and slim, with closely cropped black hair and a preference for bright red lipstick, Kate Fallon was dressed in a pinstriped waistcoat with matching flared trousers, a pair of black leather platform shoes, and a bright orange shirt with a wide collar.

She stopped in front of my desk and pushed her wide-framed glasses back on her long nose, a time-consuming gesture that allowed me to ponder whether Kate was the type of woman that Peter's wife had expected me to date after Claire's death.

"Hi, Kate. How did your birthday party go on Saturday night?" I asked her.

"Great, thanks, Killian," she replied. "I'm sorry that you couldn't make it. And thanks again for the present, it was very generous."

Kate Fallon had joined the advertising agency after a spell working in New York. Back in Dublin, Kate's sharp-witted attitude and no-nonsense approach had soon created problems with some of our clients and her position was in jeopardy until I had reassigned her to the Jasper's Chicken Restaurants Account, and she had soon marshalled their vacuous marketing personnel and unruly franchisees into something approaching normality.

"You deserved that present," I said and then switched tone. "I'm sorry, Kate, I can't tell you why right now, but I need to know where Dave is performing today."

"That's no problem," Kate replied and then flipped open the manila folder in her left hand and looked down at the JimiJix performance schedule. "He's in the Jasper's Restaurant in The O'Malley Centre this morning, and then in their Kilkenny Restaurant this afternoon," she said.

"Thanks," I said, and then decided to tell Kate why I had asked her about Dave's schedule. "According to Louise, Dave was acting strange last night and I can't get hold of him now," I said. "When is his show at The O'Malley Centre taking place?"

"At eleven-thirty," Kate answered. "Do you want me to go there and talk to him?"

I shook away her offer, looked up at the railway clock on the wall to my left, calculated how long it would take me to drive to The O'Malley Centre, and then stood up and swept my car keys from the desk.

"No thanks, Kate, this is personal stuff. So, he probably just wants to have a quick chat with me about something. The last thing we need right now is anything that will mess up Jasper's Telethon on Thursday, so I'll go out there and check on him," I said. "I'll talk to you later, okay?"

"Thanks," Kate replied, looked as if she was going to say something and then shuffled out my office.

When Kate was gone, I picked up my desk phone and told Linda that I was going out for a while.

"Something has come up, so I have to go out for a while," I told her. "I won't be back until after lunch but will be on the mobile if you need me."

MONDAY — FOUR

"**N**ice? He actually used the N word?"

I had called Ted O'Shea from my black Audi as I drove out to meet Dave at The O'Malley Centre. Once the advertising agency's owner, and then its chairman when I took over as its chief executive, Ted was the man who was responsible for getting me into the Irish advertising industry, the man who sold his advertising agency to Peter and me when he decided to accept the role of heading up the advertising education unit at the Dublin Institute of Communication, and the man who I considered to be my mentor.

"Yes, that's exactly what Peter said," I replied. "That I had become nice."

"Well then, you know what you have to do, don't you, Killian?" Ted declared. "You have to go right back in there and fire the fucker."

"Jesus, Ted," I protested. "I can't just do that. How will that look?"

"Good, it will look good," Ted stated firmly. "Because if you don't make a big gesture, then you're finished in this industry. No one who is successful in advertising was ever described as nice. Nice is the last thing that we are. Doctors, nurses, and teachers are nice. We're over-paid, evil scum from the dark side who hypnotize people into buying shit that they don't need. We play mind games, overwhelm people's willpower, and then raise their expectations to the point where they spend too much money and their lives are ruined. Some people even kill themselves because of us. So, the last thing that we are is nice," Ted said. "I'm sorry, Killian, but if the nice perception of you is already out there then you're fucked because there are no nice people in advertising. That's why you have to fire Peter. He's leaving anyway, so go for it."

"Sorry, Ted, but I can't do that. Peter has been with me for ten years," I explained. "We work well together and everyone knows that."

"You used to work well together," Ted corrected. "I'm telling you that you need to get rid of him. Go back into the agency and start a row. Tell him to fuck off or something, and then punch him in the face and fire him. After that, nobody will think that you're a nice guy anymore."

When a few seconds had gone by in which I didn't respond to his suggestion, Ted spoke again. "Okay, so you're not willing to do that," he relented. "If only you were a woman, then this whole thing would be so much easier," he said. "Then all you'd have to do is get a makeover, go back in there with a skirt up to your ass and blow some young guy. Suck him dry. Hey, what about this? Why don't you hire a couple of young female interns and fuck them both at the same time? Everyone loves the old three-in-a-bed angle. That would sort the nice thing out."

"Stop it, Ted, please." I lowered the Audi into third gear and applied its brakes as I came to a set of traffic lights. "I'm not going to go down that route, okay?"

"Okay," Ted surrendered. "But you still have to do something big to get rid of the nice perception. You know that, don't you, Killian? That's what you would advise your clients to do if they had to change the perception of one of their brands in a hurry, isn't it?"

"Yes," I admitted. "But it doesn't feel like I have to do something that radical. Maybe if I just harden my attitude then people will notice a difference."

From Ted's prolonged silence, I knew that I had said the wrong thing.

"I'm sorry, Killian, but you don't seem to fully comprehend what's going on here," he eventually said. "If you are already perceived as being nice, then you don't have any time to ease into being seen as firm. You're in a bad and dangerous place."

"Then what do you suggest?" I asked him.

"I already told you that," Ted replied. "But you didn't like it. Maybe we should park this conversation for the moment. Are you free to meet up later?"

"Yes, I'm free this evening," I replied.

"Good. Then why don't you call me again later and we'll arrange something?" Ted said. "In the meantime, there's something that I want you to do."

"What's that?" I asked and then checked the digital clock on the car's dashboard as the traffic lights changed to green and I drove forward again.

"Start acting tough," Ted said. "Be a bit more bolshie. The last thing that you need right now is for anyone else to think that you've gone soft, or are nice."

"Thanks Ted, I'll try that," I said. "Talk to you later."

Our call over, I thought back over what Ted had said to me.

It was obvious from Ted's tone and his ready advice that my mentor wasn't too surprised that I was already being perceived as nice.

The fact that Ted had asked so little about Peter's plans also concerned me. Had he known about what was going to happen in the advertising agency? Had Ted also noticed that I had become soft and nice since I had lost Claire and Sarah?

The last thing I wanted to do was to disappoint one of my late father's oldest and closest friends, a man who had always helped me with my career, and yet I couldn't help feeling that's what I had just done.

MONDAY — FIVE

It was Ted, after the sudden death of my mother, who had convinced my father to change the positioning of his chain of underperforming electrical stores. Back then, the strategy that Ted proposed was simple. That his advertising agency would produce a series of brash, low-budget TV commercials, that made my dad's electrical stores look cheap and conveyed the perception that they sold stuff that was only available for a limited time.

Ted persuaded my father that if the commercials were delivered with raw excitement, they'd get punters fired up.

"We'll aim the advertising at people who never thought that they'd be able to afford the items on offer. New televisions, new dishwashers, new vacuum cleaners, all at prices that will amaze them," he told my dad. "And we'll make you a famous hero."

My dad thought about Ted's strategy for a while, bought into it, and the new advertising campaign for his electrical stores that Ted's advertising agency produced started a month later.

An instant success, the new commercials featured my father in rolled up shirt sleeves as he punched his right fist into his left palm and ranted on about the buzz in his stores that week as the prices of the electronic products on offer were highlighted with price-blast graphics that flew onto the screen.

A few weeks into the campaign, my father brought me along to a shoot for one of those television commercials. That was how I first met Ted, who hired me during my school holidays the following summer, and how I got into an industry that had treated me so well. It was also how I came to meet Claire, who was to become my wife, and the mother to my daughter, Sarah.

A young model back then, Claire had paid her way through art college by appearing in advertising for everything from soft drinks to high fashion, and had considered it hilarious that my nickname, Buzz, had come from my father's appearances in the TV commercials produced by Ted's advertising agency.

As I drove to meet Dave, the memory of meeting Claire that first time made me realize something else, that what Peter had told me that morning was both true and incredibly revealing.

Peter had pointed out that from the time that I lost my wife and daughter, my life had stalled. He told me that I had buried myself in work and had become immune to everything and everybody around me. Peter had claimed that I had carried too much emotional baggage for too long, and had let it wear me down until I had become a changed individual that even my friends didn't like any more. As usual, Peter was right, and had told me that I needed to move on and restart my life.

As energy surged through me, and I thought about what that new life could offer me, I accelerated to overtake a slower driver in front of me and considered my options.

I decided that I would sell the business, travel the world, meet new people, and then come back to Ireland to try something new.

While conscious that I needed to get to The O'Malley Centre in time to talk to Dave before he performed his show, I now felt more refreshed and energized than I had at any point in the last three years. No longer would I need to bury my grief in work, no longer would I have to explain the concept of advertising to people who didn't understand it, or didn't want to. I could now become my own person and enjoy life again.

Yes, I had earned a good living in advertising, but there were few people who believed that the world would be a worse place if advertising went away. No one would question why I had left an industry that they view as the nasty part of capitalism.

Most people believe that without advertising they would keep their jobs and still be able to afford all the mass-produced goods that were once considered a luxury. And most people never pause to think that without advertising, the sales of some items would go down, and don't appreciate that without advertising they might never know that there are products out there that could improve their lives. Most of the people who hate advertising don't accept that increased sales generate the taxes that allow governments to spend more money on things like schools, hospitals, and the police.

Yes, few people would ever question my decision to leave the advertising industry and start a new career in some other profession that they view as more noble, so I could turn the music off on that ice cream van, claim that I was always against free speech for organizations, and say that I never believed that advertising really worked.

I would cite all the advertising campaigns that I had worked on that had tried but failed to get people to stop smoking, drive carefully, or get fit, and would announce that advertising never really got anyone to change their behavior, their attitudes, or to rein in their desire for instant gratification.

Just after I had decided to leave advertising and make big changes to my life, a red Toyota Corolla shot out of a side street, smashed into the rear wing of my Audi, and spun it into the path of an oncoming Coca-Cola truck that screeched to a noisy halt just inches away from the passenger side of my car. Relieved to be still alive, I restarted the Audi's engine, steered it to the side of the road and then got out and stormed back towards the red Toyota Corolla which lay across the road at a right angle.

"Are you fucking blind?" its agitated young driver shouted at me from beside the Toyota Corolla and then looked down at its broken headlight glass on the road's surface.

I ignored his question. "There are two ways we can do this," I said, took out my mobile phone, activated its camera and stooped over the front windshield of his car, snapping a photograph of his out-of-date tax and insurance discs. "Either we call the cops and wait until they get here," I said. "Or we just drive away. That way, we'll save time and you won't have to answer any tricky questions. It's up to you, which way do you want to play it?"

"Don't try that fucking rich guy shite with me," the other driver responded aggressively. "You crashed into me, so you have to pay for all the damage."

Up close, I detected a stench of stale cigarettes from his breath and saw that the other man wasn't as young as I had first thought.

Clad in a sleeveless black T-shirt that displayed his muscular and tattooed arms, the man had a hostile face that featured a saddle nose and small, squinting eyes that were framed between a flat tweed cap and a brown bushy beard, a combination favored by men who lose their hair prematurely and then grow a beard and wear a cap to mask their naked crown.

"Okay, we'll get the cops," I said and began to use my mobile phone. "But just so that you are aware, I'm going to tell them that you crashed into me and that the footage from that security camera over there will back me up," I said and nodded at the video camera mounted on the side of a nearby building.

The face between the beard and the cap angled towards me.

"Fine," he said. "But before you call anyone, you should know that this car belongs to my brother. When he hears that you fucked it up, he's going to come after you. And he'll sort you out, big time."

"I look forward to that," I replied. "Now, will I get the cops or not?"

The young man looked down at his brother's damaged Toyota Corolla for a moment as if trying to remember something and then shook his head. "I suppose not," he said. "But, as I said, Anto is going to be really pissed off."

"Then Anto should never have let you have his car," I replied, turned away and walked back to my black Audi, satisfied that my firm interaction with the driver of the red Toyota Corolla had set the tone that Ted had advised me to adopt.

MONDAY — SIX

After my interaction with the driver of the red Toyota Corolla, I drove faster than usual in an attempt to reach The O'Malley Centre before Dave's show started, but despite my disregard for the posted speed limits, was still late and arrived at the Jasper's Restaurant just as the JimiJix show was about to start.

Forced to stand inside the restaurant's entrance, I took in the scene as Dave high-fived his way to the party area in a jester's distinctive purple and orange costume, as young mothers and their preschool children hollered out the JimiJix song:

> *Let's clap our hands together*
> *Let's clap our hands real loud*
> *Let's clap our hands together*
> *And shout his name real loud!*
>
> *JimiJix! JimiJix! JimiJix!*

When Dave reached the table that had been cordoned off for his performance, he mimicked disgust that six large, brightly colored plastic drinking cups had been left on it. Awkwardly, he began to lift them off the table, but soon found himself unable to hold them all and dropped, and then caught, one after another, until he was staggering back and forward and juggling all six cups in the air.

As squeals of high-pitched laughter reverberated around the restaurant, I spotted the pretend shock on Eddie Farrell's face as the restaurant's franchisee looked back at me from a table near the rear of the restaurant.

One of the first Jasper's Chicken Restaurant franchisees that I had gotten to know, Eddie had started his career behind the counter, made his way up through management ranks, and had then borrowed enough money to open his own restaurant in The O'Malley Centre.

A couple of years after Eddie had obtained that franchise, a new shopping center, one that boasted the presence of a German discount store, opened its doors within easy driving distance of The O'Malley Centre and many of the retail units that neighbored The Jasper's Chicken Restaurant had closed down.

I regretted that I hadn't called ahead and informed Eddie of my pending visit. Short but well-built, in a white shirt and a purple-and-orange Jasper's necktie, Eddie stood and greeted me with a strong handshake as I reached his table.

"To what do we owe this privilege?" he asked me.

"I need to have a quick word with Dave." I replied, took a seat across the table from Eddie, and then watched with a smile as my brother in the JimiJix outfit pretended to encounter difficulty as he blew up a giant yellow balloon that escaped his grasp and looped through the air until it flopped to the floor next to his curly-toed Arabian slippers.

Eddie shook his head on hearing my honest reply and then summoned a red-haired young man in a purple shirt and orange necktie over to our table as Dave picked up the yellow balloon.

"What do you want?" Eddie asked me when his assistant manager had reached us.

"I'll have a chicken sandwich, medium fries, and a black coffee," I said and then spun back around to watch Dave again as a spike of laughter from the crowd ended abruptly in a collective gasp.

I saw that Dave had let go of the big yellow balloon and had raised both of his hands as a man in a black boiler suit and a matching ski mask raced towards him, roughly grabbed hold of the motley collar of his JimiJix costume, twisted Dave around, and then rammed the twin barrels of a sawn-off shotgun under his right ear.

"Do what I say and nobody gets hurt," the man shouted in what sounded to me like a stage Dublin accent as he scanned the restaurant. "Put everything you have on top of the table in front of you. Money, watches, phones, jewelry, everything," he said.

The raider in black then directly addressed the young, red-haired assistant manager who stood next to our table.

"You, empty the money from the tills into a disposal bag and then bring it over here," he instructed.

The red-haired man ran back across the restaurant, vaulted its stainless-steel counter as his colleagues backed away, and then scurried from left to right as he emptied the money from the cash tills into a black plastic refuse sack.

"Now, put all the stuff from the tables into that bag too," the gunman commanded the restaurant's assistant manager as he tightened his grip on the collar of the JimiJix costume and tugged Dave back towards the restaurant's entrance.

Across the table, I noted the tremor in Eddie's right hand as he removed his wallet from a back pocket of his trousers and tossed it onto the table.

Following his lead, I removed my mobile phone and wallet from pockets inside my blazer and took off my watch. I placed those items on the table in front of me as the red-haired assistant manager rushed from table to table, scooped up the customers' personal possessions, and then dropped them into the black plastic sack.

The assistant manager was just two tables away from us when I turned my attention back to Dave, sought out his eyes, and shuddered when I saw him glare directly back at me. I had risen to my feet, my eyes fixed on my brother's face, when a kick beneath the table buckled my legs and forced me back down again.

"Stay the fuck down or you'll get us both killed!" Eddie snarled as the assistant manager arrived at our table to collect our personal belongings.

As he did so, I spun back around, saw that the gunman had now pushed Dave's head down lower and then jolted when I saw that the raider's eyes inside the ski mask were aimed directly at mine.

"Ready!" the restaurant's assistant manager shouted as he hoisted the half-full black plastic sack.

"Then bring it over here and leave it at the door," the robber instructed.

In anticipation that Dave would soon be released by the gunman, I stood and watched as the red-haired assistant manager scampered forward, dropped the plastic disposal sack onto the black-and-white floor tiles just inside the restaurant's entrance, and then retreated to the restaurant's stainless-steel counter with his hands held high.

At that point, the raider yanked Dave's collar as he took another step backwards towards the restaurant's entrance, looked down momentarily as his left heel connected with the black plastic sack behind him, scanned the restaurant, and then tilted the shotgun's sawn-off barrels at the base of Dave's skull and pulled both of its triggers.

Deafened by the gun blast, and with my vision blurred by the cloud of red gore in the air, I raced across the restaurant, slid to my knees, and cradled my brother in my arms.

I saw that there was little left of Dave's face and felt a surge of his warm blood wash over the back of my right hand as I threw back my head and let an involuntary guttural scream of sorrow leave me and rise towards the restaurant's brain splattered ceiling.

MONDAY — SEVEN

O dours of stale food rose from the pub's abandoned lunch counter as I was led by a Garda Sergeant from the upstairs lounge in The O'Malley House down a wide, carpeted staircase to the less comfortable but more airy public bar, where three teams of detectives had commandeered a table each to record the initial witness statements.

The broad Garda Sergeant stopped in front of the table closest to the bar counter and handed a blue clipboard across to a female detective, who gestured for me to take a seat across the table from her.

"Hello, Mr. Doyle. Before we start, I want to assure you that you have the condolences and sympathy of all the Gardai here," the detective who looked more Chinese than Irish said in a hoarse Dublin accent that was at odds with her attractive facial features. "We have a few questions that we need to go through, and then we'll have someone drive you to wherever you need to get to."

I put the pending encounter with my sister-in-law, Louise, out of my mind, nodded back my understanding of what the detective had just said and then sat still as she pointed a finger back at herself.

"My name is Detective Jill Maguire," she told me and then pointed the same slender finger at the bulky man in the tweed jacket seated to her right. "And this is Detective Inspector Cormack O'Sullivan."

At the mention of the detective inspector's name, my head snapped left as I focused on Jill Maguire's colleague. In the three years since I had last seen him, O'Sullivan hadn't changed much. Yes, he had put on some weight and lost some of his wavy brown hair, but from his smug expression and the manner by which his smile still revealed the perfect horizontal edge of his false teeth, I saw that his malevolent attitude was still fully intact.

"Hello again, Mr. Doyle," he stated in his rhythmic Cork accent. "I was so, so sorry to hear about the death of your younger brother today."

I stared back at O'Sullivan in silence for a moment and then returned my attention to his confused colleague.

"I appreciate that you need to take my statement now," I told her. "But I really need to be with my brother's wife soon, so can we please get this over with quickly?"

"Yes, of course we can," Maguire replied, obviously unnerved by my interaction with O'Sullivan, who leant forward and lifted his large nose towards me.

"I fully understand your desire to get away, Mr. Doyle," he said. "But I think that we should tell Detective Maguire here how we know each other."

Before I nodded my agreement to his suggestion, O'Sullivan turned to face Jill Maguire. "Mr. Doyle and I know each other from the investigation into the death of his wife and daughter in a failed kidnap attempt three years ago," he informed her.

"A crime which you never prosecuted anyone for," I commented and took in O'Sullivan's well-tailored tweed jacket, his white shirt, green necktie, and tan slacks.

The bulky detective stared back at me for a moment. "Unfortunately, we can't solve every crime, Mr. Doyle," he stated and shook his head.

"Maybe if you hadn't spent so much time trying to pin the kidnap on me, you might have caught the person who was really guilty," I fired back at him.

"I've explained all that to you before, Mr. Doyle," O'Sullivan replied. "We had to rule you out. Maybe, if you had given us your full co-operation, we could have done that a lot quicker."

Jill Maguire came between us.

"Please, gentlemen," she said. "That was another case. Can we just get to our questions about today's incident?"

"Fine," I replied. "But first, I want to make sure that you're both aware that my younger brother is married and has a four-year old son?"

"We're fully aware of that," Jill Maguire said before she rapidly read out my home address, my contact details, and then quickly showed me a diagram of the interior of the Jasper's Chicken Restaurant to establish where I had been seated when Dave was killed.

I studied Jill Maguire as she spoke. In contrast to O'Sullivan, her brown herringbone suit and cream blouse looked like they had been plucked from the racks of a discount clothing chain, and yet, with her wide green eyes, shiny black hair, and perfect skin, she was extremely attractive. Which made me ponder whether O'Sullivan's preference for the finer things in life had now spread to his choice of partner.

Obviously unnerved by the intensity of my examination of her face, Jill Maguire lifted her head towards me as she concluded.

"I'm sorry, Mr. Doyle, but I talk too fast sometimes," she stated. "Would you like me to repeat anything that I just said to you?"

"No, that's fine," I said. "I used to talk too fast myself but my little brother kept teasing me until I slowed down. You must be an only child."

Maguire's head shot back as if I had just slapped her, while next to her, a smile formed at the sides of O'Sullivan's lips as he lent forward again.

"I had forgotten about your amazing powers of deduction, Mr. Doyle," he said. "Detective Maguire is indeed an only child. She is the late detective Tony Maguire's daughter. You might remember him from the hunt for the people who abducted your daughter and killed your wife?"

I closed my eyes and recalled the black and white press photograph of a distressed young woman who was overcome with sorrow as she attended the funeral for her father, a detective called Tony Maguire, who had been shot dead during an armed robbery in a post office that took place ten days after I had lost Claire and Sarah in the failed kidnap.

Tall and thin, with fair hair, and the kind of strong-jawed face that you usually associate with comic book heroes, I had liked Detective Tony Maguire, the way that he had conducted himself, and the manner in which he had kept me fully informed during the search for whoever had ended the lives of my wife and daughter.

Detective Tony Maguire's daughter looked nothing like him, and yet I should have figured out who she was from her surname. When I opened my eyes again, I looked directly across at Jill Maguire and shook my head.

"I'm so sorry," I said and raised my hands. "I should have realized who you are."

Jill Maguire acknowledged my apology with a nod as O'Sullivan inched forward and, in a more formal tone, recommenced the interview.

"Now, Mr. Doyle, can you please tell us why you were here today?" he began.

"Yes, I can," I said. "My advertising agency works for Jasper's Chicken Restaurants, and Dave, my brother, is a JimiJix. His wife, Louise, called me this morning and told me that Dave was upset about something when he got home last night, so I came out here to see what that was, and to make sure that everything was okay with him. The annual Jasper's Telethon is on Thursday night, so this is a big week for us, and I wanted to make sure that everything was all right with Dave."

"And was it?" O'Sullivan queried.

"I've no idea," I replied. "I got here too late and the show had already started. I was planning to talk to Dave afterwards, but then..."

"So, you drove out here to talk to your brother but didn't?" Jill Maguire asked me.

"No, I didn't get to speak with him," I said and shook my head. "I had tried earlier to reach Dave on his mobile phone but didn't get him that way either."

"I see," O'Sullivan said. "You tried to talk to your brother but didn't. Did you have any indication about what was wrong with him? For instance, were you concerned that there was some sort of issue with him? Was he being threatened or something? Or had problems with money, drugs, drink, or a woman?"

"No, as I said, I've no idea what was up with Dave," I replied to the detectives.

Jill Maguire nodded as I fell silent and then threw a glance at O'Sullivan as she asked me another question.

"I'm sorry, Mr. Doyle, but when was the last time that you spoke to your brother?"

"Last Friday," I replied. "Dave was in the advertising agency to go through some telethon stuff and we had a quick chat after that."

"But you haven't spoken to your brother since then, and aren't aware of any problems or issues that he might have had?" O'Sullivan asked.

"No. Dave tried to get me on my mobile phone last night, but I didn't answer his calls," I answered. "Then, I missed him again this morning and couldn't get him back. So, after speaking to Dave's wife, and hearing that something was up with him, I decided to come out here and talk to him but didn't get a chance to do that."

Jill Maguire picked up on what I said, "I'm sorry about this, Mr. Doyle," she probed. "But can you explain why you didn't answer your brother's calls?"

I shrugged. "I left my mobile phone upstairs last night and didn't hear his missed calls," I said. "And this morning, I was in a meeting, so my mobile phone was silenced when he called me."

"What time was it when your brother called you last night?" Maguire asked me.

"I'm not sure," I answered her. "I didn't see his missed calls until about midnight. That's when I usually go to bed."

"And you were at a meeting when he phoned you this morning?" O'Sullivan asked.

"That's right," I said. "When Dave couldn't get me on my mobile, he tried me on my land line at the office," I replied. "And Linda, that's my personal assistant, took a message from him asking me to call him. Which I did when I got out of the meeting but didn't get him."

"So, it sounds like your brother was anxious to talk to you about something?" Jill Maguire asked.

"Yes, it does," I replied and waited for the detectives' next question.

"Tell me something, Mr. Doyle, was the JimiJix show here advertised?" O'Sullivan wanted to know.

"Yes, we placed some advertising in the local press," I replied. "And there would have been posters up in the restaurant announcing the show for about two weeks," I added.

"Did any of the advertising refer to the telethon donations?" O'Sullivan asked.

"Yes, that was the key message in both items," I replied.

"The key message," O'Sullivan echoed. "Right, so the robber might have assumed that there'd be a lot of money here today?"

"Maybe," I conceded and then remained silent until Jill Maguire leant forward to ask me another question.

"We're putting together a description of the man who killed your brother, Mr. Doyle. Is there anything you can tell us about him, anything at all?" she asked. I contemplated Maguire's query for a moment.

"Yes," I then told her. "He was about the same height as Dave but thinner than him and was more agile and younger than him too," I replied. "And it sounded like he was putting on an accent."

"What kind of an accent?" Jill Maguire asked.

"I could be wrong here, but he sounded like Bono," I replied.

O'Sullivan winced at my response to Jill Maguire's question and, with a flick of his hand, prompted her to wind up the interview.

Maguire looked flustered by her boss's gesture.

"Thank you, Mr. Doyle," she said. "If you remember anything else that you think could help us, please call this number."

I nodded, accepted the business card that Jill Maguire handed over to me and then went to give her one of my own business cards from my wallet.

"I'm sorry," I said and slapped my forehead. "My wallet and mobile phone were taken during the raid. If you need me, you'll have to call my home number."

"No problem, what is it?" Maguire asked, lifted a black biro from under the clasp at the top of the blue clipboard and jotted down my home number.

"If you can't reach me on that number, you can leave a message," I told her.

"Thanks," Jill Maguire said. "Now, where do you need to get to?"

"To Dave's house in Dunnefarnham," I said and pushed back my chair.

Jill Maguire deposited the clipboard on the table in front of her, stood up, and pointed to a uniformed police officer who was sitting near the entrance into the pub.

"That officer will organize a car for you," she told me.

On her feet, Jill Maguire was a lot taller than I had expected while her conservative brown trouser suit failed to mask the shapely figure inside of it. Conscious of spending too long looking at the detective's figure, I turned away from her as I stood up and then looked down into O'Sullivan's face.

In response, the male detective noted my assessment of his partner with a smirk.

"Thank you, Mr. Doyle," he said. "I'm sure that we'll meet again soon."

Monday — Eight

Dressed in black slacks and a mauve shirt, Louise's older sister, Betty, opened the front door of Dave's house and led me into the sitting room, where Louise was perched on the edge of the blue corduroy sofa.

A picture of grief, my sister-in-law held crumpled-up tissues in both of her hands, was clad in a grey velour tracksuit and had her curly fair hair pulled back into a severe bun.

As she rose to embrace me, I noted that even with her moist eyes and crimson nose, Louise's young looks made her appear more like a jilted teenager than a newly widowed twenty-eight-year-old. While Louise blubbered against my right shoulder, I looked around the room and saw that, in addition to Betty, it was populated by a uniformed female Garda and a stern-looking woman in a wrinkled grey linen skirt suit who held a brown leather doctor's bag. An instant later, my sister-in-law pushed me away from her.

"Will you tell Philip about his dad?" Louise pleaded as she looked into my eyes.

"Yes, I will," I assured her but was barely able to keep my emotions in check at the thought of speaking to my young nephew. "But only if you agree to do something for me."

"Only if I agree to do something?" Louise queried.

I drew Louise back to my damp shoulder and whispered.

"Yes, you really need to rest now, Louise, because when I tell him what happened to his father, Philip is going to need you to be there for him," I told her.

"I need some rest?" Louise asked as she pushed herself away.

"Yes, you need to sleep," I said, looked away from Louise and nodded to Betty.

"Come on my love, the doctor is going to give you something to help you sleep," Betty said as she stepped forward, reached out, wrapped her hands around her sister's shoulders, and then guided her away from me.

Followed by the doctor and the police officer, Betty led Louise out of the sitting room into the house's hall and towards its staircase.

I went with them to the base of the carpeted stairs and remained there as they escorted Louise up to her bedroom.

When they were gone, I made my way into the kitchen, where three women were seated around the table in the middle of the room. I didn't recognize two of them and presumed that they were Louise's neighbors as the third woman jumped up from the table and embraced me.

"I'm so sorry, Killian," Kate Fallon wailed into my right ear as she wrapped herself around me. "I can't believe what happened to Dave."

"Me neither," I replied and nodded to the two other women as the tearful Kate forced me to retreat out into the house's hallway.

"Did you talk to Dave before he died?" she asked me anxiously in the hallway as she pulled the kitchen door closed behind us.

"No, I was too late," I told her. "I was going to speak with him after the show, but then he was…"

My incomplete response resulted in an outburst of grief from Kate, who tried to shake away the tears that streamed from her eyes.

"So, you never spoke to him?" she said.

"No, I didn't," I said and then gripped Kate's shoulders. "Kate, I really appreciate the fact that you're here, but, if you don't mind, I'd like you to sort out a few things."

Kate stepped back, wiped her eyes, and then nodded.

"Of course, Killian, what do you want me to do?" she asked.

"Well, the first thing that you can do is arrange to get me a new mobile phone," I said. "The phone that I had was taken in the restaurant earlier, and I'm really going to need one over the next few days. Can you please arrange to have a replacement sent to my apartment? I'll be back there tonight."

While Kate looked disappointed by the nature of my request, she reacted keenly. "Absolutely, no problem," she replied and then started to cry again. "I'm really sorry about all this. It's just that…"

I reached out and placed a finger across Kate's red lips.

"It's okay," I told her and recalled how much I had suffered from my exposure to despair and sadness when Claire and Sarah had been murdered.

"Thanks," Kate said when I took my finger away, and then remembered something. "Oh! I nearly forgot," she said. "Frank is looking for you. He doesn't feel that it would be appropriate to proceed with the telethon on Thursday night and wants you to call him."

"What do you think?" I asked Kate. "Do you feel that it should go ahead now?"

Before Kate answered me, she took a step back in the hallway and removed her glasses. When she had puffed a breath onto their lens and wiped them clean, she put them back on, looked at me and shook her head.

"No, I don't feel it would be right to hold the telethon now," she replied. "Why?"

I pulled a troubled expression. "Because I think the opposite," I said. "I feel that Dave would have wanted the telethon to go ahead," I said. "Otherwise, we'll just be giving in to the scumbag who killed him."

Kate shrugged. "If that's your view then you need to talk to Frank," she replied.

"Fine, I'll call him now. Do you have his number?" I asked Kate and stepped towards the semicircular telephone table in the hall.

In response, Kate extracted her mobile phone, scrolled down through her list of contacts and scribbled down Frank Hennessy's mobile phone number on a notepad next to the telephone. She then made her way down the rest of the hallway, opened the front door, and let herself out of Dave's house without saying goodbye to me.

Monday — Nine

After Kate's sudden departure, I picked up the telephone's receiver, dialed the number that she had given me and turned back to the small table as Frank Hennessy answered my call.

"Hi, Frank, it's Killian," I said, conscious that my father-in-law wouldn't recognize the number being displayed on his caller ID. "I'm at Dave's house."

"How are you, Killian?" Frank quizzed in his deep baritone.

"Shattered," I admitted, lifted the telephone and sat on the fourth step of the stairs.

"I heard that you were there when it happened. Is that true?" Frank asked me.

"Yes," I confirmed. "Louise called me this morning and said that Dave was acting odd, so I drove out to The O'Malley Centre to see what was wrong with him."

"And what was it?" Frank asked.

"I never found out," I answered. "The show had already started by the time that I got there so I didn't get a chance to talk to him. Though, when the robbery was in progress, Dave gave me this really strange look."

"A really strange look?" Frank repeated.

"Yes. Dave looked like he knew what was about to happen to him and was startled to see me there," I said. "It was like he was angry with me over something."

"Angry with you?" Frank queried.

"Yes," I said. "It was like Dave knew that he was about to be killed and felt that I had something to do with that."

There was a pause before Frank spoke again. "Please, Killian, don't do this to yourself again," he said. "You don't know what was going through Dave's head before he died, and never will, so please just leave it that way, okay?"

"Okay, and I'm sorry, Frank," I said and then stood up and stepped aside to let the doctor and the female Garda pass me as they returned down the stairs.

"How about Louise and Philip," Frank asked. "How are they?"

"Louise had to be sedated," I said, and then hesitated for a moment. "And Philip hasn't heard about his dad yet." I said and closed my eyes at the thought of the conversation that I had promised Louise that I would have with her son, my young nephew.

"Jesus. Philip doesn't know about his dad yet?" Frank sighed.

"No, but he soon will," I replied. "Because, I'm about to tell him."

"Jesus," Frank repeated and then asked another question. "How about the cops?" he asked. "Do they have any idea who did this?"

"I don't know," I replied, sat down on the stairs again, and then watched as the female Garda let the doctor out of the house. "That guy O'Sullivan was there, and from the questions that he asked me, I got the impression that he thinks that Dave was just an innocent victim in an armed robbery."

"I can't say that I blame him for that," Frank said. "We're a cash business and get robbed all the time. Do you have some reason to doubt what O'Sullivan thinks?"

"No, I saw what happened," I said. "I just hope that they get the guy soon."

"Don't worry," Frank assured me. "I'm sure that they will."

"Yeah," I replied. "Just like they did after Claire and Sarah were murdered." Frank took a deep breath. "Killian, I know how hard this is for you, but please don't do what you did after Claire and Sarah were murdered. I'm with you if you need to ramp things up, but let's just see where this goes first, okay?"

"Fine," I agreed and then adopted a sharper tone. "Sorry, Frank, Kate told me that you want to cancel the telethon?"

"No, I don't," Frank replied. "I talked to Kate about postponing it, not cancelling it. Under the circumstances, I feel that it might be better to hold off on the telethon until after Dave's funeral. What's your view?"

"My view is that Dave would have wanted the telethon to go ahead," I replied. "The guy who killed my brother will get to dictate our schedule if we postpone it, so I feel that the telethon should go ahead on Thursday."

Obviously surprised by the brevity and intensity of my response, Frank capitulated immediately.

"Point taken," he said. "Let's go ahead with the telethon on Thursday, but the media are going to be all over this, so we'll need a press statement and a tribute to Dave to run on the show."

"Agreed," I replied. "I'll get someone working on them."

"Thanks, Killian," Frank said. "We'll talk again later. In the meantime, look after Louise, Philip, and yourself. Please tell Louise that I'll talk to her tomorrow. In the meantime, you know where to find me if you need anything"

"I appreciate that, Frank," I managed to reply and then lowered the receiver back to the telephone and stood up again.

My next call was to the advertising agency, a number that I knew by heart. As usual, Eva was on switchboard duty and was shocked when she heard my voice.

"Killian! Oh my God!" she stated loudly, no doubt to alert those within earshot of her that I was on the line. "We were just talking about you. Everyone here is so shocked."

"Thanks, Eva," I said. "Please give everyone there my regards, I'll see them all soon, but right now I just need to talk to Linda. Is she around?"

"Yes," Eva told me. "I'll get her for you."

Two seconds passed before I heard a call tone at the other end of the line.

"Hi Killian, it's Linda," my personal assistant declared in a voice that was stretched by emotion. "I honestly don't know what to say."

"Please don't say anything," I said. "Linda, I'm sorry about this, but there's something that I need you to do for me. Kate was here earlier, but she's gone now and I don't have her mobile number. I want you to call her and say that Frank has agreed that the Jasper's Telethon should go ahead on Thursday night as planned. Please tell Kate that she needs to get a press release and a tribute to Dave prepared for that. Okay?"

"Yes, of course, Killian," Linda answered. "Is there anything else?"

"No, not for now, thanks, Linda," I said. "I'll call you again tomorrow. Please tell Peter and everyone else that I'll talk to them soon too."

"Sorry, Killian," Linda said to keep me on the line as I was about to hang up. "Ted called a few times. He told me that you two were talking earlier and said that he needs to speak to you urgently. Do you want his number?"

"Yes, please," I answered, took down Ted's phone number, and then ended the call with Linda.

I had just replaced the telephone on the semicircular table when the kitchen door was pulled open and the two women who I had taken to be Louise's neighbors stepped towards me.

The first of the two women had shoulder-length brown hair, was clad in a long navy pullover that covered her hips, and wore denim jeans that were tucked into her brown leather calf-high boots.

"I'm sorry for your loss," she said and stretched out her right hand towards me.

"Thank you," I replied to an expression that I had heard too many times before.

Dressed similarly in a wine pullover over black jeans, the second woman was heavier with longer and lighter-colored hair.

She took hold of my right hand in both of hers as she stepped forward, repeated the same expression of sympathy as the first woman, and then relayed a piece of information to me.

"Philip is in the Redmonds," she told me. "It's the house with the blue door down the road."

I held the front door open for the two women as they left the house and then waited in the kitchen for Betty to come back downstairs from what used to be Dave and Louise's bedroom.

"She's out for the count," Louise's sister announced when she came into the kitchen a minute later and strode across its hardwood floor. "I need a coffee. Do you want one?" she asked when she reached the sink and began to fill the kettle.

A makeup artist employed with a national TV channel, Betty was a bustling, unmarried woman in her late thirties who wore high-heeled shoes, doused herself in too much perfume, and flirted with them in a manner that unnerved young men.

"We need to agree on what gets done around here over the next few days and who is going to do what," she said and flicked the kettle on.

"Right," I agreed and sat down at the table. "Maybe we should make a list."

"Good idea," Betty replied. "I'll get a pen and some paper."

When we had finished our coffees and compiled a list that included the funeral arrangements, I pushed my chair back from the kitchen table and stood up.

"I think it's time that I went and got Philip," I told Betty, who nodded as I left to travel the brief distance to the house with the blue door that I had been directed to by Louise's neighbor.

The woman who opened the blue door was a lot older than I had expected. Dressed in a long beige woolen cardigan over a faded brown dress, her face took on a look of sadness when I introduced myself to her as Philip's uncle.

"You'll find Philip in the back room with my grandson, Tommy," she responded and drew the front door fully open to let me enter her son's home.

I had just taken my first step inside the house when two young boys peeked out from a doorway at the other end of the hallway.

"Uncle Killian!" Philip roared and tore towards me.

I bent down, hoisted up the young boy with the mop of blond hair, and folded him over my right shoulder. "It's okay, young man, I've come to take you home," I announced in a superhero voice and then spun around and carried him out of the house.

At the gate to the front garden, I turned and nodded back to Mrs. Redmond as tears began to run down her powdered cheeks. Barely able to contain my own grief, I then jogged back to Dave's house as Philip hollered in joy over my shoulder.

Back in the sitting room, I lowered Philip to the carpeted floor and then stood back from him as he looked around the room, spotted Betty and the uniformed female Garda, and then turned back to me with a quizzical look on his young face.

"Where's Mummy?" he asked me.

Before I had time to respond to Philip, Betty leant forward towards him.

"Your mother is fine," she told my nephew. "She's just taking a little nap upstairs."

I dropped to my knees. "I'm sorry, Philip, but I have some terrible news for you," I began. "A bad man shot your daddy today and he won't be coming home."

Philip didn't scream or cry out and looked more confused than anguished. "He won't?" he asked me.

I shook my head. "No, I'm sorry, Philip, but he won't be," I said.

Philip stared back at me. "Will you please take me to my Mummy?" he asked me.

"Yes, of course I will." I said, stood up, and then led my nephew by the hand up the stairs and into his parents' darkened bedroom where the only illumination was provided by the glow of fading sunlight that penetrated the bedroom's tan curtains.

Louise remained asleep as I lifted Philip and laid him on the bed next to her. The young boy snuggled up to his mother's back and then turned his face to me as I retreated from the bedroom.

"Uncle Killian," he asked as I reached the bedroom door. "Are you going to get the bad man who killed my daddy today?"

"Yes, I am, Philip, I'm going to get him," I vowed.

TUESDAY — ONE

A white padded envelope was propped against the bottom of the front door when I finally got back to my apartment in the early hours of the morning.

I carried it into what was once the apartment's TV room, switched on my laptop on the coffee table, and slumped down onto one of the room's two brown leather couches to open the parcel.

I found that Kate had included some handwritten instructions with my new mobile phone. Written on four pages that had been torn from a notebook, she informed me that my new mobile phone was fully charged, that it had been synced with my e-mails, that it had the same number as my last mobile phone, and that it contained all my contact details.

Following her comments about my new phone, Kate repeated her sorrow about Dave's death and expressed an apology for her earlier behavior. Weary of being wallowed in sadness again, I stopped reading Kate's notes at that point and pulled the laptop closer.

It took me less than a minute to locate the press photograph of Jill Maguire that I had scanned into the computer folder that contained the various newspaper articles and photographs about my wife and daughter's murders.

I saw that my earlier recollection had been wrong, the photograph was in color but contained so many black and grey tones that I had recalled seeing a monotone image.

Now enlarged to fill the computer's screen, under examination, I saw that the photograph had been taken from an angle and contained the two people who Jill Maguire was walking behind.

One of those people was O'Sullivan, who was walking next to a frail-looking Chinese woman, who I hadn't paid any attention to before but now realized must have been Jill Maguire's Asian mother, and, as such, was the late Detective Tony Maguire's wife.

I looked at that image for another few seconds, shook my head again, and then closed and pushed away the laptop, wandered out of the TV room into the apartment's lounge, and gripped its brass banisters wearily as I ascended the sweeping staircase that led up to my bedroom on the floor above.

On reaching my bed, I deposited my new mobile phone on the locker and sat down to stare at my reflection in the mirrored closet doors. Apart from the obvious need to shampoo and comb my unruly hair, and shave away the shadow of beard that had grown on my face, what worried me most were my eyes, which seemed to have darkened, sunk back into my skull, and looked like they belonged to someone else.

I continued to examine myself in the mirror for another moment, and then removed my blazer, took off my shoes, lay back on the bed, and closed my eyes as I thought back over the day's awful events.

An hour later, I shot up into a sitting position, reached out to gather up my new mobile phone, and tried to identify the noise that had awoken me. That was when the strident buzzing noise sounded again and I realized that it was the apartment's external doorbell.

I felt a stab of grief about Dave's passing, listened as the buzzer sounded twice more, and then got off the bed and shouted unnecessarily as I made my way down to the video-intercom mounted on the wall next to the apartment's front door.

Tuesday — Two

Detective Jill Maguire stared back at me when I activated the intercom's speaker.

"Open the door, Mr. Doyle, I need to talk to you," she demanded and held up her identification card at the intercom's spherical lens.

"There's a lift across the lobby, take it up to the sixth floor," I told her, pressed the button that unlocked the building's entrance, pulled the apartment's front door open, and then went out onto the corridor to wait for her.

When the lift's doors opened and the detective arrived on my floor, I directed her towards my apartment, followed her purposeful strides as she made her way into my home, and was closing my apartment door behind us when she spun around and thrust a piece of torn newsprint into my face.

"Tell me why my late father wrote down your name and home telephone number on this newspaper cutting?" she shouted and extracted her handgun with her free hand.

"I've no idea why he did that," I gasped, jolted back in shock as Jill Maguire aimed her gun at my face and then raised both my arms.

"Right, so you don't have any idea why my father wrote down your name and home telephone on a newspaper that was published the day before he died?" Detective Jill Maguire yelled and tossed the piece of newsprint at me.

Unsure of what to do next, I stood with my hands raised and waited until the detective shouted at me again.

"Pick that up!" Jill Maguire said, nodded towards the piece of newspaper that had fluttered to the floor between us, took a step backwards, and then used both of her hands to steady the gun that was aimed at me.

I kept my eyes on the detective's gun as I stooped down, slid my left hand along the varnished floor boards, and then brought the piece of newsprint up slowly in front of my face to review it in detail.

Torn from the top right-hand corner of a newspaper page, the press cutting contained a head and shoulders photograph of Frank Hennessy, over which some words and numerals had been scribbled in blue ink.

I recognized my surname and home telephone number amongst those scribbles, plus the word Reid, and 4:00 pm, but had never seen that piece of newspaper before. That was why I shook my head at Detective Jill Maguire when I had examined it in detail and lowered it.

"I don't know anything about that," I told her.

"Really?" she snapped. "That's amazing, because that cutting was found on my father's desk after he was killed. Can you explain why he would have noted your name and home telephone number, and those other details, in his own writing, on a newspaper that was published on the day before he was shot dead?"

"No, I can't," I said, examined the piece of newsprint again and re-read Maguire's father's notes. "If your dad had listened to the telephone message that I left for him on the day that newspaper was published then he might have written those notes," I said and shook my head. "But he told me that he never got my message when he came here that Sunday night."

"My father was here the night before he died?" Jill Maguire shrieked.

"Yes," I replied. "He came here to tell me about Declan Reid."

"Declan Reid?" Jill Maguire queried.

I pointed to the other surname that her father had written on the piece of newspaper.

"Yes," I said. "Declan Reid was the private detective that I hired to find out who was behind my daughter's kidnapping. Your father used to work with Declan Reid and recommended him to me. He told me that Reid was the best detective in Ireland."

"My father recommended a private detective to you?" Jill Maguire asked.

"Yes," I confirmed. "He even brought Declan Reid here to introduce him to me."

Jill Maguire shook her dubious head. "My father encouraged you to hire a private detective to work on a case that he was assigned to?" she asked me.

"Yes," I confirmed again. "Your father suspected that certain people were involved in Sarah's kidnapping and got me to hire Declan Reid to get answers to questions that he couldn't ask."

"To get answers from who?" Jill Maguire asked and then smiled. "You know, Cormack warned me about you," she said. "He told me that my father always suspected that you were behind your daughter's kidnapping and told me that you didn't seem to care too much about your wife's death either. That was why I went through the records about that kidnapping when I got back to the station tonight and found that," she said and indicated the piece of newspaper that I now held in my left hand.

"Really, and what else did O'Sullivan tell you?" I asked.

"Cormack told me to stay away from you because you manipulate people," Jill Maguire replied. "Now I know what he meant by that."

"And yet here you are, Detective Maguire," I said and noted that she was still wearing the same trouser suit that she had worn earlier. "Luckily for you, O'Sullivan was wrong about that. I don't manipulate people, all I do, is motivate them to change their behavior," I said, and then asked her another question. "Tell me, Detective Maguire, when you were talking to him earlier, did O'Sullivan tell you why he had your father killed?"

Jill Maguire stepped back, steadied her aim, and looked like she was about to shoot me.

"How dare you!" she snarled. "Cormack O'Sullivan was my father's best friend. He even shot the guy who killed him."

"Yes, and how very convenient that was," I said drily, and then tossed the piece of newspaper back at Jill Maguire's feet. "Johnny Callaghan was the twenty-two-year-old who killed your father," I stated. "His friends nick-named him Beep-Beep because he was such a fast runner. And yet a bulky, middle-aged, detective like O'Sullivan chased after him on foot, caught up with him, and then shot him dead at close range," I said and raised my eyebrows. "I'm sorry, Detective Maguire, but if that's what you want to believe then go right ahead," I said. "Otherwise, I strongly suggest that you check out what really happened to your dad, and see if all the facts about his death add up."

Jill Maguire kept her gun aimed at me but narrowed her eyes.

"Why do you think that Cormack O'Sullivan had my father killed?" she asked.

"If you want an answer to that question, then you're going to have to put that gun away," I said. "Otherwise, I think that it's time that you left my home, don't you?"

Maguire stared back at me for a few seconds and then lowered her handgun, slipped it into a holster attached to the back of her waistband, and stooped down to snatch up the piece of newspaper that I had thrown down to the wooden floor.

"Okay," she said. "Why do you think that Cormack had my father killed?"

"To shut him up," I said and flexed my fingers as I lowered my hands.

"To shut him up about what?" Jill Maguire asked.

"Your father told me that he suspected that O'Sullivan knew what had really happened to my wife and daughter. That's why he got me to hire Declan Reid. To find out what O'Sullivan really knew about that kidnap."

Jill Maguire looked undecided.

"Tell me more about Declan Reid?" she asked.

"Declan Reid and your father used to work together. Reid was the strong, silent type but didn't like using phones much. He said that they weren't secure. The morning before your dad was killed, Declan Reid phoned me and said that he had found out who was behind Sarah's kidnapping but wouldn't tell me who that was over the phone. That's why we arranged to meet here at four that afternoon."

"And who did Reid tell you was behind the kidnap?" Jill Maguire queried.

"Declan Reid never showed up here that afternoon," I said. "His car was found just around the corner but he had fallen into the Liffey and drowned before he got here."

Jill Maguire's face expressed doubt as she thought over what I had just said.

"Only you don't believe that, do you?" she asked me.

I shrugged. "No, I don't," I said. "Declan Reid drank a lot, and your dad told me that he couldn't swim, so it's possible that he just fell into the river. But I doubt that's what really happened to him. But no one saw anything, so no one really knows about his death."

Jill Maguire paused again before she asked me her next question.

"Do you think Declan Reid told my father about what he discovered?" she asked

I shook my head. "No," I said.

"Why not?" Jill Maguire asked.

I shrugged again. "Because Reid told me that he hadn't said anything about the kidnap to anyone else, and your father said that he didn't get my phone message that day. So, your father wouldn't have known that Declan Reid was coming here to tell me who organized the kidnap."

Jill Maguire mulled over what I had said.

"Did you ever tell anyone else that Cormack might have had my dad killed?"

"Like who?" I replied.

"I don't know," Jill Maguire said. "Whoever you share your suspicions with?"

I nodded. "Three years ago, I told someone else what I just told you."

"Who?" Jill Maguire asked me.

"I'm sorry," I said. "I'm not going to tell you that."

"I see," Jill Maguire said. "But whoever it was, they told you to stay quiet, didn't they?"

"Yes, they did," I said. "They pointed out that I didn't have any proof against O'Sullivan, so if I spoke up, I could be putting myself in harm's way."

"I see, so you just kept your little head down and stayed quiet about my father's death," Jill Maguire mocked.

I spun around to the apartment's front door and opened it.

"That's it," I told the detective. "Get out!"

In response, Jill Maguire smiled at me and then brushed past me towards the open door.

"Don't worry, this won't be the last time that we talk," she threatened.

"Great, I'm really looking forward to meeting you again," I replied as she passed me. "I presume that you recognized the man in that photograph too?" I asked her.

"Yes, of course I did," Jill Maguire responded. "That's your father-in-law."

TUESDAY — THREE

Two thoughts ran through my head as the lift's doors shut to bring Jill Maguire back downstairs and I stepped inside my apartment, closed, and then locked my front door. One of them was why Jill Maguire's Dad had told me that he didn't get my phone message when he had noted down the contents of my call?

The second was if Jill Maguire had spotted that I had shared my suspicions about O'Sullivan's role in her father's death with Frank Hennessy.

The next time that I woke up, a digital version of the bland corporate tune that featured in the TV commercial for my new mobile phone was ringing. I hadn't selected a ringtone from the mobile phone's settings, so its operating system had defaulted to a polyphonic rendition of the soundtrack from the forgettable lifestyle TV spot that was used to support its sales in various markets. That was one of those obvious multi-market television commercials that was populated with a mixed-race cast in brightly colored clothes who danced, chatted, and joked around with each other on a sunlit beach.

"Hi Killian, it's Frank," My father-in-law said in his voluminous voice when I answered him. "Kate told me that you had a new mobile phone."

"Hi, Frank," I answered, wondered if Kate had remained in the odd mood she had displayed just prior to her departure from my late brother's house, and then shuddered on spotting from my bedroom's clock radio that it was already twenty minutes to ten.

49

After Jill Maguire had left my apartment, it had taken me two hours to get back to sleep and I had slept well past my usual wake-up time.

"I'm sure you're that you'll be busy today, so I won't keep you for long," Frank said, as though reading my thoughts. "I just wanted to let you know that your car is here. I had it brought back from The O'Malley Centre last night. We had a tow truck going out there for the JimiJix Jeep, so I got them to do another run. I thought that your car would be safer here."

"Thanks, Frank," I said. "Where is it parked?"

"In front of the building here," he answered me. "Do you want me to get someone to drive it to you?"

"No, that's okay, I'll pick it up myself later," I told him. "Will you be around?"

"Yeah, I'm here all day," Frank said. "I'm expecting O'Sullivan and that detective woman you met yesterday at ten, but apart from that, I'm free."

Frank's mention of the female detective reminded me of Jill Maguire's visit to my apartment. I wondered what she had told O'Sullivan about that, but decided not to say anything about it to Frank.

"See you later," I told my father-in-law, and dialed the number for Dave's house.

Betty told me that Louise had woken up during the night in a bad way and had to be sedated by the doctor again. The female Garda had also returned to the house an hour earlier. She informed Betty that some detectives would call to Dave's house later in the morning to talk to Louise.

"I'll try to be there by then," I told Betty. "My car is out at Jasper's Head Office, so I'm going out there to collect it and have a quick word with Frank. When I get to the house, you should take a break," I said.

"I need one," Betty replied. "It was a strange night."

Minutes later, I was on my way back from the bathroom when the apartment's landline telephone rang and the words 'Private Number' appeared on its caller display. I let the call ring four more times before answering it.

"Good morning, Mr. Doyle. We only met once, so you probably won't remember me," an elderly woman said. "This is Anne Reid, Declan Reid's widow."

I remembered Declan Reid's widow, and our only encounter three years earlier, and wrongly assumed that her call had something to do with Jill Maguire's visit to my apartment. That the detective must have followed up on our conversation by contacting Anne Reid about her father's death.

"I remember you," I replied. "What's this about?"

There was a pause before the woman spoke again. "We saw you on the TV last night and thought that it would be a good idea to meet up," she said with the clipped tone and authority of age.

"We?" I queried.

"Sorry, Vincent Lynch and me," Anne Reid replied apologetically.

"Who's Vincent Lynch?" I asked.

"Vincent used to be one of Declan's detective partners, he's retired now," the elderly woman explained. "He spotted something during the TV News Report about your brother that didn't add up."

Conscious of the time, I was more abrupt with Anne Reid than normal.

"I'm sorry, Mrs. Reid, but I'm in a hurry," I said. "So, you're going to have to tell me what this Vincent guy saw before I agree to meet you?"

"As I said, Mr. Doyle," Anne Reid replied. "This is about your brother's murder. Vincent wants to tell you what he thinks really happened to him and isn't willing to discuss that with you over the telephone."

I hadn't heard the 'over the telephone' excuse since Anne Reid's husband, Declan, had drowned and wanted to end the conversation immediately. And yet, the reference to what had really happened to Dave intrigued me.

"Where and when do you want to meet?" I asked her.

"At my house this evening," Anne Reid replied. "Is that all right?"

"Yes, that's fine," I said. "What's the best phone number to reach you on later?"

I jotted down the telephone number that Anne Reid gave me and then entered it into the contacts on my new mobile phone as I walked to Pearse Street and hailed down the taxi that would take me to Jasper's Head Office.

TUESDAY — FOUR

Apart from two queries about our destination, the taxi driver maintained his silence during our drive to Jasper's Head Office.

I sat in the back of his Volkswagen Passat, listened for a few minutes to a heated debate on the radio about increased property taxes, and then called Ted O'Shea from my new mobile phone.

"I disagree entirely," I told my mentor when he urged me to ignore the advice that he had given me the previous day about firming up on my attitude. "You said that I needed to change people's perceptions of me and you were right," I said.

"Please Killian, please just put the whole nice thing on hold for a while," Ted said. "We can talk about it later. Right now, you really need to be just you," he added. "You've lost your only brother and are the victim of a horrible crime. If you try to be tough now, people might misjudge you and think that you're just an asshole and not somebody who is grieving for his dead brother."

"Thanks, Ted," I replied. "I hear what you're saying, but I'm not going to let this one go. Not this time. When I lost Claire and Sarah, I thought that the cops would take charge of everything and that they knew their way around what had happened. But they didn't behave like that and I let them roll all over me. That isn't going to happen this time. This time, I'm going to be much tougher with them and make sure that everything is looked into. I'm going to make sure that whoever killed Dave isn't going to get away with it."

I heard Ted cover his telephone's mouthpiece and bark at someone who had entered his office. When he came back on the line, there was a plea in his voice.

"Please, Killian, please don't do that," he begged. "The cops know what they're doing. They do this every day. That's their job. If you talk down to them, or go to the media behind their backs, you'll only get in their way and slow things down, and, believe me, no one is going to think that you're being strong or smart if you do that."

"So, your suggestion is that I just sit on my hands and do nothing, is that it, Ted?" I replied and saw that while he was trying to ignore the content of my heated telephone conversation, the back of the taxi driver's neck had taken on a deeper shade of pink.

"No, that's not it at all, Killian," Ted replied. "I just don't think that your brother's death is a good opportunity for you to try and turn around how other people see you. That's why I'm suggesting that you should wait until things cool down a bit before you address the nice thing," he said.

"Maybe you're right," I agreed. "Can I call you later?"

"Yes, of course, Killian," Ted replied. "You can call me at any time. In the meantime, please take care of yourself. Do you hear me?"

"Yes, I hear you. Thanks Ted," I muttered, ended the call, and then listened to the car's radio again as the talk show was interrupted by the ten-thirty news bulletin.

The lead item on the news was Dave's murder. According to the radio station's crime reporter, the Gardai had recovered the burned-out getaway car that had been used by the killer the previous day, a white Mazda 626 that had been stolen near The O'Malley Centre shortly before Dave's death but had only used to transport the killer a short distance away from the crime scene.

I tuned out the rest of the news items as the taxi pulled into the car park in front of the shimmering steel and glass building that was Jasper's Head Office in Ireland. When I had paid and tipped the taxi driver, I saw that my dented black Audi was parked in Frank's usual space, immediately to the right of its front entrance.

The interior of Jasper's Head Office building was constructed in the style of a huge courtyard with casual seating areas, open work spaces, and lots of meeting rooms that were located on balconies that ran on the four floors that surrounded its central atrium.

Jenny, one of Jasper's Chicken Restaurants receptionists, spotted me as soon as I came through the building's automated front doors, donned a sad face, and then stood up to lean forward and embrace me.

Next to her, Leanne, another receptionist, remained seated until her colleague had released me and then stood up, took my head in her hands, kissed my right cheek, stepped back, and shook her head as tears began to run from her eyes.

"Everyone in here is devastated," she told me. "We just can't believe what happened to your brother, Dave, he was such a nice guy."

There was that horrible nice word again.

A moment later, when Jenny had repeated her colleague's sentiments, she informed me that Frank was unavailable.

"He's with some people right now," she said. "They should be finished soon. Can I get you something while you wait?"

"No, I'm fine," I replied as Jenny handed me a self-adhesive visitor's pass and activated the sliding glass turnstile that allowed me access to the atrium.

Inside the turnstiles, I crossed the marble floor to one of the purple leather couches in the waiting area, sat down, looked around me, and saw that a small Jasper's Restaurant was located directly ahead of me. To the right of that restaurant was a well-stocked convenience store, while an automated banking machine and a dry-cleaning outlet were located to its left. All facilities that were intended to lessen the need for any of Jasper's employees to have to leave the building during working hours.

Across the atrium, I also saw that a wiry, middle-aged black man in navy overalls with an orange J embossed over his breast pocket was erecting a folding ladder next to a huge potted palm tree.

Satisfied that the ladder would support his weight, he then climbed up to one of the palm tree's fronds, gripped its tip, and used a soft cloth to wipe its serrated surface clean before unhitching a plastic spray bottle from the belt around his waist and covering the frond with a fine mist of chilled water.

The man's concentration on the task reminded me of how my late wife had often devoted her full attention to her collection of houseplants, a practice that she claimed both calmed her mind and increased her emotional control.

For a moment, I tried to recall why I gotten rid of those plants so soon after Claire's death but then was disrupted by Frank's secretary, Susan, as she sashayed in front of me as if she had just reached the end of a catwalk.

Now in her early forties, Susan wore a shiny olive-colored business dress that accentuated the effort that she had made to maintain her swagger, her once-blond hair had been dulled through the use of dye, and I saw that the expensive anti-aging creams that Susan bought to deliver that all-important second glance were no longer money well spent.

In the past, there had been some rumors about Frank's relationship with Susan and the likelihood that he would dump her after it ended and hire a younger secretary. I had never given any credence to that scenario and had never witnessed any evidence that the relationship between my father-in-law and his secretary was anything other than professional.

Besides, given the longevity of Frank's marriage, and his loyalty to his friends and family, I considered any concerns that Frank would replace his secretary with a younger model to be unfounded and somewhat ridiculous.

"Hi, Killian, are you okay?" Susan asked and shook her head on halting in front of me. "I was so upset when I heard about Dave. I am so, so sorry for your loss."

"Thanks Susan," I replied, got to my feet, and began to follow her across the atrium towards the lift station.

On our way there, a descending lift arrived and I watched Jill Maguire and O'Sullivan step out of it and turn right towards the building's exit. Neither of them noticed us or looked in our direction.

Moments later, Susan and I arrived on the fourth floor, where she rushed ahead of me, pushed open one of the double doors into Frank's corner office, and stepped back smartly.

"Killian, come in," Frank's voice boomed as he got up from his desk and approached me. "I'm sorry you had to wait downstairs, but Cormack O'Sullivan and Tony Maguire's daughter were here longer than I expected."

A former head of Garda Detectives, Frank Hennessy had left the force ten years earlier, had headed up Jasper's security team, and had then worked his way up the company ladder into its top job, a position that he had acquired by the time that I married his daughter.

TUESDAY — FIVE

A huge, bearded man in his early sixties, Frank was dressed in an immaculate double breasted pinstripe suit, white shirt, and wine-and-grey striped necktie.

After he had pumped my right hand with both of his, Frank led me across to the informal meeting area on the other side of his office, where a matching pair of black leather two-seater couches were separated by a low coffee table.

"Did the detectives have any news about the hunt for Dave's killer?" I asked Frank and sat down on the couch that he directed me to with one of his enormous hands.

"If they did, they didn't share it with me," he replied as he pinched up the trouser legs of his suit and slowly lowered himself into the center of the couch opposite mine until his outsized frame covered most of it.

"How are you doing?" Frank then asked.

"All right, I suppose," I said. "Just a bit light-headed. I feel as if something is about to happen, yet it never does. Do you know that feeling?"

"Unfortunately, I do," Frank replied. "I know it all too well."

For a moment we sat in silence and then Frank jerked forward.

"Sorry, Killian, can I get you anything, a coffee, a tea, or some water?"

"No thanks, Frank," I said. "I promised Betty that I'd relieve her, so I better head up to Dave's House soon. Thanks for having my car brought back here," I added. "I see that it's parked in your usual space. Where's your car?"

"It was being serviced yesterday," Frank told me. "I was supposed to collect it from the garage yesterday evening but…"

I nodded and then changed the subject. "What did O'Sullivan and his sidekick have to say?" I enquired.

"Not much, they just had lots of questions," my father-in-law replied.

"About what?" I asked

"About everything," Frank replied. "Our restaurants, the JimiJix program, how much cash we take in, the telethon," he paused. "And you."

"And me?" I asked. "What did they want to know about me?"

"A number of things," Frank answered in his deep voice. "Like why you were at The O'Malley Centre yesterday, how you got on with Dave, stuff like that."

"Did Jill Maguire tell you that she called to my apartment last night?" I asked him.

"No, she didn't," a surprised Frank retorted. "What did she want?"

"She was all flustered and had a press clipping from a newspaper that came out on the day before her dad died," I told him. "Apparently, Jill Maguire checked the records about Claire and Sarah's deaths when she got back to her office last night and discovered that her dad had noted down my home telephone number and Declan Reid's name over a photograph of you that he tore from a newspaper," I said. "She seemed to think that I would know why her father did that and then got annoyed when I told her that I knew nothing about it," I added.

"You didn't say anything to her about your suspicions about Cormack, did you?" Frank asked as his eyes narrowed and he creased his forehead.

When I didn't respond quickly enough to his question, Frank covered his face with his big hands. "Oh no! What did you say to her?" he groaned through his fingers.

"Nothing much," I replied. "She annoyed me, so I might have put a doubt in her mind that Cormack O'Sullivan was her late father's best friend."

"Jesus," Frank responded and lowered his hands. "How did she react to that?"

"She didn't believe me," I said and shrugged. "She reminded me that O'Sullivan had killed the bloke who shot her father and told me that he had warned her about me. Don't worry, Jill Maguire would probably get into trouble if O'Sullivan ever found out that she had called to my apartment, so she's unlikely to say anything to him."

Frank nodded. "You can say that again. She wouldn't still be on the case if O'Sullivan found out that she called to your home. In fact, knowing Cormack, she'll be lucky to still have a job if he finds out about that," he added. "Which is good, because we don't ever want O'Sullivan to find out that you suspect that he was involved in her father's death. You didn't tell her that, did you?"

"No, I didn't," I lied. "All I did was suggest to her that she should check out the facts about her father's death."

"Have you told anyone else about her visit to your home?" Frank asked.

I shook my head. "No, why?"

"Because you should keep it that way," Frank told me. "You accusing O'Sullivan of having anything to do with his partner's death is the last thing that we need right now."

I nodded to acknowledge Frank's wisdom and was about to ask him if he remembered a retired detective called Vincent Lynch when Susan knocked on one of the double doors into his office and quickly stepped inside it without waiting for a response.

"Hi, can I get you guys anything?" she queried.

"No thanks, Susan," Frank answered too quickly.

"Sorry, Frank, but I need to go now," I said and stood up when I surmised that Susan's intrusion into Frank's office had been prearranged.

"Really?" Frank asked me as he stood up and put a big hand on my right shoulder to walk me out of his office. "You know where I am if you need anything," he offered. "And don't worry about the telethon. Kate is playing a blinder there."

"I'm glad to hear that," I said and then examined one of the framed photographs on the wall next to the office's double doors.

Familiar to me from previous visits to Frank's office, the color image had been captured at the Royal Griffith Golf Club in Sutton on the day after the Jasper's Telethon two years earlier.

In the photograph, three men smiled into the camera with their arms wrapped around each other's shoulders while, behind them, a well-tended lawn was bordered by a natural stone wall, and beyond that the deep blue sea of Dublin Bay sparkled in late summer sunshine. The three men in the photograph were Frank, Dave, and me.

"Happier times," Frank said when he noted my line of vision.

"They certainly were," I agreed, shook Frank's hand again and left his office.

Back outside in the warm sunshine, I unlocked my Audi, examined the damage to its rear wing, took off my blazer, spread it on the car's backseat, and then recalled what Frank had said about the JimiJix Jeep being brought back to Jasper's Head Office.

When I had wandered around to the rear of the building, I saw that the JimiJix Jeep was in its usual spot next to the JimiJix storeroom, and that Dave's blue midrange Hyundai was parked next to it. That was when an officious male voice sounded from behind me.

"Hi, Sir, can I help you with something?" it asked me.

I turned to face my inquisitor. No taller than five-foot-four, no heavier than ten stone, and no younger than sixty-five, the man in the black security uniform sauntered into the bright sunshine.

"Hi, my name is Killian Doyle and I was just in with Frank Hennessy. That's my brother's car," I told him and pointed towards Dave's blue Hyundai.

The older man looked over at the blue Hyundai and then back at me.

"You're Dave's brother?" he asked as his face softened.

"Yes," I said. "And that's his car, right?"

"Yes, that's Dave's car all right," the security man commented. "He always parked it there. I'm Jim Cahill. I look after the security around here during the day," he told me.

"During the day," I repeated. "Who looks after it at night?"

"Nobody," he replied. "The security firm that I work for sends a van around here to check on the place every half hour after six pm, but since no one works here at night, Jasper's don't pay us for full-time security."

I pointed up at one of the security cameras attached to the steel girders on the edge of the building's roof. "I presume that they help at night time too," I said.

Cahill followed my finger and looked back at me. "Those cameras haven't worked for years and aren't connected to anything," he said and shook his head.

"They're just there for show?" I asked.

"A lot of security cameras are," the older man said and nodded as if he was sharing a secret with me. "I even find it hard to spot the real ones myself."

I turned back to the Hyundai. "How long has Dave's car been here?"

"Since yesterday morning," Cahill answered.

"Were you talking to him before he left here?" I enquired

The security man nodded. "I met Dave most days," he said. "He wasn't in good form yesterday morning though and hardly even acknowledged me."

"Did you ever see him like that before?" I asked.

Cahill shook his head. "No, most of the time Dave was in good form and used to slag me about United. Yesterday, he must have had a row with his wife, or something."

"Maybe," I said, bid Cahill farewell, and returned to my car.

I had left Jasper's Head Office and driven half a mile towards Dave's house when I realized that Dave had probably taken the same route back home on Sunday night after he switched from the JimiJix Jeep to his own car. Apart from a silver Nissan about a hundred yards behind me, there were no other cars in my rear-view mirror, so I slowed down, pulled over, and took out a road map of Dublin from the Audi's glove compartment.

According to the map, I estimated that the journey between Jasper's Head Office and Dave's Home would take about thirty minutes to complete, which was similar to the length of time that Louise had said elapsed between Dave's call home on Sunday night and his arrival there in a foul mood. Whatever had upset Dave must have been something that he had encountered on his drive home on Sunday night, so I decided to look around closely as I drove to his house, put the map away, and pulled back out onto the road ahead of me.

That was when I noted that the silver Nissan had also parked at the side of the road ahead of me. The other car suddenly sped away from me as I approached it, and then faded out of sight around a curve ahead.

The erratic behavior of its driver might have been purely coincidental and yet I had an uneasy feeling about it.

TUESDAY — SIX

The drive to Dave's house took him about thirty-minutes to complete and yet took me fifty as I stopped to jot down the reference numbers on advertising hoardings, note the location of shops or pubs, or list the zebra crossings that Dave would have passed on his way home.

Having completed the journey, and on reaching Dave's house, I decided to call the advertising agency's media department and get details of any communications or messages that Dave could have seen or heard as he drove home on Sunday night.

Apart from the posters in three bus shelters that featured Dave in his JimiJix costume and promoted the televised broadcast of Jasper's Telethon on Thursday night, I had noted nothing of any relevance that could have affected my brother's mood as he drove home.

What I would never be able to access about Dave's journey was any footage from the security cameras that had captured the roads that he had travelled home, or any information on anyone or anything that he might have seen as he drove past them on Sunday night.

I accepted that most of that information would be available to Jill Maguire and O'Sullivan as I reached Dave's house and parked behind a recently registered grey Ford Mondeo that I had seen earlier outside Jasper's Head Office.

From that car's metallic paint, its wide alloy wheels, and its tinted glass, I guessed that it belonged to Cormack O'Sullivan.

My assumption proved correct when Betty opened the front door to let Jill Maguire and O'Sullivan out of Dave's House after their interview with Louise. The two detectives had reached the house's front gate before they noticed me.

"Good afternoon, Mr. Doyle," O'Sullivan stated, while next to him, Jill Maguire managed a nod in my direction. "We just met with your sister-in-law," he told me and then compressed the key fob that unlocked his Ford Mondeo. "The poor woman is heartbroken," he declared and shook his head before getting into his car.

Dressed in a dark-blue trouser suit, Jill Maguire paused before she got into the car after O'Sullivan, caught my eye, and mouthed a silent 'thank you'. I presumed that her gesture was related to the fact that I hadn't mentioned her early morning visit to my apartment to her boss.

I watched as O'Sullivan maneuvered his car across the road in a tight circle and drove off at speed, and then, when the detectives were gone, continued into the house and felt guilty when I saw that Betty was still wearing the same mauve shirt and black slacks that she had worn the day before.

"Are you okay?" I asked her and stepped inside the house.

"Yes," she replied and then signaled for me to follow her into the kitchen.

"How did that go?" I asked when she had closed the door.

"All right, I think," Betty told me and then made her way to, and sat back, against the kitchen table. "The detectives didn't want me present while they talked to Louise. Apparently, they were afraid that I would contaminate the witness. I told them I hadn't contaminated anyone for ages," she said.

"Did they ask you many questions when they were finished with Louise?" I probed.

"Yes, they did," Betty admitted. "Most of them were about Dave. When I first met him? Did I know if he was in any trouble? Was he happily married? That kind of stuff."

I nodded. "And how's Louise now?"

"Not good," Betty responded. "She needs some more sedatives. The doctor left a few tablets for her, so I'll give them to her and then get Louise back to bed. Once I've done that I'm going home to get some sleep for myself." she added. "That way, you'll be here if needed during the day, and I'll come back later."

"Good idea," I said. "Where's Philip?"

"Some woman called here with a friend of his about an hour ago," Betty said. "She took the two boys out to see a movie and is getting them something to eat afterwards. She said that Philip will be back at about six."

"Right," I said and nodded. "And how is he today?"

Betty made a rippling effect with her right hand.

"So-so," she said. "I don't think he fully understands what's going on yet. Now, the sooner that I give Louise those tablets and get her back to bed, the sooner that I can get out of here."

"I hear you," I said. "But I'd like to have a word with Louise first. It will only take a minute, I promise."

"Fine," Betty said as I turned to leave the kitchen.

TUESDAY — SEVEN

Dressed in a simple green cotton dress, a tearful Louise was perched on the edge of the corduroy sofa again as I walked into the sitting room. I kissed the top of her head and then pulled an armchair in front of her as she tightened her grip on the tissues that she held in both hands.

"I hope that your talk with the detectives wasn't too difficult," I began and then spotted an envelope on the sofa next to Louise. I knew that it would contain all the detective's contact details and would tell Louise how to reach the police if she needed to talk to them. I had received similar written material from the detectives after Claire and Sarah were killed.

"They're just doing their jobs," Louise replied and lowered her vision to the carpeted floor. "Trying to catch whoever killed Dave."

"Yes, and I hope that they do that," I said and then inched the armchair forward until our knees almost touched. "I'm sorry about this, Louise, but to get some things clear in my head there are a few questions that I need to ask you too, okay?"

Louise snuffled and nodded back to me as I realized that it would be some time before she recovered from the loss of Dave, if she ever did.

"When you phoned me yesterday morning, you said Dave was in a really bad mood when he got home here on Sunday night," I began. "Do you have any idea why he was like that?"

After Louise had executed three well-spaced sniffles, she responded to me in a shaky voice.

"Dave was Dave," she told me. "If you annoyed him, then he mightn't tell you what you did wrong but he would get into a really bad mood. But, if you asked him what was bugging him, he never held back," she said. "That's why Sunday night was so different," she added. "When he got home, Dave wouldn't tell me what was up with him."

"Do you think that Dave was in some kind of trouble?" I quizzed. "That he owed money to someone dodgy, or something like that?"

"This is about another woman, isn't it?" Louise said and glared at me. "You're trying to find out if I knew that Dave was having an affair. That's it, isn't it, Killian?"

I threw my hands up. "No, that's not it at all, Louise," I said. "There was only one woman in Dave's life and that was you. I'm just trying to find out what was wrong with him on Sunday night," I emphasized. "Why Dave tried to reach me and yet wouldn't tell you what was up with him."

"Dave tried to reach you on Sunday night?" Louise asked as her head snapped up.

"Yes, he phoned me twice," I admitted. "I missed both of Dave's calls and missed him again when he tried to get me at work yesterday morning. I was in a meeting, so didn't talk to him."

Louise was astonished. "You never said anything about that to me until now," she said. "What did Dave want to talk to you about?"

"I've no idea, because I never got to speak to him," I said, reached out and took hold of Louise's hands. "You have to believe me, Louise," I beseeched. "There is no one more upset or sorry that I didn't take Dave's calls on Sunday night or yesterday morning than I am. My brother wanted to talk to me and I wasn't there for him. I let him down."

For a moment, Louise didn't say anything. She just sat still and looked back into my face. "You didn't speak to Dave even though you knew that he was upset about something?" she asked and shook her head.

"No, no, it wasn't like that!" I spluttered. "As soon as you called me yesterday, I left work and drove to the Jasper's Restaurant in The O'Malley Centre to talk to Dave, but I got there too late."

Louise pulled back her hands as a teardrop ran from the corner of her left eye, dripped from her chin, and stained the front of the green dress.

"What's going on, Killian?" she whispered to me. "There's something that you're not telling me, isn't there?"

I reached out and took hold of my sister-in-law's hands again.

"No, Louise, I'm just trying to find out what upset Dave so much on Sunday night," I said. "Please don't do this to yourself, if Dave wanted to talk to me rather than discuss what had annoyed him with you, then it must have been something to do with his job. Did he say anything about his work recently?"

"No," Louise said. "Dave loved his job and would have told me about any problems that he had with it, not you."

A moment passed in silence between us.

"I'm really sorry, Louise," I said and tried to rein in my anger as I let go of my sister-in-law's hands and pushed my chair back. "I had a chance to talk to Dave on Sunday night and I blew it. Now he's gone, and no one will ever know what he wanted to talk to me about," I said. "When Claire and Sarah were murdered, I didn't do everything that I could and should have. But this time, things are going to be different, I'm going to make sure that Dave's killer is caught and I won't rest until that happens."

Louise's expression changed to one of fear as she looked into my intense face. My grieving sister-in-law then appeared relieved when the door into the sitting room opened and Betty entered it with a glass of water in her left hand and a couple of yellow tablets in the palm of her right.

When Betty had put Louise to bed, and had gone home to catch up on her own sleep, I sat alone on the sofa in Dave's sitting room for a few minutes, got used to the silence around me, and then took out my new mobile phone and scrolled down through its list of contacts.

TUESDAY — EIGHT

Tom McNulty, the franchisee who owned and operated the Jasper's Restaurant in Wexford, was surprised by my call and expressed his sorrow to me about Dave's death.

"We're all really gutted down here," he told me.

"I appreciate that," I replied and then cleared my throat. "Tom, I know that this might sound odd to you, but how did you find Dave on Sunday, mood-wise, I mean?"

"Flying," McNulty answered. "And he put on a mighty show for us."

"Was in good form when he left there?" I asked.

"Yes, powerful," McNulty replied. "That's what I told that detective woman too."

"Detective woman?" I asked Tom, although I had already guessed who he meant.

"I have her name here somewhere," McNulty said and sounded distracted for a moment. "Here it is. Detective Jill Maguire. That was her."

I thanked McNulty and then called Kate Fallon at the advertising agency. After I had answered her inevitable query about my well-being, and we had discussed the preparations for the Jasper's Telethon, I asked the question that was my real reason for calling.

"Kate, I know that this might sound odd," I said. "But you had more dealings with Dave than anyone else in the advertising agency, are you aware of anything that might have upset him on Sunday, anything at all?"

"What exactly do you mean by that, Killian?" Kate replied.

"I'm sorry that I didn't tell you this sooner, Kate, but Louise phoned me yesterday morning," I said. "According to her, Dave was in a really strange mood when he got home from Wexford on Sunday night. There was something up with him but he wouldn't tell Louise what it was. I tried but couldn't get Dave on his mobile yesterday morning, that's why I went out to The O'Malley Centre to see him. Obviously, I was too late getting there. Do you know what might have upset him?"

"I'm not sure," Kate said after a pause. "Maybe something happened to him while he was driving home on Sunday night," she said.

"Maybe," I agreed. "But whatever it was, I can't understand why Dave wouldn't have told Louise about it, instead of phoning me on my mobile."

"Sorry, it was just a thought," Kate said.

"You have access to Dave's company credit card records, don't you?" I asked her.

"Absolutely," Kate answered. "They're available online."

"Great," I said. "Can you check if Dave spent any money on his way home from Wexford on Sunday night. Maybe he stopped off to get petrol or something?"

"I've already checked that," Kate replied. "He didn't."

I waited a beat. "Why did you do that, Kate?" I asked her.

"Because I got a call from a detective earlier who asked me to check out the same thing," Kate answered. "When she had me on the phone, that detective also asked me lots of other questions too."

Once again, I surmised who the detective was.

"Questions like what?" I asked Kate, stood up, and moved across to the window, where I drew back one of the curtains and let bright sunlight into the room.

"Questions like whether I knew if there were any issues in Dave's life, or if any threats had been made against him or JimiJix," Kate said and then adopted a more conspiratorial tone. "She also seemed quite interested in you," she whispered as I reached up to the narrow shelf above the aging TV set. The shelf that Dave kept his travel books on.

"Really? Why, what did she want to know about me?" I replied, located a road map of Ireland, and lifted it down from the shelf.

"Just general stuff," Kate answered. "How you got on with Dave? What you're like to work with as a boss?" she hesitated. "That kind of stuff."

"And what did you tell her?" I asked, looked down at the map and then sensed from her silence that Kate had taken exception to my question.

"Just the truth," she replied.

I flinched. "I'm sorry, Kate, I shouldn't have asked you that question," I said. "I'm not thinking straight today. I'll call you again later, okay?"

"Okay, talk to you then," Kate said and hung up.

When my call with Kate was over, I opened and spread the road map of Ireland across the corduroy sofa's cushioned seats, knelt on the floor, and ran a finger along the line that represented the motorway between Dublin and Wexford.

Then I sat back on my haunches, thought about my telephone conversation with Kate, and began to worry about the questions that Jill Maguire had asked her.

What was on the detective's mind? Did the cops suspect that Dave had advance knowledge of the robbery? Did they assume that was the reason why Dave was in such a strange mood on Sunday night? Was that the reason why Jill Maguire thought that Dave hadn't told Louise or me what was bugging him, that he knew about the robbery, and was in on it?

I now regretted what I had said to Jill Maguire about O'Sullivan in my apartment. I had lashed out when it would have been better to stay quiet.

I looked down at the road map again and realized that Jill Maguire would be able to get the precise time and location of Dave's phone call to Louise, and then check to see whether my brother had made or received any other phone calls before he had arrived home on Sunday night.

I got back to my feet, called the advertising agency again, and was put through to its accounts department.

Noel Collins answered my call to his department and professed his commiserations to me by way of a lengthy monologue that included a reference to the tragic washing machine accident that had ended the life of his family's pet cat.

"I'm sorry, Noel," I interrupted. "I fully appreciate your kind thoughts, but I'm under a bit of pressure here. I know that this might sound odd," I warned him. "But you can access the calls on Dave's mobile phone from Sunday night, right?"

"Yes, that's correct," Noel Collins replied. "But only the calls that Dave made, not the ones that he received. The mobile calls that we make get logged and the costs are detailed on the phone company's itemized bill each month, but not the calls that we get."

"Right," I said. "So, you can only look up the calls that Dave made on Sunday night not the ones that he got?"

"Yes," Noel Collins replied. "But it usually takes me a few minutes to log onto our account. Can you wait that long, or will I call you back?"

"No, that's okay, I'll wait. Thanks, Noel," I replied and grimaced.

There was a pause while I listened to Collins's meaty fingers tap on a keyboard, and then a gap in time before he came back to me.

"I can see that Dave made three calls from his mobile phone on Sunday night," Noel Collins told me. "One to a landline and two to a mobile phone."

"What time did he call the landline at?" I asked.

"At seven-thirty-two," he replied. "For twenty-eight seconds."

"Thanks, Noel," I said and hung up.

Noel Collins was smart, so I presumed that he would check out the mobile phone number that Dave had called twice on Sunday night and see that it belonged to me. There was nothing that I could do about that and considered it worthwhile to receive the data about Dave's call to Louise on the landline.

I knelt back down, bent over the road map of Ireland again, and then got up and returned to the narrow shelf above Dave's TV until I had found a map of Dublin.

According to the timing that Noel Collins had provided, Dave had called Louise in an upbeat mood from the car park at Jasper's Head Office, and yet had arrived home in a bad mood just half-an-hour later.

To try to establish why Dave's mood had changed so significantly during that period, I called the advertising agency again and talked to Jimmy Nixon, the long-haired media strategist with a fondness for torn jeans, cowboy shirts, and scuffed sneakers. The type of clothing that put some of our clients on edge, and forced me to tell them how good Jimmy was at his job.

Jimmy was as blasé as usual as he delivered his brief condolence.

"What can I do for you?" he then asked in his usual aloof drawl.

"This might sound odd, Jimmy," I cautioned him. "But I need information about anything that Dave could have seen or heard as he drove home from Jasper's Head Office on Sunday night. Any posters that he could have seen, any commercials that he might have heard on his car's radio, everything."

"That does sound odd," Jimmy remarked. "What time frame do you want me to cover and where are we talking about?"

"Time-wise, I need the information from seven-thirty to eight o'clock on Sunday evening," I answered. "And geographically, I need to know about anything that Dave might have seen or heard between Jasper's Head Office and on reaching his home in Dunnefarnham."

"That's going to take me a while," Jimmy replied. "When do you need it?"

"The sooner, the better," I replied. "Please call when you have it."

After I had ended the call to Jimmy, I folded up the map of Dublin and the road map of Ireland, sat back down on the sofa when I had reassigned them to the shelf, and closed my eyes and listened to the sounds around me. A relaxation method that Claire had once suggested.

The first sound that I made out was a distinct hum. I listened for a few seconds to that sound and then recognized that it was being generated by a car's engine.

That was when I opened my eyes again, jumped up from the sofa, scrambled over to the window, and saw that a silver Nissan was idling outside the house.

The car's driver was a fair-haired young man with sunglasses. When he turned and spotted me looking out at him, he drove away at speed.

The wall into Dave's front garden was too high for me to make out its license plate but I had little doubt that it was the same car that I had seen earlier.

TUESDAY — NINE

It was nine o'clock that night by the time that Betty returned to Dave's house to relieve me. She looked rested, wore a wine-colored polo shirt over sand-colored jeans and was carrying a blue sports bag that she had prepared for her overnight stay.

"It looks like you've been busy," she commented when she saw the untouched plate of food on the table in front of Louise, who sat motionless on the sofa and stared absently at some property show on the television.

"I made that dinner for Louise about two hours ago but she didn't eat any of it," I told Betty. "Please try to get Louise to eat something before she goes to bed or she'll get weak, and we don't need that, do we?"

"No, we don't," Betty said. "How about Philip. Is he okay?"

"Yes, he's fine," I said. "I brought him up to bed about an hour ago and stayed with him until he was asleep. I doubt if he'll wake up until the morning. If he does, and you need me here, then please just call and I'll come right over."

"I don't think that will be necessary," Betty assured me and then nodded towards the door. "Come on, Killian, you need to take some time out for yourself too. Just be back here in the morning to relieve me, and remember that we still need to sort out a few things."

"Thanks," I said, pecked Betty's left cheek and then kissed the top of Louise's head.

Inside my Audi, I noted that the shorter night was a clear sign that the summer was coming to a close, started the car's engine, turned on its headlights, and then groaned loudly when I recalled phoning Anne Reid and arranging to meet her and her friend Vincent Lynch when Betty had returned to Dave's home.

Despite my tiredness, my depression about Dave's death, and my desire to get back to my apartment, during my call to Anne Reid, I had agreed to call to her house when I was on my way home.

Fifteen minutes later, I steered my Audi left, drove another three hundred yards and then negotiated a sharp right-hand bend before entering the narrow, tree-lined avenue of semi-detached houses where the private detective's widow lived.

Apart from the installation of double-glazed windows and an up-and-over garage door, the core structure of Anne Reid's house appeared unchanged, and looked outdated when compared to the dwellings on either side of it, both of which boasted enclosed porches and an additional bedroom above their garages.

Anne Reid opened the green painted door of number forty, peered up and down the quiet road, beckoned me inside of her home, and then led me into the house's front room.

"Vincent will be here in a few minutes," she told me and then gestured towards a cream chair that was embellished with a floral pattern and had curved wooden armrests.

"What's this about?" I asked, sat down, and looked around Anne Reid's front room, which, apart from the addition of some recent titles on the bookshelf above the sideboard, seemed to have changed little since the last time I'd been there. Which was about a week after Anne Reid's husband had drowned on his way to meet me.

"Vincent called me after he saw the TV news last night," Anne Reid told me. "He shared a theory about your brother's death and I reminded him that I knew you. Vincent was reluctant when I first suggested that the three of us should meet but eventually came around to my idea."

"He was reluctant that we meet," I repeated. "Let me get this straight, Mrs. Reid, this Vincent guy had no problem telling you his theory about my brother's death but didn't want to meet me to discuss it?"

Anne Reid looked hurt. "I'm sorry," she said from her matching armchair on the other side of the fireplace. "I thought it would be a good idea for you to meet Vincent and hear what he has to say."

I nodded, glanced at my watch, scanned the room again, and focused on the faded framed photographs on top of the brown-tiled mantelpiece.

"Those photos haven't changed in years," Anne Reid informed me when she saw where my attention was aimed, lifted a strutted silver picture frame from the mantelpiece and handed it across to me. "You might recognize some of the people in this one," she said.

I brought the frame closer to my face and studied the photograph.

In it, a beautiful young girl with short, shiny black hair parted in the center was wearing a bright orange dress, white socks, and light brown leather sandals as she sat happily on top of a picnic table between two delighted adults.

When I eventually recognized the little girl as Jill Maguire, I leant forward and examined the smiling man seated to her left.

Tony Maguire's sandy-colored hair was longer and darker than it had been when I had got to know him, while his green polo shirt in the photograph exposed a pair of pale muscular arms that he had never revealed in my company, and yet it was definitely him.

"That photograph has been sitting on the mantelpiece for twenty-two years," Anne Reid told me. "Declan took it in Dublin Zoo on Jill's third birthday."

"He did?" I asked and examined the woman with the oriental features on the other side of Jill Maguire. I saw that she was the same woman from the photograph that had been taken at Tony Maguire's funeral.

Anne Reid nodded. "Back then we knew the Maguires well," she said, took back the faded image from me, and looked down at it. "Tony and Mei were a nice couple, but it was always a bit of a strain being in their company," she said. "If you know what I mean."

"No, I'm sorry, but I don't know what you mean," I replied thinking that Anne Reid was being racist about Tony Maguire's wife. "What exactly are you saying?"

"What I'm saying is that none of us ever really knows what is going on in someone else's marriage," Anne Reid elaborated. "There was a lot of talk at the time that Tony Maguire and his wife didn't get on, but that was only because they didn't talk much."

"Is that what you meant when you said that it was always a bit of a strain being in their company?" I asked Anne Reid.

"Yes, that's exactly what I meant," she replied. "Unless you were talking about Jill, who they both worshipped, it was difficult to have a conversation with Tony and Mei."

"But they had no problem talking about their daughter?" I asked.

"No," Anne Reid said and smiled. "Jill was always laughing and giggling back then. She was good fun to be with and an easy subject to talk about."

"Have you spoken to Jill Maguire recently?" I asked Anne Reid.

The widow shook her head of short blond hair.

"I'm afraid not. Jill is a detective these days, so I see her on the news now and again but not in person. Did you meet her yesterday?"

"Yes, I did," I said.

"I don't know if you agree with me," Anne Reid said. "But if it's possible, I think that Jill is even prettier now than she was when she was a child."

"I'm not sure about that," I said. "I never met her when she was a child."

"Of course you didn't," Anne Reid said and then nodded towards the framed photograph. "We met the Maguires a few more times after that day, but once Robbie came along, I never met Jill or her mother again."

"Robbie?" I queried.

Anne Reid picked up and handed me a smaller silver frame from the mantelpiece.

In the faded colour photograph that it contained, an anxious-looking Anne Reid and a tall, slim man with long hair combed back from his forehead, that I recognised as her late husband, Declan, leant back against a rural stone wall. Between them was a young boy with sloped shoulders, a round face, a small chin, and almond-shaped eyes.

"When Robbie was born with Down's Syndrome, Declan went all strange," Anne Reid told me. "He didn't want to have any more children, refused to meet our friends, and started to drink heavily. Over time, we lost touch with everyone that we knew including Tony and Mei. Declan continued to work with Tony for a while after Robbie was born, but we never got together with Mei or Jill again. And then Declan lost his job and neither of us saw Tony again either."

"Where is Robbie now?" I asked Anne Reid and handed back the photograph.

"He died of a heart condition last summer," she answered.

"I'm sorry to hear that," I said and fell quiet until Anne Reid spoke again.

"You know, I spotted that you were lying the last time that you came here," she stated. "You didn't owe that money to Declan that you gave me, did you?"

I shook my head. "No, I didn't," I admitted. "Tony Maguire told me that Declan had a drink problem and had left you with a young son to look after."

"I see, so you decided to call here and give me some money," Anne Reid said. "Did you think that I believed your little story back then?"

I shook my head again.

"No," I said. "I sensed that you knew that I was lying."

"And yet you gave me all that money anyway," Anne Reid said.

"Yes," I replied. "Did you ever tell anyone that I did that?"

"Only a few people," Anne Reid answered. "I don't like discussing Declan's drinking or that he left me penniless," she explained. "How about you, did you tell anyone that you gave me that money?"

"No," I said as the smile dropped from Anne Reid's face.

"You gave me that money because you felt responsible for Declan's death, didn't you?" she asked me in a more forceful tone.

I lifted my hands and let them drop back to the chair's wooden armrests.

"Maybe," I admitted. "I felt responsible for lots of things back then. Your husband's death being one of them."

Anne Reid continued her interrogation. "Declan was on his way to tell you who had kidnapped your daughter and murdered your wife when he died that day, wasn't he?"

"Maybe," I repeated. "Declan phoned me that morning and told me that he had found out who had killed the Gilroy Brothers. They were the two guys who had killed Claire and kidnapped Sarah. Their dead bodies were found next to Sarah's, so it was presumed that whoever had hired the Gilroy Brothers had killed them when they messed up," I said and paused. "So, I presumed that your husband knew who was behind Sarah's kidnapping. He wouldn't talk to me over the telephone that morning, so we agreed to meet in my apartment that afternoon."

"Only Declan never showed up there, did he?" Anne Reid stated.

"No, he didn't," I agreed.

"Did anyone else know that Declan was coming to see you that day?" Anne Reid asked me in a premeditated manner.

"No," I replied. "I had called Tony Maguire after Declan phoned me to arrange our meeting but didn't get him. I left a message on his phone but he told me later that he hadn't listened to it."

"So, if he had accessed the messages on his phone, Tony Maguire would have known that Declan was going to see you that day to tell you who was behind the kidnap?" Anne Reid said.

"Yes," I replied. "Why?"

"Because I think that someone else must have heard your message that day," Anne Reid said. "What did you think when you heard that Tony Maguire was shot dead during a post office robbery the next day?"

"I was shocked," I said. "Tony Maguire had been in my home hours earlier."

"Was that when he told you that he hadn't heard your message?" Anne Reid asked me.

"Yes, it was," I said and stood up. "I'm going to leave now, Mrs. Reid," I added. "I'm tired and didn't come here to go back over what happened to your husband three years ago. The only reason why I came here was because you said that there was something that I should know about Dave's death, but you don't seem willing to talk about that until your friend Vincent gets here and he hasn't arrived yet."

Anne Reid looked both surprised and disappointed.

"You're going now?" she asked me.

"Yes, I am," I replied and made for the door.

"Do you not want to hear what Vincent has to say?" Anne Reid queried.

"No, maybe I'll meet him some other time," I replied and then jolted when a loud bell rang out in the hallway.

"That's probably him now," Anne Reid announced from behind me. "Please stay here and listen to what he has to say."

I paused at the door. "Okay, but only for a few minutes," I said.

"Thanks," Anne Reid said, got to her feet, and passed by me to answer the door.

Tuesday — Ten

In his early sixties, Vincent Lynch was of medium height but broad-shouldered. He had pale skin and a thin moustache, wore gold rimmed glasses over intense grey eyes, and had a severe mouth that looked like he didn't use it to smile too often.

Dressed too warmly for the summer weather in a well-tailored brown leather jacket, a navy zip-up sweater, and dark green corduroy slacks over a pair of well-polished brown leather brogues, Lynch projected the presence of someone who had once enjoyed the physical side of his job, and was the kind of detective that I never wanted to be interviewed by.

He gripped my right hand firmly as he stepped inside the house.

"I'm sorry for your loss," he said and examined my face.

"Thanks," I replied, and then stepped forward when Lynch indicated for me to walk ahead of him as Anne Reid opened a door into her kitchen at the other end of the short hallway.

When she flicked on two light switches, I saw that I had been wrong about the renovations to Anne Reid's home and that her kitchen had been extended into a long and wide room that featured floor to ceiling windows that revealed a well-kept back garden.

"This is where I spend most of my time," Anne Reid said as she directed Lynch and me towards a glass-topped table below a skylight in the center of the room and then moved to a countertop. "Drinkers love strong coffee," she declared when she had carried a chrome coffee carafe and three blue mugs over to the table and sat down next to Lynch across from me.

"Vincent told me something last night that I felt that you needed to hear," she stated as she filled the coffee mugs and pushed one of them across to me. "But there's something that you need to understand before he speaks," she stressed. "That what Vincent says is strictly confidential and stays between the three of us."

I pulled my head back to register my surprise and then turned to Lynch as he sipped his coffee, nodded approval of it to Anne Reid, and then leant forward and began to talk across the table at me in a dull monotone.

"If you're going to murder someone, you either kill them someplace away from prying eyes, or you display what you're doing right out in the open," he told me, as I smelt a waft of peppermint on his breath. "The best way to display a crime is to hide it within another crime," he continued. "That way no one suspects what's really going on. I think that's what happened to your brother yesterday. That he was killed deliberately in what appeared to be a robbery."

When Lynch finished talking, he took another sip of coffee, and I shook my head and leant back from the table.

"I'm sorry, Mr. Lynch, but I don't fully understand what you mean?" I questioned him.

The former detective glanced at Anne Reid and then turned back to me.

"Obviously, I didn't make myself clear enough," Lynch said. "What I'm saying is that I don't buy the theory that your brother was an innocent victim who got killed in a robbery. It's my view that what happened to him was a premeditated murder."

I shook my head again. "I'm sorry, Mr. Lynch, but I was there yesterday and saw what happened to Dave," I said. "He was shot during a robbery."

"You saw what you were meant to see," Lynch retorted. "Not the murder of your brother that was hidden inside the robbery that you witnessed."

"Why would anyone kill Dave like that?" I asked and sat forward again.

"I don't know," Lynch replied and spread his hands. "Was there a reason why someone wanted your brother dead?"

I stayed silent for a moment. Lynch didn't look deranged, and while Anne Reid still harbored some issues about her late husband's death, it didn't appear that either of them were using Dave's death simply to get me there. Nonetheless, I regretted phoning Anne Reid from Dave's house.

"I'm sorry, but you're going to have to explain to me how you reached your conclusion about my brother's death," I told Lynch.

Lynch shook his head and leant in closer over the kitchen table.

TUESDAY — ELEVEN

"**T**here are lots of things that don't add up about that restaurant robbery yesterday," Lynch began. "That type of cash hold-up is usually a spur of the moment thing carried out by some opportunistic loser or dope-head who needs a quick fix," he said. "But what happened yesterday was different. The guy who killed your brother was well-prepared, well-disguised, and got everyone in the restaurant to hand over their personal possessions. That's an old trick. When you get the eyewitnesses wrapped up in their personal stuff, they don't remember much else afterwards."

"You don't think it was a straightforward robbery?" I asked Lynch.

"No, I don't," the retired detective said. "You saw what you saw yesterday, Mr. Doyle, but professional robbers don't usually hit fast-food restaurants and I believe that the real crime that was committed yesterday was your brother's assassination."

"My brother's assassination," I repeated as Lynch drank more coffee.

"Yes, was your brother into drugs, owed a lot of money, or was having an affair?" Lynch asked when he had put down his mug.

I gave him an incredulous look. "No, not that I'm aware of," I said. "And anyway, I still don't get why someone would go to the trouble of killing Dave."

"I'm sorry to have to tell you this, Mr. Doyle," Lynch replied. "But people kill each other for all sorts of reasons, so you're going to have to find out what was really going on in your brother's life. That's the only way you'll get hard evidence against his killer."

I thought back over what Lynch had just said. If his theory was correct and Dave knew that his life was in danger, then it might explain his strange mood on Sunday night. If Dave feared that he was going to lose his life the next day then he would have acted odd and Louise might have misread his anxiety. Lynch's theory could also explain why Dave had tried to get hold of me on Sunday night and Monday morning, and why he gave me that odd look just before he died. Did Dave think that I knew he was about to be murdered?

"Have you shared this theory with any of your former colleagues?" I asked Lynch.

The retired detective shook his head. "No, and there are reasons for that," he said.

"Which are?" I asked.

"Firstly, I left the force two years ago," Lynch replied. "So, the last thing that anyone on that case wants to hear are suggestions from a retired cop."

"Even if it helped them to solve a crime?" I queried.

"The detectives who are trying to find your brother's killer are smart people," Lynch replied. "That's why I'd be surprised that they haven't already spotted what I just told you."

"What other reasons have you got for not talking to them?" I asked.

Lynch stirred uncomfortably. "What happened to your brother yesterday reminded me of another case three years ago," he answered. "Even though it happened a while ago, some people still don't like anyone asking questions about that case."

"Which case?" I asked. "And what people are you talking about?"

Lynch and Reid exchanged a glance before he proceeded.

"The other case was Tony Maguire's murder," the retired detective told me. "That was also a crime within a crime. Tony was shot dead during what was supposed to be a post office robbery, and the people that I'm talking about are Cormack O'Sullivan and Jill Maguire, both of whom you met after your brother's murder yesterday."

"How do you know that I met them yesterday?" I asked.

"I just do," Lynch stated.

"Do you think my brother's murder yesterday had something to do with Tony Maguire's death?" I asked him.

"No, and I never said that," Lynch replied. "What I said was that those two crimes are similar and that there are a number of direct connections between them."

If it was Lynch's intention to intrigue me, then his tactic had worked.

"What connections?" I asked him.

"You, for one," Lynch said. "Plus, Jill Maguire and Cormack O'Sullivan."

I sat back, digested what Lynch had just told me, and then looked from him to Anne Reid, who had been monitoring the conversation between Vincent Lynch and me closely.

"That's really why I'm here, isn't it?" I asked Anne Reid. "You believe that O'Sullivan had something to do with my brother's death, and that he was involved in your husband's death too. Do you want me to go after him?"

"Are you aware that Cormack O'Sullivan claims that Declan committed suicide?" Anne Reid asked me as the expression on her face hardened.

"No, I didn't know that," I replied. "I thought that he drowned."

"Not according to Cormack O'Sullivan," Anne Reid stated. "He has told people that there was a suicide a note in Declan's car but that he got rid of it because he didn't want me to bear the stigma of my husband's suicide and claimed that I would have been denied any of my drunkard husband's life assurance if the truth about his death ever got out."

"Why did he do that?" I asked.

"So that nobody would ever ask any questions about Declan Reid's death," Lynch answered. "Cormack O'Sullivan also killed the guy who shot Tony Maguire during a Post Office robbery and, by doing so, ensured that there weren't too many questions asked about that crime either," he added. "I think that he did something similar yesterday, that he hid your brother's murder inside a robbery. Now, do you see where we're coming from, and why we asked you to respect the privacy of this conversation?"

"Yes, I do," I replied. "Does anyone else know about this?"

Anne Reid hoisted her thin shoulders. "We don't know," she said. "Most people are too afraid to speak up about anything to do with Cormack O'Sullivan. When Vincent called me last night and shared his theory about your brother's death, I felt that you needed to hear what he had to say."

"I see," I said. "So, you figured that if I heard that O'Sullivan had something to do with my brother's death, then I would go after him."

"Something like that," Anne Reid admitted. "Will you?" I sat back from the table again and sighed heavily.

"I'm sorry, but no," I said. "I still don't have any reason to believe that O'Sullivan was involved in Dave's death, or even why anyone would want Dave dead, so I'm not going to do anything yet."

Lynch shot forward. "Would you change your mind if it was proven to you that Cormack O'Sullivan was involved in your brother's death?" he asked me.

"Yes, I would," I replied.

TUESDAY — TWELVE

Maybe it was the effects of Anne Reid's strong coffee, or what I had just heard from Vincent Lynch, but, as I drove home to my apartment, I did so carefully and paid more attention to my car's rear-view mirror than usual.

When I got to the apartment's underground car park, I sat still, waited until my Audi's interior lights had dimmed to blackness and then looked around me. There was no one else in the car park and yet I exited my car swiftly and made my way across the echoing concrete floor to its lift at a fast pace.

Once I had locked the apartment's front door from the inside, I went into the TV room, switched on my laptop computer, and walked into the kitchen to prepare a ham and tomato sandwich.

An hour later, most of which I had spent thinking about what Vincent Lynch had told me, the sandwich still lay untouched on its plate as I examined, downloaded, and then printed out the last photographic image of the road that Dave would have driven home on Sunday night.

In addition to the advertising that he was exposed to as he drove home, the media list that Jimmy Nixon had supplied to me by e-mail that afternoon had also included the songs played, the topics discussed, and the news items on the radio on Sunday night.

Information that had allowed me to note, in black marker on the printouts, what Dave would have seen or heard at any specific point of his journey home.

As detailed as my analysis was, I still hadn't spotted anything that would have affected my brother's frame of mind on Sunday night, and became increasingly anxious that Vincent Lynch knew something that he hadn't shared with me.

Tired and frustrated, I sat back, shook my weary and disappointed head, and then checked the time in the bottom right-hand corner of the computer screen. I saw that it was twelve minutes to midnight and decided to take a couple of tablets to relieve the headache that had pulsed into life between my ears.

If, as Vincent Lynch had predicted, Jill Maguire and O'Sullivan had reached the same conclusion as him, that Dave had been murdered deliberately and not by accident, then the detectives might suspect that Dave had advance knowledge of the restaurant raid and could have changed my brother's status from victim to villain.

Once again, I regretted that I hadn't answered Dave's phone calls on Sunday night, and was just about to put the computer into sleep mode when the apartment's video-intercom issued three angry pulses.

When I had made my way to the video-intercom mounted on the wall next to the apartment's front door, I saw that its small screen had flickered into life and was displaying a reduced and grainy image of Detective Jill Maguire as she stepped back from the main entrance into my apartment building and looked up towards my balcony.

I pressed the intercom button. "Do you want to come in?" I asked.

Jill Maguire rushed back to the intercom. "Yes, please open the door, Mr. Doyle."

I deactivated the lock on the building's entrance, left the front door into my apartment ajar, and was in the apartment's black-and-red-tiled kitchen when I heard Jill Maguire enter my home and call out my name.

"I'm in here," I replied and then held up a finger as the detective entered my kitchen. "I'll be with you in a second," I told Jill Maguire and continued to rifle through the drawer beneath the one that I kept the cutlery in. "I've got a bad headache, and need some pain killers," I explained as she strode forward and then stopped next to my granite-topped kitchen island.

"Found them," I declared a second later and held up a red and silver packet.

I noted from Jill Maguire's stance as I crossed to retrieve a drinking glass that the detective was keen to say something, and saw that she had changed into faded denim jeans, a turquoise cable-knit sweater, and a pair of powder blue tennis shoes since I had last seen her.

The casual clothes emphasized Jill Maguire's figure and, I felt, suited her better, although the large flesh-colored bandage adhered to her forehead did worry me a bit.

"You obviously have something to say," I pried, filled a tall glass with water, and then plopped two soluble tablets into it. "What do you want this time?"

"To apologize for my behavior last night," Jill Maguire replied. "Plus, I need to know if you told anyone else that I was here last night?"

"I accept your apology, but you're going to have to tell me why you want to know if I told anyone that you were here last night," I replied

"I'm not a hundred percent sure about this yet," Jill Maguire answered. "But I think that I've been removed from the investigation into your brother's death."

"Do you think that's because I told someone that you were here last night?" I asked, peeked down into the fizzing liquid, and saw that the two pain killers had almost dissolved.

For a moment, Jill Maguire looked reluctant to answer my question. "I didn't say anything to Cormack about being here last night," she said. "But this afternoon, I took a tumble down a railway embankment," she pointed to the fresh bandage on her forehead. "And, as I was dusting myself off, Cormack took a call on his mobile phone. His attitude towards me changed after that call and he used my fall as an excuse to get rid of me and insisted that one of the uniformed guards take me to a doctor and then bring me home."

"So, you presumed that someone must have called O'Sullivan to tell him that you were here last night?" I asked. "If you don't mind me saying so, Detective Maguire, that sounds like you have leapt to a big conclusion. Maybe O'Sullivan was just following personnel protocol when he ordered you home?" I suggested and then drank the dissolved pain killers down in one continuous swallow.

Jill Maguire shook her head. "Cormack doesn't follow protocol," she told me. "And he had already warned me to stay away from you. That's why I didn't tell him that I was here last night. If he found that out..."

"He would take you off the case," I interjected. "Do you really expect me to believe that, Detective Maguire? Did you really come here tonight to accuse me of getting you taken off the case, or do you just want to find out if I told anyone that you were here last night? Maybe I should have complained that you pointed a gun at me."

Jill Maguire stared back at me as if I had a comprehension issue.

"You don't seem to understand," she said. "When I tried to get Cormack on his mobile phone after I was in the doctor's surgery, he didn't answer my calls, and he doesn't do that. Since then, I've tried him a number of other times and he hasn't taken my calls or returned any of my messages," Jill Maguire said. "Cormack believes that no response is a response, so I believe that he is giving me the silent treatment for a reason."

"Why, because he heard that you were here last night?" I asked her.

"Yes," Jill Maguire said and then tilted her head to the right and slanted her eyes. "You didn't tell Frank Hennessy that I was here last night, did you?" she queried.

The detective's use of Frank Hennessy's name threw me off guard momentarily. "I might have," I replied. "I was with Frank this morning and we discussed lots of things. One of them might have been your visit to my home last night. Why?"

Jill Maguire shook her head. "Was Frank Hennessy the person who you shared your suspicions about Cormack's involvement in my father's death with?" she questioned.

"Yes, it was," I conceded. "Why?"

"So Frank Hennessy told you to stay quiet about my father's death three years ago," Maguire said and nodded.

"I respect Frank's advice," I said in my defense.

Jill Maguire shook her head again and smiled. "You don't know much about Frank Hennessy, do you," she said. "Do you even know that he used to work with Cormack?"

"Yes, I do," I said. "But that was a long time ago, right?"

"Yes, a long time ago," Jill Maguire said and then ignored me as she looked down at the kitchen's black-tiled floor.

When the detective remained silent, I decided to move the conversation on.

"Did you check the records about your father's death?" I asked her.

"Yes, but I didn't find anything unusual there," Jill Maguire said as she looked back at me again. "Where did you hear about Callaghan being a fast runner?"

"I read about it in a newspaper interview with some of his friends," I replied.

"That could explain why there's nothing about that in the records," she said. "I also looked at the file on Declan Reid's death," she added. "There was nothing much there either. The cause of his death was listed as drowning but no one saw what happened to him. Does that sound about right to you?"

"Yes, it does," I said. "Did the records that you looked at state that he was on his way here when he drowned?"

Jill Maguire shook her head. "No, there was nothing about that," she said, relaxed, and then let her eyes wander around my kitchen. "I better go," she added. "I'm supposed to be at a case conference about your brother's death first thing tomorrow morning, but I expect that Cormack will talk to me before then and let me know that I've been taken off the case."

I followed Jill Maguire out of the kitchen into the apartment's lounge and then halted when she stalled to look out through the glass doors that led to the balcony.

"Your father liked that view too," I said, gripped the handles of the two glass doors and slid them apart. "Do you want to look outside?"

Jill Maguire lingered at the threshold to the balcony and then stepped out through the open glass doors onto the teak decking and walked across to the chrome railings at the apex of the large triangular balcony.

I followed her out into the night air and then stood in silence behind her as she looked across the gleaming Samuel Beckett Bridge at the huge illuminated glass barrel that fronted the National Convention Centre on the other side of the river.

"I can see why my father liked it here," she said. "It's some view from this balcony."

"You were close to your father, weren't you?" I asked.

"Yes, I was," Jill Maguire said and turned back to me. "He seemed really interested in the things that I was into, and was always showing me stuff and telling me about its history. He was also a real rock of support when my mother had cancer," she said and then seemed to realize she had let her personal enthusiasm get the better of her usual investigative mode. "How long have you lived here?" she then asked in a more inquisitive tone and turned back to look out at the view again.

"I bought this apartment off the plans about five years ago," I replied as a ripple of colorful reflections from the river was mirrored onto Jill Maguire's glossy black hair. "It was supposed to be an investment but then things changed and I never rented it out."

"Right," Jill Maguire said. "So, you moved in here full time back then. When was that?"

"Not long after Claire and Sarah died," I said. "Back then, I thought that moving away from the family home that we used to share would help me to get over their loss."

"And did it?" Jill Maguire asked as I registered the scent of her perfume on the warm night air.

"No," I said. "I work just across the river, so I didn't have to drive in and out of town anymore and seemed to have even more time on my hands to think about them."

"Moving in here wasn't such a good idea, was it?" Jill Maguire asked.

"No, it wasn't," I said, and then remembered that Peter didn't think that some of the other things that I had done since Claire and Sarah had died were good ideas either.

To banish those thoughts quickly, I asked Jill Maguire another question.

"Where do you live?" I asked her. "If it's acceptable for me to ask you that."

Jill Maguire smiled as she turned back to me again. "Of course, it's acceptable for you to ask me that," she replied. "I inherited my parents' house when they died. It's a typical three-bedroomed, semi-detached in Whelanton.

Until a couple of months ago, my boyfriend lived there with me. Then he moved back in with his wife and two kids. Any other questions?"

"No," I said. "And it wasn't my intention to pry into your personal life."

"That's okay," Jill Maguire said. "But please let me give you some advice."

"Go on," I said as we walked back inside the sliding glass doors.

"Your brother's murder was a terrible crime," Jill Maguire stated when we reached the apartment's front door. "But I strongly suggest that you don't meddle in this investigation."

I smiled back. "You're more like your father than you realize," I told Jill Maguire. "He gave me similar advice the last time that he was here. He warned me that my life was in danger if I stayed here and tried to convince me to run away."

"But you decided not to take his advice back then," Jill Maguire asked. "Why?"

"Because I don't run away," I replied. "And I'm not going to run away this time either. So, thanks for your advice but if I want to get involved in the investigation into my brother's death then that's my business," I said and opened the front door. "Goodnight, Detective Maguire."

"Goodnight, Mr. Doyle," Jill Maguire replied in a warmer tone than I had used with her, walked past me, left the apartment, and made her way down the corridor to the lift.

I stayed at my front door until the lift's doors had closed to bring the detective back downstairs and then entered my home again.

I wasn't sure if Jill Maguire had told the truth about still being on Dave's case but felt guilty about telling Frank Hennessy about her previous visit to my apartment.

I had been stimulated by the detective's presence in my home, and yet couldn't allow my feelings towards Jill Maguire to dilute my determination to find out if someone had been behind Dave's death, or to derail my plan of getting away from advertising and Ireland.

WEDNESDAY — ONE

Dressed in a light blue T-shirt, black shiny shorts, and white trainers, I completed thirty bicep curls with each arm in the morning sunshine on the apartment's balcony and then carried the twenty-kilo dumbbells back inside the apartment.

When I had lowered and stacked them carefully on the wooden floor inside the glass doors, I wandered into the apartment's kitchen, filled a glass tumbler with chilled water, returned to the spacious balcony and drank down most of it.

I had just deposited the tumbler on the glass-topped wicker dining table and had sat down on one of the cushioned wickerwork chairs that were arranged around it when the buzzer on the apartment's video-intercom sounded.

This time, when I looked into its screen, I saw that another woman was standing at the entrance to my apartment building.

"Hi, Killian," Kate Fallon said when I answered her call. "Can I please talk to you?"

"Of course you can," I answered, even though I was surprised by Kate's presence at my home. "When I unlock the building's front door, cross the foyer, take the lift up to the sixth floor, and I'll meet you there," I instructed her.

Kate's visit to my home puzzled me.

Apart from Peter, few of the people that I worked with in the advertising agency had ever called to my home, although they had often resorted to pointing my apartment out while making small talk with clients and prospective clients.

"That's where Killian lives," they would say and point to my home.

"Sorry about my clothes, I was just working out," I said and led the image-conscious young account director into my home.

"Don't worry about that," Kate replied in a disinterested tone that alerted me to the fact that what she had come to my home to share wasn't going to be pleasant.

"If it's okay, we'll talk out on the balcony," I suggested and then gestured for Kate to go through the sliding glass doors and walk out onto the balcony ahead of me.

Clad in a light grey, knee-length business dress, Kate stepped out onto the balcony, made her way over to the wicker table, sat down on one of the cushioned wickerwork chairs that I had motioned, and deposited her black leather satchel on the seat next to her as she responded to the coffee that I had offered her.

"No, thanks," Kate replied and then looked intently into my eyes. "Killian, I'm really sorry about this, but there's something I have to tell you."

"Go on," I said and sat down across from Kate.

The account director shook her head of short black hair.

"I'm really sorry about this," she told me. "It's about Dave and I should have said this to you before now. In fact, I thought that you'd start this conversation after you read the note that I included with your new mobile phone on Monday night."

"I'm sorry, Kate, but I didn't read the whole note that you included with my new mobile phone," I admitted. "I was tired by the time that I got home on Monday, so I started to read but never finished it. What exactly did you say in it?" I asked her.

"I said that there was something that you needed to hear about Dave," Kate replied.

"Which is?" I asked.

"That he was having an affair and was going to leave Louise," Kate said. "That's what I think was on his mind on Sunday night."

"How do you know about this?" I probed.

"Because I was the one who Dave was having his affair with," Kate said.

I sat in silence for a moment, shook my head, and then asked Kate another question. "How long were you two…seeing each other?"

"For more than a year," Kate replied and swallowed as her eyes misted up. "That's why I gave him an ultimatum last weekend, and why Dave promised to speak to Louise and move in with me."

"Jesus," I said. "Who else knows about this?"

"A few people," Kate said. "Liz in the office might have overheard a thing or two, and I told my sister about Dave," she added. "But I'm pretty sure that she has never said anything to anyone."

"And there's no one else who knows about this?" I asked Kate who shook her head.

"No, why?" she asked me.

I looked out across the balcony towards the prominent stone building that housed the advertising agency on the other side of the river as I thought about the implications of what Kate had just told me.

"Why didn't you tell me about this before?" I asked and turned back.

"I tried to," Kate replied. "I was going to say something to you in Dave's house on Monday until I saw how upset Louise was," Kate added as her voice broke. "That's why I left Dave's House in such a hurry, and then wrote that note to you. That was also why I so was taken aback when you asked me yesterday if I had any idea why Dave was in such strange mood on Sunday night. I knew then that you hadn't read my note."

"Once again, I'm sorry for not reading all of your note," I said and noticed the bags under Kate's eyes. "Did Dave promise that he was going to tell Louise about leaving her when he got home on Sunday night?"

Kate shook her head. "Not exactly," she replied. "But Dave and Louise were at my birthday party on Saturday night, and he whispered soon to me as they were leaving. I assumed that's what was going through Dave's head on Sunday night."

"Maybe your affair was on Dave's mind on Sunday night," I said. "But he didn't say anything to Louise about it and you know that now, don't you?"

"Yes, I do," Kate admitted and bit down on her bottom lip before continuing. "But that was why I got so anxious when you said that you were going out to The O'Malley Centre on Monday morning to talk to Dave. Because I thought that he was going to tell you what was going on, and I didn't know how you'd react to that."

"And yet yesterday, you didn't tell me what was really going on between Dave and you when I asked you directly," I stated and shook my head.

"I'm sorry about that," Kate said as tears began to leave her eyes. "But you have to realize that I had just lost Dave too, and wasn't thinking clearly."

"When Dave phoned me on Sunday night, I didn't take his call," I said. "Did he call you on Sunday night too?"

"No," Kate said. "And Dave didn't answer any of my calls to him that night or on Monday morning either. That was why I had no way of knowing if he had talked to Louise about us when you left to talk to him."

I looked across the river again, thought about the news of Dave's affair and how it would change how his loved ones, the cops, and the media, would talk about him.

I turned back to Kate. "Why did you decide to wait until this morning to tell me about your affair with Dave?" I asked her.

"I'm not sure," Kate replied. "Maybe it was because I remembered this morning how much Dave always looked up to you and how he had told me to talk to you if anything ever happened to him," Kate stated. "Dave once told me that his big brother, Killian, would know what to do if he wasn't around. I suppose, that's why I'm here now."

I reached across the table and took hold of Kate's hands.

"There's nothing that we can do about the past," I told the tearful young woman, and gently turned her hands over. "Dave is gone, and there's nothing that we can ever do to bring him back," I said. "All we have to treasure now is our memories of him. That's why there's one thing that you should never do now, or at any time into the future."

"Which is?" Kate quizzed.

"Don't ever tell anyone else what you've just told me," I said. "Dave wouldn't have wanted that to ever happen, and Louise and Philip will be really hurt if they ever find out about it. So please just keep your affair with Dave a secret."

"I promise that I'll never say a word about my affair with him to any-one." Kate replied.

"Thanks," I said, let go of Kate's hands and sat back. "Now, do you need to take some time off from work?" I asked her

"Yes, but I can't," Kate replied. "The Jasper's Telethon is on tomorrow night and Frank is real jumpy about it, so he'd go mad if I wasn't around."

"Of course he would," I said. "But once the telethon is out of the way, we'll see what we can do," I said, stood up and pointed inside my apart-ment. "There's a bathroom across the lounge," I told Kate. "You need to freshen up in there before you go into work. I'll be in the advertising agency later, so we can talk about this again then, okay? In the meantime, please remember that you're never to breathe a word about your affair with Dave to anyone else, okay?"

"Don't worry, I won't, and thanks, Killian," Kate said and stood up too.

Five minutes later, Kate looked composed when she exited the bathroom and thanked me for my advice again.

When Kate had left my apartment for the advertising agency, I went back out onto the sunlit balcony, sat down at the wicker table again, angled my unshaven face up to the strong sunshine, and then closed my eyes as I thought about what she had told me.

I was convinced that what Kate had said about her affair with Dave wasn't the reason why my brother had been killed, and yet I saw that her admission had the ability to send the investigation in a totally new direction.

I didn't want that to happen, so opened my eyes again, leant forward to pick up my mobile phone and made a call.

WEDNESDAY — TWO

My call rang six times, and I was about to hang up, when Ted O'Shea answered. "Hi, Killian," he said. "Can you hold on for a moment, I'm at a meeting."

"No problem," I replied, relieved to hear that Ted's voice harbored none of his anger from our previous phone call.

"If you can believe it, we were just having a meeting here to agree the timetable for next term," he told me as his footsteps echoed along a marble-floored corridor. "It never fails to surprise me how time passes faster as one gets older," he said. "Anyway, what can I do for you? I presume this is about Dave?" he asked in a lower, more personal tone as the echo ceased and he entered a room that I surmised was his office.

"Yes, it is," I replied. "I just heard something that changes everything."

"Heard what?" Ted asked.

"That Dave was having an affair and was about to leave Louise when he was killed," I stated.

"Shit," Ted said. "Do you know that for certain?"

"Yes, I just talked to the woman who Dave was having the affair with," I said. "She told me all about it. I know her well and she wouldn't lie to me about something like this."

"Shit," my mentor repeated. "What happens now?"

"I promised to keep her out of it," I said. "But I'm going to have to tell the cops about this. Louise too. She'll be devastated, as will Philip. I'm also going to have to tell Frank. A JimiJix screwing around goes against Jasper's family values and Dave's affair will be all over the media."

"Fuck him and Jasper's family values," Ted replied. "It's Louise and Philip that you should be worried about. Are you sure you have to tell them, or anyone else, about this?"

"Yes, I have to tell people about this," I retorted. "This explains why Dave was in such a weird mood on Sunday night. If I keep quiet about his affair then I could be accused of withholding vital evidence."

Ted paused and then spoke slowly. "Please listen closely, Killian. If you tell the cops about Dave's affair they will go after Louise as their prime suspect and will charge you for keeping evidence from them unless you give them the name of the woman that Dave had the affair with. Also, everyone will have a completely different opinion of your brother Dave when they hear that he was fucking around. If you tell people about Dave's affair, the media will paint him as a love cheat, and there will be some people who feel that he deserved to die. Do you want that?"

"No, of course I don't want that," I answered. "Why, what do you think I should do about this news?"

There was another pause before Ted spoke again. "Nothing," he said. "Unless you think that this affair was the reason why Dave was killed then you should pretend that you never heard anything about it. And you don't think that this was the reason why Dave was killed. Do you?" he asked me.

"No, I don't," I said. "There's no jilted husband or lover on the woman's side, and I'm pretty sure that Louise knew nothing about what was going on. Even if she did, she's not the type who would do anything to Dave. Plus, there's something else."

"Something else?" Ted asked me.

"Yes, one of Dave's traits that drove me mad when we were kids was that he would always think things through," I said. "He retained that habit when we grew up and never made a quick decision. Even if you asked him what drink he wanted, Dave would take forever analyzing his choice. That's why, if Dave had to decide which woman to choose, his wife or the woman that he was having the affair with, then he would have considered that if he left Louise that his job would be over, that he wouldn't get to see much of his son, Philip, that he would be dumping me in the shit with Jasper's, and that the woman who he was having the affair with would probably lose her job too. That's why I feel that Dave wouldn't have chosen the woman that he was having the affair with. Like lots of other guys, he would probably just have strung her along until their affair ended. That way, Dave would never have to make a big decision. Anyway, my brother would never have done anything that would harm me without talking to me first, and he wouldn't have done that over the phone. It was always face-to-face with Dave, especially when it came to his personal decisions and their consequences."

"I see, so you don't think that he was going to tell Louise about his affair, and don't believe that's what got Dave killed," Ted said, and then paused again before asking me another question. "Who knows about Dave's affair?"

"Five people," I replied. "The woman that he had the affair with, her sister, another woman who might have heard something, me, and now you. Why?"

Ted hesitated before answering me. "Because if you don't believe that his affair got Dave killed, and you can keep a lid on it, then I feel that you should try to do that," he said. "At least until you've talked this through with Greg."

"Talked this through with Greg?" I repeated.

"Yes, he's your solicitor," Ted replied. "So, he'll know what to do. I presume that you've been talking to him since Monday?"

"No, I haven't," I replied. "Greg has tried to get hold of me a few times, but I haven't had the time to get back to him yet."

"Then you need to talk to him right now," Ted said.

Greg Moore was a close friend and had been my solicitor since he had qualified from law school. Before that, we had grown up in the same neighborhood, had played soccer and tennis together, went to the same secondary school, and both began dating girls at the same time. We had remained friends into adulthood, and Greg was my best man when I had married Claire. Three months later, I returned the favor when he wed, Nikki.

"You need to hear what Greg has to say before you say anything about Dave's affair," Ted said. "He might have a completely different view to mine."

"Okay, I'll meet him," I promised Ted. "Will I call you afterwards?"

"Yes, or I'll call you," Ted threatened.

I ended the call, checked the time on my mobile phone, and then rang Greg's office. My call was answered by Anne-Marie, his officious-sounding receptionist, who told me that Greg was out at the courts.

When she had agreed to get him to call me back, Anne-Marie offered me her commiserations about Dave and said that she was sorry for my loss. When I had hung up the phone, I went back inside the apartment and got showered and dressed.

WEDNESDAY — THREE

Twenty minutes later, I was about to leave the apartment when my new mobile phone rang. The caller was Betty.

"Hi, Killian, how are you today?" she asked me in a tone that was approaching normality.

"I'm fine, Betty, and you?" I replied, took my hand away from the lock on the front door of the apartment and turned back into its lounge.

"The same," she said. "That fat cop girl just called. The detectives are coming back here again at ten this morning and she wanted to know if you'd be around."

"That fat cop girl is called Frances," I reminded Betty. "She's our family liaison officer, so you need to be nice to her as she's our main link with the police. Did Frances say which detectives would be calling to the house?"

"Yes, she did," Betty answered. "The same two who were here yesterday. That chinky young one and the culchie guy. Why?"

"No reason." I said and shook my head. Jill Maguire had lied to me. O'Sullivan hadn't taken her off the case and she would be at the family briefing in Dave's house later that morning.

"Will you be here by ten?" Betty enquired.

"No, you'll have to count me out," I said. "I need to call into the advertising agency to catch up on some stuff," I said. "I'll be there as soon as I can, but won't make it to Dave's House by ten," I told Betty. "I'm sorry."

As soon as my call with Betty ended, I scrolled down through the list of contacts on my new mobile phone.

"I need to talk to Lynch now," I said when Anne Reid answered me.

"I'll see if he's around," she replied calmly. "I'll have to call you back."

Seven minutes later, Anne Reid rang me back. "Vincent will meet you in O'Keefe Square at twenty-minutes passed ten," she told me. "He'll be on a bench on the south side of the park. If he's with anyone, don't go near him. Plus, he stressed that you're not to bring your mobile phone with you."

I kept myself busy by going online and unearthing more information about O'Sullivan and Jill Maguire. Then, when it was time for me to leave, deposited my new mobile phone on the kitchen island and headed to the rendezvous with Lynch.

Despite the strong sunshine, the retired detective was dressed in the same brown leather jacket and dark green trousers that he had worn at Anne Reid's house the previous night. He sat alone on a park bench and held a lead attached to a small dog's collar. The dog looked up and yelped at me when I neared where Lynch was sitting.

"What's with the dog?" I asked the retired detective.

"He's the reason why you just stopped to talk to me," Lynch replied as he looked down at the dog and then scratched its furry neck.

"I see," I said and then stooped down to pet the brown Border Terrier, which barked at me and then shied away beneath its owner's legs.

"You never had a dog, did you?" Lynch commented.

I shook my head. "No, my dad claimed that he was allergic to dogs. The truth was that a dog would mess the place and he knew that my brother and I wouldn't clean it up."

Lynch nodded. "My Dad wouldn't let my sister and me get a dog either," he said. "He used to say that there were enough dumb animals in the house already."

I straightened up. "I have two questions for you," I told Lynch. "Firstly, I need to know why you agreed to meet me last night? Is this about money?"

"No, I don't need any of your money," Lynch replied. "It was Anne Reid's idea that we got together last night, not mine. As you saw, she's the one who really wants to get O'Sullivan. Now, what's your other question?"

"Why all the secrecy?" I asked. "For instance, what's with not bringing my mobile phone here? Who are you afraid of?"

Lynch leant forward, reached down, and tickled his dog behind its ears. "Mobile phones are easy to trace," he told me without looking up. "So, if someone followed you by scanning your phone, they might see me here," he explained. "And I don't ever want to be seen with someone like you."

"Why don't you want to be seen with someone like me?" I enquired.

"Because whoever killed your brother is still out there," Lynch replied without making eye contact with me. "Because Cormack O'Sullivan is involved, and because you work in advertising."

I nodded and then looked around the park to make sure there was no one watching us. Apart from three elderly men who were sitting on another bench, and a couple of East European women in T-shirts and track suit bottoms who lay on the grass next to baby buggies, there was no one else present in the small south city park.

"You don't like me, do you, Lynch?" I asked when I turned back to him.

Lynch made a clicking sound to the dog before answering my question.

"It's not that I don't like you," he said. "It's that I don't trust you. That's why I was reluctant to meet you in Anne Reid's house last night, and why I didn't want to meet you here today either."

"Why don't you trust me?" I enquired.

Lynch sat back and rattled off his answer. "Because you were married to Frank Hennessy's daughter. Because Declan Reid was working for you when he got killed. Because Tony Maguire told me that he suspected that you were involved in your wife's murder. And because you gave Anne Reid a big chunk of money but are so stupid that you don't think that anyone else knows about that." He raised his left index finger to silence me when I was about to interrupt him. "And then there's your job," he added. "You work in advertising, so you're a professional liar."

"A professional liar," I repeated and sat down next to Lynch on the park bench. "I haven't heard that one for a while," I said. "If you don't trust me then why did you promise to get proof that O'Sullivan was involved in my brother's murder?"

"Because that's what Anne Reid told me to tell you," Lynch replied. "And I want to help her. Now, what do you need to know so urgently that you got me here?" He asked.

I stooped forward and smiled down at his dog as I spoke. "When I got home last night, Jill Maguire called to my apartment. She tried to trick me into believing that she was no longer on Dave's case but I've since found out that isn't true," I told Lynch. "What's the story with her and O'Sullivan?"

"The story?" Lynch repeated. "The story is that Maguire's dad and Cormack O'Sullivan were close," he said. "Jill Maguire was already a cop by the time that her father was killed and Cormack O'Sullivan took care of her. He had her fast-tracked into the detective division and then made her his new partner."

"So, they're an item," I said.

"Something like that," Lynch said, tickled his dog behind its ears some more, and then continued. "There's also other stuff between Cormack O'Sullivan and Jill Maguire too," he added. "Tony Maguire, who was Jill Maguire's dad, lived close to Cormack O'Sullivan, who has two daughters. They were Jill's closest friends when she was growing up, so she was always in O'Sullivan's house."

"They have this father and daughter thing going on," I concluded.

"Yes. Why, did you think there was something else going on between them?" Lynch asked. "Is that why I'm here, because you fancy Jill Maguire and were concerned that Cormack O'Sullivan might be banging her?"

"No, that's not it at all," I replied. "I sensed that Jill Maguire can't be trusted and wanted to know more about her, that's why I asked you to meet me here."

"You sensed that Jill Maguire can't be trusted," Lynch snorted and shook his head. "Why the fuck would anyone trust the likes of her? Cormack O'Sullivan probably got her to call to your home last night because he knows that a sap like you can't resist a nice bit of ass and would tell her anything."

Stung by Lynch's words, my cheeks reddened as I sat back and thought of something else to ask him. "What do you know about Frank Hennessy?"

Lynch made some clicking noises at the dog and then answered me. "Considering that you're Hennessy's son-in-law, I'm surprised that you have to ask me that question," he said. "Then again, we don't always know much about our in-laws, do we?" he said. "Before Frank Hennessy was employed by Jasper's, he was a cop and used to head up the detective unit. He was my boss, Tony Maguire's boss, Declan Reid's boss, and Cormack O'Sullivan's boss too."

"Right," I said. "And did Frank Hennessy treat O'Sullivan any differently from the rest of the detectives under his command?"

"Yes, in all sorts of ways," Lynch replied.

"Which were?" I queried.

Lynch sat back. "Hennessy always acted like he was Cormack O'Sullivan's big brother," he replied. "He let him get away with things that he didn't with the rest of us, and taught him everything that he knew. They soon became good friends and still have a special bond today."

"They're still friends?" I asked.

"Yes," Lynch replied. "Frank and Cormack play golf together and meet up for drinks too," he said as his dog spun around and strained at its leash to reach a small bird that had landed on the grass in front of the bench that we were sitting on. "Did you not know about that?"

I looked into the distance. "I knew that Frank and O'Sullivan used to work together," I said and shrugged. "But not that they were still friends and met up." I added.

"Yeah, well they're still pals," Lynch said and stood up. "Was there anything else?" he asked and looked down at his dog. "I need to get going."

"Yes, there was actually," I said. "Is there a number where I can contact you?"

Lynch was about to answer my question when a loud clatter sounded from the other side of the square as the contents of a wheelbarrow were dumped into a metal skip. The noise upset the retired detective more than it should have, and a moment passed before he appeared to be fully in control of his senses again.

"Sorry," he said and turned back to me. "What did you just ask?"

"For a phone number where I can contact you directly," I replied.

Lynch took a step away from me. "I don't think that would be a good idea," the retired detective said. "We wouldn't be here now if I hadn't phoned

Anne Reid and given her my interpretation of that story on the TV News the other night. She's been leading things ever since, so, if you've more questions, then I suggest that you get in touch with her," he said. "It would be better if we kept things that way, if you know what I mean."

"No, I don't know what you mean," I said and pulled my head back.

Lynch tugged gently on the dog's leash and then turned back to me. "Anne is still upset about losing her husband, Declan, she thinks that O'Sullivan had him killed and that you're going to get vengeance for his death," he told me. "That's why she got us together last night. She believed that you'd go after O'Sullivan if I told you my theory about your brother's death. Unlike me, she trusts you, and thinks that you're going to get O'Sullivan for her. If that's not the case, then you need to let her down softly, the last thing that Anne needs right now is for someone like you to disappoint her."

"Someone like me?" I replied. "I'm sorry, Lynch, but you seem to underestimate me. I'm going to get to the bottom of this, whether that involves O'Sullivan or not," I said. "My brother was killed in front of me on Monday, and I'm going to make sure that whoever did that gets brought to justice."

Lynch appeared unmoved by my declaration. "Yeah, well the best of luck with that," he said. "But from where I'm standing, I think that it would be better if you just let things go. When you get to my age, you'll realize that there are times when we just have to accept things and move on," he said and then nodded in agreement with his own words. "That's what you should do here. You should be grieving for your brother right now, not running around the place meeting people like me."

"So that's it, is it, Lynch," I said in a voice that was obviously louder than Lynch expected. "According to you, I should just grieve for my brother, stay quiet, don't ask any questions, and let people like Jill Maguire and O'Sullivan look after everything?"

Vincent Lynch looked like he wanted to be somewhere else. "Yes, I'm sorry, Doyle, but that's how I see things," he said and then glanced down at his dog again.

I got both louder and angrier. "Then I'm sorry for you, Lynch, because your crap advice sounds exactly like the shit that I got three years ago when my wife and daughter were murdered," I yelled and pointed a finger at his chest. "Back then, I didn't do anything about what I suspected and just kept my head down because that's what someone like you told me to do. This time, things are going to be different," I shouted. "This time, I will find out who killed my brother and sort them out myself if I have to."

When I had finished talking, Lynch stared back at me in silence for a few seconds and then spoke again. "If that's the case, then I'm even more sorry for you, Mr. Doyle," he said. "Because you need to wise up. Right now, you're just a fucking amateur who is going to get into a whole world of hurt if you continue on with this nonsense," he stated and then turned away and walked off with his dog across the park towards the nearest gate.

I watched Lynch's departure as I thought about his nasty assessment of me, brought my breathing back under control, and then made my way out of the park in the opposite direction.

I had probably learnt more from Vincent Lynch than he realized.

Wednesday — Four

On my way to the advertising agency, I stopped off at my apartment to pick up my mobile phone. Shaded its display from the bright sunlight as I walked across one of the bridges over the Liffey and saw that I had received two missed phone calls from Betty.

"Hi, Betty, what's up?" I asked her when she answered my call.

"Hi, Killian," she replied. "When are you going to get here?"

"I'll be there in about an hour," I replied and stopped walking. "Why?"

"Because we need to talk about what the detectives said to me this morning," Betty replied. "Their investigation into Dave's death seems to have changed."

"In what way?" I asked Betty and made my way to the side of the bridge.

"Hold on a minute," Betty instructed me and then went silent for a few seconds. "Sorry, I was with Louise there, and didn't want her to get upset if she heard what I'm about to say to you," she said.

"Upset? Why would Louise get upset?" I queried.

"Because the cops are now saying that Dave was murdered deliberately," Betty replied. "According to that culchie detective, O'Sullivan, their investigation has moved on, and they now think that the guy who shot Dave wasn't working alone."

"What!" I said and looked down into the river.

"He told me that the cops now know that the killer abandoned all the stuff that he took in the restaurant in his getaway car, made his way into town, and was picked up in a fake taxi," Betty said. "So, the robbery that Dave was murdered in might have been just a pretend job and Dave mightn't have been just an innocent victim."

"What?" I exclaimed again as I thought back on what Vincent Lynch had said. He had described Dave's murder as a crime within a crime. "Did the detectives say why anyone would want to kill Dave like that?"

Betty took a deep breath. "Not really," she said. "According to O'Sullivan, you know why Dave was killed but haven't told them the truth yet. He said that they'll never catch the scumbag who killed Dave unless you're honest with them."

"Honest!" I shouted. "The truth is that I don't have a fucking clue why Dave was killed. Did O'Sullivan tell Louise that I know who killed Dave too?"

"No," Betty replied. "That other detective, the chink woman, was with Louise while O'Sullivan was with me," she said. "Afterwards, Louise told me that she asked her some strange questions about Dave," she added.

"Some strange questions about Dave?" I repeated and placed my left hand on the bridge's warm metal railings to steady myself.

"Yes," Betty said. "Louise told me that the detective asked her lots of questions about Dave and his money. She wanted to know if Louise knew how much money Dave earned, and if Louise was aware of what he spent it on. That sort of stuff."

"Did she tell Louise why she wanted to know about that?" I asked.

"No," Betty said. "But there must be a reason for those questions."

Based on Jill Maguire's questions to Louise, and what O'Sullivan had said about me, I was convinced that the cops knew about Dave's affair, ended the call to Betty with a promise to be at the house soon, put away my mobile phone, and jogged the rest of the way across the bridge towards the advertising agency.

WEDNESDAY — FIVE

O'Sullivan's claim to Betty about me withholding evidence, must have meant that the cops had become aware of Dave and Kate's affair and thought that I knew all about it but had kept that information from them.

Maybe the cops hadn't worked out who Dave had his affair with yet.

That would explain why Jill Maguire had asked Louise about the money that Dave earned and where he spent it. Maybe she was trying to find out if Louise knew that her husband was spending his money on another woman. Her questions indicated that there was still time, if I hurried, to stop the cops from finding out that Dave had his affair with Kate.

I ran left at the end of the bridge, dodged right, and then saw that the entrance to the advertising agency was in front of me.

Once a quayside warehouse where wines and spirits were stored until the duties were paid by the people importing them, the landmark granite building had housed the advertising agency for the past four years.

Back when Peter and I bought it, the girth and solidity of the old building's walls made the new premises for our advertising agency expensive to rewire, while the installation of air conditioning and additional lighting in its layered interior was a major investment.

All those costs were soon recovered after we moved in and our business expanded rapidly to make us one of the top three advertising agencies in Ireland.

I stopped running inside the building and then made out the sad expression on Eva's face as she stood up behind the reception desk.

"Hi, Killian," she said. "I'm so sorry for your loss."

"Thanks Eva," I replied and crossed the ground floor to the black metallic staircase that led up to my office on the mezzanine level.

Monitored closely as I walked across the agency's open-plan interior, I responded with a polite nod and a closed-mouth smile to the many messages of sympathy directed at me, and then saw that my personal assistant, Linda, had left her desk in the office next door to mine.

"Hi Killian," Linda said as she closed my office door. "I didn't expect you to come back here so soon. Obviously, I was devastated by the news about Dave."

"Thanks, Linda," I told her. "And thanks for that too," I added and pointed to the neat pile of paperwork stacked on my desk. "I'm only going to be here for a short while today, so I'll go through it all another time, okay," I said.

"That's fine," Linda agreed but didn't retreat from my office. "Killian, I'm not sure about how to broach this subject," she said and swayed slightly. "But lots of people have been asking me about Dave's funeral. What do you want me to tell them?"

"Tell them that the cops have asked us for more time to complete their forensic tests, so we haven't been told when Dave's body will be released yet," I said and stepped behind my desk. "Please tell them that you'll confirm the funeral details as soon as they've been finalized."

"Thanks," Linda replied and edged out of my office.

When she was gone, I reached for the telephone on my desk, called Kate's internal number and asked her to join me in my office immediately. Seconds later, Kate rushed into my office, closed the door behind her, and took a seat on the opposite side of my desk.

"What is it?" She asked.

"I think that the cops know that Dave was having an affair," I told her. "Do you have any idea how they might have found that out?"

"No," Kate replied as her face contorted into misery. "But I knew that this would happen. Do you want me to call the cops?"

"Not yet," I replied. "I don't think that the cops know who Dave had his affair with yet or they would have questioned you by now. Could they have found out about his affair from his mobile phone records, or from his credit card?"

Kate shook her head. "I don't think so," she said. "We were really careful about those things. Other than our normal work calls, we used call boxes, paid for things in cash, and didn't go to the same places more than once. That way, there was no mobile phone records, no credit card receipts, and no one who would recognize us as frequent visitors."

"Do you have any idea who might have tipped the cops off?" I asked.

"No," Kate said. "Would Louise have said anything?"

"I don't think so," I said. "Louise asked me if Dave was having an affair yesterday, but I'm pretty sure she didn't say anything to the cops. I'm going to talk to Liz now and make sure that she hasn't said anything either, and try to get her not to say anything in the future," I told Kate. "In the meantime, please stay quiet and keep your head down, even if the cops do know about Dave's affair, you can be assured that I'm not going to give them your name."

"Thanks, Killian," Kate said as she got up from the chair.

WEDNESDAY — SIX

I waited until Kate closed my office door behind her and then picked up the receiver from my desk telephone and called Liz O'Mahony.

Twenty-two years old with long blond hair, a figure that turned a lot of men's heads, and an attitude that reflected the sentiments of a generation that claimed to have watched its parents mess up their world, Liz strolled into my office, sat down on the other side of my desk before I had invited her to do so, and told me how sorry she had been to hear about Dave's death.

"Thanks, Liz," I said. "And thanks for coming here so quickly."

"No problem, how can I help you?" the young account manager asked as she fanned her long blond hair out over the shoulders of her white woolen sweater.

I glanced towards the glass door for a moment, and then leant across the desk. "I'm sorry, Liz, I know that this is going to sound odd," I told her. "But the cops keep asking me about Dave's private life. They seem to think he was having an affair, but I keep telling them that they're wrong about that. What do you think?"

Liz considered my question for a moment before responding to me.

"I think that they're wrong about that too," she replied. "Dave was a happily married man with a young son and I'll tell the cops that if they ask me about him."

"Thank you, Liz, that's how I'd like my brother to be remembered," I said. "If you know what I mean."

"I know exactly what you mean," Liz said, winked across at me, and then stood up on her high-heeled feet and brushed down the front of her skirt with both hands as if a cat had just been sitting on her lap.

I made another internal call when Liz had left my office. Hired two years earlier, when his female predecessor had gotten married and moved to Canada, Rory Shields was in his early forties, had slicked-back brown hair, a well-trimmed goatee, and headed up our production department.

The only man in the advertising agency who wore a suit, shirt, and tie to work every day, Rory was also one of the few people that I worked with who I completely trusted. This time, I wanted Rory to acquire a copy of the full newspaper article that Jill Maguire had produced a cutting from on Monday night. If Jill's father, Tony Maguire, had been reading that page as he listened to my message, I wanted to see what else he could have read about Frank as he wrote down notes over his former boss's face.

Rory arrived into my office less than a minute later, closed the glass door behind him, and then carefully lowered his slim frame into a seat on the other side of my desk so as not to spill any of the water from the glass he was carrying in his right hand. Once seated, he offered me his sympathy about my brother's death.

I thanked Rory for his commiserations, warned him that what I was about to ask him to do might sound a bit odd, and then instructed him to obtain a copy of a Sunday Globe article from three years earlier.

"That article was about a man called Frank Hennessy from Jasper's," I said. "If you get a copy of it, I want you to have it delivered to my apartment."

Rory nodded his acceptance of my request. "By when?" he asked me.

"By tonight," I replied.

"Anything else?" Rory asked.

"No, that's it," I told Rory and then jolted when I saw that Peter had arrived outside of my office door, looked really angry, and was about to enter the room.

"I heard that you were in here," Peter shouted and barged into my office just as Rory rose from his seat to leave it. "I presume that you got all my calls, texts, and emails over the last few days?" he then enquired loudly as he ignored our production director and pulled back the chair that Rory had just vacated.

"Yes, I did, Peter, and I swear that I'm not ignoring you. I've just been really busy," I replied as my partner sat down heavily across my desk. "I was going to call you later and arrange for us to meet up."

Peter pulled a surprised face. "Really?" he asked. "You were too busy to talk to me but had enough time to come in here and meet with Kate, Liz, and Rory?"

I stared back at my business partner for a moment and then pushed my chair back, got to my feet, took a quick look down the corridor, made sure that the door into my office was closed tight, and then sat down at my desk again.

"I'm sorry, Peter," I said when I had done all that. "I'm not going to tell you why I had to speak to them today, but there were urgent reasons why I needed to talk to Kate, Liz, and Rory. Believe me, Peter, I really wanted to talk to you, particularly after what we discussed on Monday, but I just didn't have the time to do that. Things have been crazy since Dave was killed, and I only plan on being here for a few more minutes, so can I please call you later to set something up between us?"

Peter exhaled. "I'm sorry too," he said. "I understand that things must be crap for you at the moment. But over the past few days, things have been fairly shitty for me too, and some stuff that I need your advice on has come up. That's probably why I was so annoyed with you for not returning my messages or getting in touch. It was like you had suddenly disappeared, or something."

"You know that I wouldn't do that," I said and looked up at the railway clock. "I would never just disappear. What do you need my advice on?"

"Nothing much," Peter said. "The biggest thing is that an issue has come up on the Kelly account again," he said. "They've rejected our latest campaign proposals and have given us just four days to come up with some new stuff."

"To the same brief?" I asked.

Peter nodded. "Yes," he confirmed. "Kelly's still want us to tell their consumers how they make their products."

"Then we should fire them," I answered.

"Fire them?" Peter queried and narrowed his eyes.

"Yes," I said. "If the clients at Kelly don't understand that consumers want to know what their products will do for them, how they'll make them feel, and not how they're made, then they don't understand anything. So, if we don't get rid of them soon, then they'll call a pitch and get someone else to do the kind of advertising that they think will increase their sales. Do you want me to call them and get rid of them, or will you do that?"

"Are you sure about this?" Peter asked. "It will put a big hole in our finances."

"A hole that we will fill quickly," I said. "Now, do you want me to call them?"

"No, I'll do it as there are some people in here that I need to talk to first," Peter replied and then examined me as if trying to determine if I was sober.

"Anything else that's pressing?" I asked him.

"Yes," Peter said. "We can discuss this in more detail later, but despite what I said on Monday, I've decided not to leave here. I'm going to stay and want to apologize to you for what I said on Monday."

Now it was my turn to look surprised. "I really appreciate that you had the courage to say those things to me on Monday," I said. "I've thought about everything that you said and have decided that I need to change."

"Change?" Peter said. "In what way?"

"After what you said, I decided to leave here and take some time out," I said. "You told me that you wanted to leave the advertising agency to get away from me. Now you can do that without having to leave here."

"What!" Peter shut his eyes and shook his head, as if trying to dispel what he had just heard. "You're leaving here?"

"Yes, I am," I replied. "We can talk about this in more detail. But what you said to me on Monday got me thinking. You were right, I've changed. So, when Dave's funeral is out of the way, I'm going to leave here, get out of advertising, and head off to someplace else."

An obviously shocked Peter was about to say something when Linda appeared outside my office and knocked on its glass door.

"I'm really sorry about this, Killian," she said and donned a tortured expression as I beckoned her inside the room. "But there's a woman on the phone. She says that she's a neighbor of yours and insists on talking to you urgently."

"Thanks, Linda, please put her through," I replied and pointed down at my desk telephone as an obviously shocked Peter sat back in his chair, shook his head again, and waited for my phone conversation to end.

"Is that Mr. Doyle?" a haughty female enquired seconds later.

"Yes, this is Killian Doyle," I replied. "Who am I talking to?"

"Your neighbor, Ruth Collins-Forrest," the woman said. "I thought that there was something that you should know about your apartment."

Stunned that the buxom middle-aged woman in the flouncing floral dresses who lived in the apartment beneath mine had phoned me at work, I sat forward.

"Yes, Ruth," I said. "What is it?"

"There are a lot of Gardai in your apartment right now," my neighbor replied. "When I asked him, a plain-clothes policeman informed me that they are conducting a search of your home and told me not to worry about any of the noises that they make."

"Thank you, Ruth." I said, slammed down the phone and sprang to my feet.

"I'm sorry Peter, but I'm going to have to dash," I explained to my startled business partner as I ran out of my office.

WEDNESDAY — SEVEN

I ran back to the apartment but was forced to halt when I reached the front door into my home and found that my route was blocked by a muscular male detective in a grey T-shirt and wraparound sunglasses.

"Can I help you?" he asked when I stumbled to a stop in front of him.

"Yes, this is where I live," I replied. "Who's in charge here?"

"That would be Detective Maguire," he said and pointed towards the TV room.

Jill Maguire was wearing a navy windbreaker with the word Garda emblazoned across the back of it in large yellow letters, and wasn't fazed by my arrival as I stormed into the TV room and yelled at her, despite the presence there of two of her colleagues.

"Why are you doing this?" I demanded. "And why wasn't I notified?"

"I'm sorry, Mr. Doyle, but we don't have to provide advance notice of a search," Jill Maguire said as she extracted a folded document from a pocket inside the windbreaker. "This is your copy of the warrant giving us the authority to search your home and seize your property. As you'll see, it's connected to your brother's murder and has been signed by a judge," she said. "You're welcome to watch us conduct our search, or, if you'd prefer, wait somewhere close-by until we have completed it. But please don't interfere with us, or try to prevent us from confiscating anything. We have the power of arrest if you do that."

I snatched the document that the officious-sounding Jill Maguire prof-fered, spun around, and walked out onto the balcony, where I used my mobile phone to call Greg Moore's office again.

"Hi, Killian," Anne-Marie answered me. "Did Greg get back to you?"

"No, he didn't," I replied. "And now I need him urgently."

"Sorry, Killian, but he's still not back from the courts," Greg's receptionist told me. "He knows that you're looking for him. How about Shane, would he be able to help you?"

"Yes," I said. "Please put him through."

Greg's assistant listened to what I had to say and then cleared his throat with a light cough.

"I'm sorry, Killian, but if the Guards have a court-approved search war-rant then there's not much that anyone can do," Shane advised me. "Just make sure that you keep your copy of the search warrant and get a list of anything that they take from your home. Also make sure that you jot down the details of anything that you feel that the police have damaged," he added. "I'll get Greg to call you as soon as he's back here."

"Thanks, Shane," I said, hung up, and then took a deep breath before calling Betty again.

"I'm sorry, Betty, but I'm not going to be able to get there anytime soon," I told her. "Please don't tell Louise this, but I'm back at my apart-ment because it's being searched by the cops who are being headed up by that detective woman, Jill Maguire."

"Did she tell say why they're doing that?" Betty asked me.

"No, and, apparently, she doesn't have to. All Jill Maguire said was that it has something to do with Dave's murder," I told her. "She gave me some standard bullshit, but it now looks like I've become an official suspect in Dave's murder."

"That's ridiculous," Betty said. "Have you spoken to your solicitor?"

"Yes, but, apparently, there's not much that I can do," I said. "I'll call again later when I know more."

When I had hung up my call to Betty, I heaved one of the balcony's wicker chairs around so that I could sit and face the sliding doors into my apartment.

For the next ten minutes, I watched Jill Maguire and three other detectives carry various bagged items out of my home. Then the attractive Chinese-Irish Detective sauntered out onto the balcony, looked around her as if she had never been there before, and advised me that the search of my home had concluded.

"This is a list of all the items we have removed from your apartment," Jill Maguire told me as she gave me a form. "You have the right to check everything before we leave here."

I looked down at the list and saw that it contained my laptop computer plus numerous books, files, and folders.

"When will I get all this stuff back?" I asked her.

"When we're finished with it," Jill Maguire replied for the obvious benefit of her smiling colleagues at the glass doors to the balcony. "Hopefully, cleaning up after us won't be too much of a headache for you," she then added, winked, and rejoined them.

I waited until the apartment's front door had been closed, and then hurried over to the balcony's railings and looked down into the street below at the white unmarked Garda van that was parked in front of the entrance to the apartment building.

When the cops got back inside it and the van pulled away, I raced into to the apartment's kitchen and pulled open the drawer that Jill Maguire had watched me use the night before.

Her message was written inside the top flap of the red-and-silver carton of dissolvable tablets.

"Meet me in Greenway Lane at 4:00 pm."

WEDNESDAY — EIGHT

reg Moore was a foot and a half taller than me and yet weighed twenty pounds less. His nickname, when we had been at school together, was Your Honor, in reference to his father, a well-known judge whose comments when sentencing people from economically challenged parts of Dublin attracted a lot of media coverage.

My friendship with Greg started on a football pitch and solidified at our local tennis club, where, as a teenager, I benefited greatly from his ability to attract and amuse young female club members with his bombastic wit.

"I presume that you're aware that I've tried to reach you on a number of occasions since Monday?" Greg enquired in his precise and booming accent when I met him in the Georgian house on Fitzwilliam Square that he and his older sister, Ciara, had inherited when their father had died.

"Yes, I know," I said. "I'm sorry for not getting back to you."

It had been a year since I was last inside the large first floor meeting room that Greg led me to and yet I instantly noted the only change to its antique furnishings.

"That's new," I said and pointed towards the large framed painting on the wall above the marble mantelpiece at the far end of the room, a space that was previously home to a dour landscape painting of some village in the West of Ireland.

Greg took a seat on the other side of the room's bog-oak conference table, positioned his Mont Blanc fountain pen on top of a lined yellow notepad, and then angled his head and squinted at the big painting over the rims of the round spectacles perched on the end of his nose.

"Yes, it is to this room," he conceded. "That painting belonged to my father and used to adorn his study. Ciara insisted that we hang it in here," he said and shook his head. "She claims that my father always liked that painting because it represents the sense of justice that he used to uphold. To my mind, it does nothing of the sort, and I feel that the man featured in it looks nothing like him."

Greg's mention of his sister prompted me to reminisce about an ill-tempered meeting that Ted and I once had with a client who was unhappy because our company's work was what he considered to be "too edgy."

"If you feel that your advertising is too edgy then that's a good thing, because we don't do dull advertising," Ted said. "Dull advertisements are like dull people," he added. "They don't get noticed."

Ciara was so dull that she would fail to attract much attention in a home for the blind if she made a lot of noise.

I acknowledged Greg's assessment of the painting and then realized with a start that he was waiting for me to comment on it.

In the painting, a handsome and robust middle-aged man in a legal wig and gown stood dramatically amid slanting sunrays in a courtroom. The man's left arm was raised high, and his right index finger pointed at something out of the frame in front of him.

I admired the painting as a visual representation of man's dedication to justice and yet concurred with Greg. The main character in it bore no resemblance whatsoever to his short and portly late father.

"You're right," I said to Greg. "He looks nothing like your dad."

"I knew that you'd agree with me," Greg said and then picked up his pen and checked its nib. "Right, we should commence," he added.

In response, I took the silver-and-red carton of painkillers out of my jacket pocket, held it in both hands, flipped open its lid, and leant forward to slide it across the table to where Greg could read the message that Jill Maguire had written on it.

"Who wants to meet you in Greenway Lane at four?" he asked me.

"A detective lady called Jill Maguire," I said and then continued when Greg gave me a baffled look. "Do you remember Tony Maguire and Cormack O'Sullivan, the two detectives who failed to find whoever had murdered Claire and Sarah?" I asked him. "Well, Tony Maguire's daughter, Jill, wrote that. She's Cormack O'Sullivan's partner, and led the search of my home today."

"And she left this message for you?" Greg asked as he rotated the cartoon around and re-read what Jill Maguire had written on it.

"Yes, in a drawer in my kitchen that she saw me use last night," I replied.

Greg looked over his glasses at me. "This detective was in your home last night. Why?" he asked, as if addressing a court witness.

"To tell me that Cormack O'Sullivan had found out that she was in my home on Monday night, and had taken her off Dave's case as a result," I replied.

"I see," Greg said and nodded slowly. "Sorry Killian, is there something going on here that I should know about?"

"No, no, it's not like that," I explained. "Jill Maguire called to my home on Monday night because she had checked the files about Claire and Sarah, and had found a note that her late father had written. It led her to conclude that I knew more about Tony Maguire's death than I had revealed."

"And do you know more about his death than you have revealed?" Greg asked me.

"Not exactly," I replied. "When Jill Maguire's father was killed, I suspected that Cormack O'Sullivan was involved, but there was no evidence to back up my suspicion."

Greg pushed his glasses back nearer to his eyes. "How come you never disclosed anything about this to me before?" he asked.

The confidentiality rules between a solicitor and their client meant that I could say anything to Greg, and yet there were still some things I had kept to myself when talking to my closest friend.

"Because I didn't want you to get involved in something that was never more than a suspicion of mine," I said. "Tony Maguire was killed the day after Declan Reid died on his way to tell me who was behind Sarah's kidnapping, so I saw a connection between those two deaths."

139

"The connection being Cormack O'Sullivan," Greg stated. "Why?"

I shrugged. "I spotted that there were some inconsistencies around that post office robbery. But as I said earlier, I have no evidence that O'Sullivan was involved in either Declan Reid's death or Tony Maguire's murder."

"So, it's just a hunch of yours," Greg said. "Did you ever share your suspicions with anyone else?" he asked me.

I nodded. "I told Frank what I was thinking."

"And what did he say?" Greg asked me.

"Not much," I replied. "I had no evidence against O'Sullivan, so Frank advised me to just stay quiet and not cause any trouble."

"That makes sense," Greg said. "Did you do as he suggested?"

"Yes, until Monday night when Jill Maguire called to my home," I answered. "I was tired and she annoyed me, so I said some things that I probably shouldn't have," I admitted. "I think she told O'Sullivan what I said about him and that he's after me as a result."

"Hence the search of your apartment today?" Greg guessed.

"Maybe," I replied. "I might be jumping to conclusions here but when Jill Maguire called to my apartment last night, she insisted that she hadn't told O'Sullivan that she had been there on Monday night too, and demanded to know if I had told anyone else that she was there."

"And had you?" Greg asked me and pushed his glasses back again.

"Yes," I replied. "I met Frank briefly yesterday and told him about Jill Maguire's visit to my home on Monday night. When I told Jill Maguire that, she surmised that it was Frank who had told O'Sullivan about her presence in my apartment on Monday night. Frank and O'Sullivan are friends, so she could be right."

Greg didn't comment on my response, lowered his fountain pen down onto the yellow notepad, took off his glasses, and massaged the bridge of his nose. He then picked up the carton of pain killers again.

"I'm sorry, Killian, but it's obvious to me that you like this Jill Maguire woman," he said. "First, you hand me this carton like it was made out of some precious metal, and then you refer to her as a lady. If there's something going on between you and Maguire then I need to know about it, because

140

it could be clouding your judgement," he said. "And there's no point in us continuing with this conversation."

I stared back at Greg. "Okay, despite everything that's going on, I do like Jill Maguire," I concurred. "But I don't think that's clouding my judgement."

Greg put his glasses back on. "Really? Because it sounds to me like your fondness for this detective has made you reluctant to accept what's really going on here. That O'Sullivan has learnt about your suspicions from her and is pissed off. I think that's why your home was searched."

"Jesus," I said.

"Yes, Jesus," Greg said and then looked down at the pack of pain killers and checked the time on his wristwatch.

"Do you plan to meet this detective lady at four?" he asked me.

"I'm not sure," I replied. "What do you recommend?"

"As your solicitor, I advise you not to meet her, or have any more conversations with the cops unless I'm present," Greg said as he slid the red-and-silver carton back across the table towards me. "But as your friend, I sense that you're going to ignore my advice and meet her anyway."

WEDNESDAY — NINE

I grinned back at Greg, thought, from what he had just said, that our meeting had ended and was about to stand-up when he picked up his pen again and then touched its nib against the writing pad.

"Now, seeing as how you didn't answer any of my calls," Greg stated. "Please tell me exactly what happened to Dave on Monday. The media said that you were there. Was that true?"

"Yes, I was there and yet I didn't see what really happened," I replied. "That Dave was murdered deliberately."

"Really?" Greg said. "I thought that Dave was a victim during a robbery?"

"That's the way it was supposed to look," I said. "But Dave was actually killed in a crime that was hidden within a crime, because someone wanted his death to look accidental."

"Really?" Greg repeated. "Who wanted Dave dead? Was he into drugs or gambling, or have an affair with some bad guy's wife?"

"No, Dave wasn't into drugs or gambling," I said and sighed. "But he did have an affair, although I'm pretty sure that's not what got him killed."

"Really, who was Dave's affair with?" Greg asked and took note of what I had just said.

"A woman called Kate Fallon," I replied. "Kate works in the advertising agency, isn't married, isn't in a relationship with anyone else, and doesn't have connections that I know of with the sort of people who would kill Dave."

"I see," Greg said. "Apart from this Kate woman, who else knows about Dave's affair?" Greg asked and then overrode his own question. "Forget what I just asked you. More importantly, apart from this Kate woman, who else knows that you are aware that Dave was having an affair that might talk to the police?"

I thought about Greg's revised question before answering it.

"No one," I replied "I talked to a girl who works with Kate this morning, but didn't reveal to her that I knew about the affair between Dave and Kate. And I told Ted about it, but he won't say anything."

"Good. Keep it that way," Greg said and then thought of something else. "How about Dave's wife?" he asked. "Does she know about her husband's affair?"

"No, and she isn't going to hear anything about it from me," I answered. "Louise has suffered enough, so news of Dave having an affair could push her over the edge."

Greg wrote down another note and then looked back at me again. "Are you certain that Louise knows nothing about Dave's affair?" he queried. "Because if the cops find out that Dave was having a fling with this Kate woman, your sister-in-law will become their prime suspect. You realize that, don't you?"

"Yes, I do, but they'd be wrong," I stated firmly. "Louise might be into causes, but there's no way that she was involved in Dave's death."

"What do you mean, Louise is into causes?" Greg asked me.

I shrugged. "You know, contributing makes Louise feel good. It provides her with purpose, so she gets into things and lends her support to the belief of the day," I said. "Louise has a strong opinion about lots of things and always had."

"So, your sister-in-law holds strong views?" Greg asked.

"Yes, and so do lots of people," I replied. "It's one of the things in life that gives us a sense of belonging. I'm sorry, Greg, but I just can't see Louise being involved in Dave's murder if that's what you're thinking. And anyway, Dave would never have left Louise for Kate."

"Why do you say that?" Greg queried.

"Because Dave always thought about the consequences of his actions," I said. "If he left Louise then his life would have been very different, and not in a good way. So I'm pretty sure that he would never have left Louise for Kate."

"Even if he was getting something from this mistress of his that he wasn't getting at home?" Greg asked.

"Yes, even then," I said and nodded. "Plus, there's something else. Dave called my mobile phone twice on Sunday night and tried to get hold of me again on Monday morning. He wouldn't have done that if it was going to tell me about his affair with Kate. Dave didn't like discussing what he considered to be private issues on the phone and wouldn't have told me in advance about his affair. If he was going to talk to me about Kate, then he would have done so face-to-face and without giving me any notice or warning."

"So, you're pretty sure that Dave wouldn't have even called you to set up a meeting about his affair?" Greg asked

"No, Dave wouldn't have done that," I replied. "That's why I feel that there was something else up with him. Another reason why Dave got so upset on Sunday night."

"Another reason why Dave got so upset on Sunday night?" Greg queried.

"Yes, I don't know what that was yet," I replied. "But Dave wanted to talk to me about something on Sunday night and, whatever it was, I feel that it might have gotten him killed the next day. Louise told me that Dave was in a foul mood when he got home on Sunday night, and yet, according to her, he had been his usual self when he had called her just thirty minutes earlier. Which doesn't sound like the affair with Kate was foremost on Dave's mind, does it?"

"No, it doesn't," Greg said. "But I'm sorry about this, Killian," he stated. "But from where I'm sitting, it sounds like Dave's affair might have been the reason why he was killed. Everything that you've told me only points in one direction, and that's towards Louise. And, unfortunately, I have some personal experience in this area."

"Personal experience, what are you talking about?" I asked my friend.

Greg took off his glasses with both hands, as if he was removing a mask, and placed them on the table in front of him.

"Nikki had an affair a few years back," he told me when he had composed himself. "It was all over by the time she confessed about it to me, but…"

"Jesus!" I interjected. "Who was the other guy?"

"I never found out," Greg replied. "Nikki wouldn't tell me his name. She claimed that the affair didn't last long, that the man was married too, and that it was all over for more than two years before she told me about it. She promised that nothing like that would ever happen again between us, and so far, thankfully, it hasn't."

"If it was over for two years then why did Nikki confess about her affair to you?" I asked.

"Nikki said that she couldn't carry the lie anymore," Greg told me. "She told me that she knew that our marriage might end, and yet she felt so guilty about deceiving me that she had to admit what she had done."

"But your marriage didn't end," I said. "Nikki and you are still together."

"Yes, we are," Greg stated as he reached down for his glasses on the table. "But I got really angry when Nikki told me about her affair. I wanted revenge, and it took me months to calm down. That's how Louise would have felt if she had found out about Dave's affair too. And that's why what I'm saying is that maybe you're being too easy on your sister-in-law. If Louise did find out about Dave's affair, then she might have decided to end it by having him killed."

"I'm sure that Louise would never do that," I said and shook my head, although Greg's suggestion that I was too easy on Louise worried me. Was what he had just said yet another example of me being nice? "On top of that, it was Louise who told me that there was something up with Dave on Monday," I added. "That's why I drove out to the Jasper's Restaurant in The O'Malley Centre. To see what was wrong with Dave."

"And what was wrong with him?" Greg asked me.

"I don't know," I said. "The JimiJix Show had started by the time that I got there, so I never got to talk to Dave before he died."

"Are you absolutely convinced that Louise had nothing to do with Dave's death, and feel that exposing his affair now will only confuse things?" Greg asked me.

"Yes, I am. I believe that there was another reason why Dave was in a weird mood on Sunday night other than his affair. I just don't know what that was yet," I replied.

"Then I suggest that you keep your mouth shut about Dave's affair," Greg said.

Wednesday — Ten

"Thanks," I said to Greg. "Actually, you might be able to help me to find out why Dave was in a weird mood," I added. "I've driven Dave's route home and checked out a few other things, but there's lots of other stuff that I can't access," I told my friend.

"What sort of stuff?" Greg asked me.

"Security footage, eyewitnesses who saw Dave drive home, and anything else that he might have encountered on Sunday night," I replied.

"Do you want me to hire someone to look into that for you?" Greg offered in a manner that reminded me of my meeting with Anne Reid the previous night, and her enduring sorrow for the last private detective that I had hired.

"Maybe. Let me think about that," I told Greg.

"Okay," Greg replied and looked down at his yellow notepad again. "Getting back to today," he said. "Why do you think that your apartment was searched?"

"I'm not sure," I said. "Maybe O'Sullivan has made me a suspect."

"For your brother's murder?" Greg probed.

I nodded again. "O'Sullivan called to Dave's house this morning and told Louise's sister, Betty, that I was holding out on them. He told her that I had information about Dave's murder that I hadn't shared with the cops."

"Was he talking about Dave's affair?" Greg asked.

"That's what I thought at first," I said. "But why would O'Sullivan have my apartment searched if that was the case? He'd just bring me in and ask me some questions. No, there has to have been another reason for the search."

Greg gave my answer some thought. "Why would O'Sullivan try to link you to your brother's murder?" he asked.

"This probably sounds too paranoid," I replied. "But O'Sullivan might be trying to discredit and undermine me."

"Unfortunately, that doesn't sound too paranoid," Greg said. "If that's the case, I'll block O'Sullivan legally if he tries anything, but you need to stay in touch with me, okay?"

"Okay," I agreed, pushed back my chair, and then noted that Greg hadn't moved.

"There's something else going on here, isn't there?" he asked me when our eyes met.

The ease with which Greg had spotted that I was troubled about something else concerned me. "There might be," I said. "But it has nothing to do with what happened to Dave or anything else that we've just discussed."

"What is it?" Greg asked.

I shrugged. "Something personal," I replied. "On Monday morning, before…"

"Dave was killed," Greg said to finish my sentence. "Go on."

I took a deep breath. "Peter told me that I had changed since Claire and Sarah had died. He said that I'd become nice and was now accepting things that I used to hate. Nobody would have described me as nice three years ago, would they?"

Greg shook his head. "No, they wouldn't," he agreed.

"Do you think I've mourned too much for Claire and Sarah?" I asked Greg. "And that my grief has dragged on for too long and made me appear nice?"

I could tell from Greg's expression that he didn't like my question.

"I'm not sure that I'm qualified to answer that," he said as he took off his glasses again. "All I'll say is that I don't ever want anyone to grieve for me in the same way that you have grieved for Claire and Sarah. When I go, I'd like Nikki and Steve to get on with their lives."

"Right," I said. "So, you do think I've mourned too much for Claire and Sarah," I concluded.

"I knew that you'd say that to me," Greg responded. "I just fear that you think more about Claire and Sarah now than you did when they were alive. Claire would have expected you to move on by now, find someone else, and not just mope around thinking about Sarah and her. You know that, don't you, Killian?"

"Yes, I do," I replied. "And I also know that you, and lots of other people, feel that I have grieved too much for Claire and Sarah too, and that my morning over them has gone on for too long."

Greg closed his eyes, shook his head, and then opened them again.

"I'm sorry, Killian, I've already told you that I'm not qualified in this area. All I know is that if you grieve for someone too much, or for too long, then there's a danger that their departure becomes about you and not about them," he said. "Maybe you need to talk to a counsellor or someone. Yes, you've changed and become nice, but only a fool would expect you not to change after you lost your wife and daughter."

I smiled across at Greg. As usual, his words had reassured me.

"Thanks, Greg, I needed to hear that," I said, and then divulged my future plans. "When all this is over, I've decided to leave advertising and Ireland. I'm going to take a break and do some travelling. Hopefully, I'll have changed by the time that I get back here."

"Hopefully, but not too much," Greg said and then checked his wristwatch. "In the meantime, unless you want to be late for your meeting with that Detective Maguire, you better leave here now. Just don't tell her anything about Dave's affair, okay?"

"Thank you," I replied. "Do you want me to call you after I meet her?"

"Yes, of course I do," Greg replied. "But please just tell me about the Dave and O'Sullivan stuff, nothing about Maguire or what you get up to with her, okay?"

"Okay," I answered.

"Okay?" Greg mimicked and then smiled. "Christ, you have changed, Killian. A few years ago, you would have told me to fuck off if I'd said that to you."

WEDNESDAY — ELEVEN

It had started to rain by the time that I parked my black Audi in front of the closed primary school at the top of Greenway Lane and made my way on foot to the small parking area at the lane's base.

A few minutes later, the wheels of Jill Maguire's Volkswagen Golf crunched to a halt on the parking area's gravel surface and I stepped out from beneath a tree and began a slow accent of the slanted lane.

One hundred and twelve yards long by eight yards wide, Greenway Lane was once a narrow avenue that ran from the seafront in Clontarf up to the quiet road where the primary school was located. Closed to motorized traffic fifty years earlier, the laneway now offered pedestrians a concrete path, a broad swath of grass, and eleven mature maple trees.

The sky darkened again, and a distant rumble of thunder made it difficult for me to make out the noise behind me as Jill Maguire shut her car door and hurried through wet grass to close the gap between us.

"Thank you. I wasn't sure that you'd be here," she told my back when she got close enough to me.

"Why, did you think that I'd be too dumb to work out your little message?" I replied and turned around to her.

"No, I've never doubted that you're very bright," Jill Maguire said and moved over from the wet grass to the concrete path to get closer to me.

"Now that I'm here, what do you want to talk about?" I asked her.

Jill Maguire paused to sweep the hair back from her forehead. "Firstly, I wanted to let you know that the search today wasn't my idea, Cormack ordered me to do that," she replied. "Secondly, I wanted you to know that I didn't lie last night," she added and took another step towards me. "And thirdly, I wanted you to know that Cormack is after you, and that your life is in danger."

"My life is in danger?" I asked and pulled a face.

The detective nodded. "Cormack is gathering evidence that will prove that you paid your brother to have your daughter kidnapped," she said. "He's going to claim that you had Dave killed on Monday because he came back looking for more money from you to stay quiet."

I smiled and shook my head. "That will never stand up in a court of law," I told her.

Jill Maguire's right hand shot out and gripped the front of my coat.

"Please don't be so naive, Killian," she said. "What Cormack claims will never have to stand up in a court of law because you won't live long enough to get to one. Once Cormack has enough evidence against you, he will bring you in for questioning and you'll disappear."

I drew my head back. "Is this another ploy of yours, Detective Maguire?" I asked. "Are you trying to scare me into saying something?"

"No, this isn't a ploy and I'm not trying to scare you into anything," Jill Maguire replied. "I'm taking a big risk just being here. If Cormack ever finds out that I met you, he'll go mad and I'll probably disappear too."

"I'm sorry, but can you explain all that to me?" I asked.

Jill Maguire swept her hair back again. "On Monday, Cormack told me that my father suspected that you were behind your daughter's kidnapping. He said that my father always hated you. I think that O'Sullivan did that for a reason," she said.

"What reason?" I asked.

"Cormack wanted to make sure that I disliked you and never talked to you. That way, I would never have heard what you said about my father or him on Monday night," Jill Maguire said. "I think that's why Cormack ordered me to lead the search today too. He found out that I had called to your apartment on Monday night, so he got me to lead the search of your home today to turn you against me. He wanted us to hate each other and never talk again."

"You're losing me," I said. "Why would O'Sullivan want us to hate each other?"

"Because then I'd disregard what you said about my father's death, and we'd always stay apart," Jill Maguire replied. "That way, you'd never find out what Cormack is planning to do to you. That he's getting evidence together that will lead to your arrest."

I scanned around the lane to make sure that we were still alone. "What evidence has O'Sullivan got against me?" I asked.

"Bank records that show that you took out a large amount of cash about a week after your daughter was kidnapped," she told me. "And phone records that prove that your brother called you on Sunday night," she said and held up her right palm to stop me from interrupting her. "Cormack is also going to claim that the reason why you were in Jasper's Restaurant in The O'Malley Centre on Monday was to make sure that your brother, Dave, was shot dead, and not to talk to him."

"Why would O'Sullivan do all that?" I asked and shook my head again. "Why would he frame me for my own brother's death?"

"I've already told you all that," Jill Maguire replied. "Because Cormack will then have you arrested, detained, and questioned. Once he does that, you will be kept for a while, asked a few questions, and then released. At that point, you'll disappear and everyone will assume that you were guilty all along and did a runner to escape justice. But in reality, it will be Cormack who makes you disappear."

"And there will be no court case," I concluded. "How long do you think I have?"

"Not long," Jill Maguire said. "Particularly after the search of your apartment today. Cormack now has lots of information, and got me to lead that search so that I'm now a witness against you too."

Another shower of rain began but I took no action to take shelter, the prospect of getting wet no longer being of any consequence to me.

"How long?" I asked more firmly.

"Tomorrow. Maybe the day after that. I honestly don't know," Jill Maguire replied.

"Tomorrow!" I yelled, turned away and continued up the laneway.

Based on what Jill Maguire had just told me, O'Sullivan had become aware of my suspicion about his role in Tony Maguire's death and had decided to come after me.

WEDNESDAY — TWELVE

I stepped away from Jill Maguire and was about to call Greg when I thought of another question and turned back to her.

"Why did you tell me what you just said?" I asked.

"Because, once you're out of the way, Cormack will come after me too," the detective said and blinked. "He doesn't know what you told me about my father's death on Monday night but he won't take any chances on that, so will get rid of me too."

"So that's the real reason why you're here," I said. "To protect yourself by getting me to stop O'Sullivan. That's it, isn't it, Detective Maguire, you only came here to save yourself?"

"No, that's not it at all," Jill Maguire replied and stepped closer again.

"Then why did you really come here?" I asked the detective as she looked up into my face.

"Because I like you," Jill Maguire replied. "Why did you come here?"

"To find out who killed Dave," I said. "And because I like you too."

Jill Maguire smiled up at me, and then glanced back down the lane before taking another step closer to me. "You could stop Cormack by using your links with the media," she said. "Tell them what you know about him, and get them to ask Cormack some hard questions. If you expose Cormack to the media, then he won't be able to go after you without looking bad in the court of human opinion, and he's not into that, it doesn't go well with his position."

I mulled over Jill Maguire's suggested plan for a moment, and thought of a journalist who I knew who worked with one of the daily newspapers. That journalist would listen to what I had to say about O'Sullivan if I called her, would investigate him, and could prevent him from seeking revenge unless he wanted to read about himself in her newspaper.

"I might be able to arrange something with the media," I replied. "Can I call you later?"

"It would be better if you didn't," the detective replied. "Cormack is probably monitoring my calls."

"Fine," I said and was about to return up the lane to my car when I noted a sad expression on Jill Maguire's face as she looked at the stretch of grass next to the damp concrete path that we were standing on.

"Now, what's the problem?" I asked her.

Jill Maguire looked back up at me as her teary eyes met mine.

"I'm sorry that I brought you here," she replied. "I read about this lane in the records on Monday night, so I knew that you'd know where I meant when I wrote that note on the headache pills packet. This is where the kidnap happened, isn't it?"

"Yes, it is," I said. "Claire was walking Sarah up to her ballet class through this lane one Saturday morning when she heard someone dash up behind her. She spun around in time to take a blow from a hammer to her head. Sarah ran off but only made it to about there," I swiveled around and pointed up the lane at the center of the lawn. "That was where she was tackled to the ground," I told Jill Maguire. "Sarah's ribs had been broken and crushed when they found her dead body, so she probably died here before she was taken away."

"And yet nobody saw or heard anything?" Jill Maguire asked me.

"No, apart from a young Polish maid who worked in that house," I said and used my right hand to point to the back of a large Georgian house on an elevated site at the top of the lane.

"A young Polish maid?" Jill Maguire asked.

"Yes," I said. "From the building's back windows, she might have seen Claire being hit and Sarah being chased," I said and shrugged. "But no one knows what she witnessed, because the Polish maid disappeared that morning and hasn't been found since."

"No one was ever charged with that crime, were they?" Jill Maguire asked.

"No, not yet," I said and shook my head. "Two days later, Sarah's dead body was found in the burnt-out wreck of a stolen van. Alongside her were the bodies of two brothers called Eddie and Liam Gilroy. From their times of death, both those men appear to have been shot in the head just hours after what had happened here."

"I see, so it looks like whoever hired the Gilroys to do the kidnapping killed them that afternoon to close the whole thing down," Jill Maguire said.

"Yes, that's what it looks like," I said. "And the day after Sarah's body was found, I was told that there was no hope for Claire either, and signed the papers that gave the hospital permission to turn off her life support machine."

"I'm sorry again that I brought you here," Jill Maguire said, and then turned away from me to make her way back down the path to her car.

"Please don't go, I've been here lots of times since that day," I said as I scrambled after the detective, reached out, and gently took hold of her left arm as she turned back to me.

"Since the kidnap?" Jill Maguire asked me.

"Yes," I answered. "In fact, the first time that I was here after what happened to Claire and Sarah was with your dad. He felt that it was important for me to see where my wife and daughter had been attacked. I was reluctant to do that, but he was a very persuasive man."

"You liked my father, didn't you?" Jill Maguire asked me.

"Yes," I said. "He was the only detective who seemed to fully understand what I was going through, and really listened to me."

"He used to really listen to me too, even when I was talking about girly stuff," Jill Maguire said, as her face took on an anxious look. "If you liked my dad so much, and believe that Cormack had him killed to shut him up, what do you think that he knew that Cormack wanted to keep covered up?"

"I don't know," I replied and shook my head. "Maybe, I'm wrong here, but I've always presumed that it was something to do with the kidnap."

"Do you think Cormack had something to do with that?" she asked.

"Yes, I do," I replied. "I think that O'Sullivan knows what happened here and doesn't want anyone to find out the truth. That could explain why

Declan Reid died when he was coming to meet me, and why your father died the next day too. Maybe, he knew something as well."

"But you can't prove any of that?" Jill Maguire asked me.

"No, I can't," I replied, and then asked the detective another question. "Do you always carry that gun around that you pulled on Monday night?"

"Yes," Jill Maguire said and smiled. "My gun is a Croatian XD-9 that my father gave me as a present when I got through Garda training. I have a problem keeping my bedroom clean, so he reckoned that I needed a gun that required little maintenance."

"Clever man," I commented and then jerked to attention when I saw Jill Maguire's eyes follow a car that passed along the road at the top of the lane.

"That was a silver Nissan, wasn't it," I said, spun around but only saw the blurred red glare of its rear lights as the car disappeared from view.

"Yes, it was and Billy King was driving it," Jill Maguire said. "That's why we need to get out of here right now."

"You know its driver?!" I quizzed her.

"Yes, I do," Jill Maguire said. "He works with Cormack and me. Why?"

"Because I think that he's been following me since yesterday," I said.

"Are you sure?" Jill Maguire asked me.

"Not exactly," I replied and turned away from Jill Maguire to walk up the path towards the top of the laneway.

When she shouted a goodbye after me, I waved a hand back to her, and then extracted my mobile phone.

"I'm not sure about you talking to the media," Greg replied after I had told him about the course of action that Jill Maguire had advised. "Now that we know more about what's going on, we should meet up again and talk things through," he added.

"Yes, we should," I said. "But before we do, there's someone that I need to talk to who has a lot more information about O'Sullivan. Are you free to meet up later this evening?"

"Yes, of course I am," Greg replied. "But it will have to be at my house. I'll be home at about eight. Will I see you there then for dinner?"

"Yes," I said. "And I hope to have more information about O'Sullivan by then."

"Good," Greg said. "In the meantime, stay safe."

Wednesday — Thirteen

This time, I didn't phone Declan Reid's widow in advance. After I had rung her doorbell, she pulled back one of the curtains in her front room and looked out to see who the caller to her house was. When she saw that it was me, Anne Reid came to the door wrapped in a light-grey cardigan with bulging pockets. The older woman wasn't wearing any makeup this time and her short blond hair lay flat on her head.

"I expected you to get in touch again, but not this soon," she said, opened her front door and led me into her kitchen. "Do you want some coffee?"

"No, thanks," I said. "I won't be here long."

Anne Reid nodded, drew back her chair and indicated for me to take the same seat that I had occupied at her kitchen table on the previous night.

"Does this have anything to do with what you and Vincent discussed in the park today?" she asked. "He told me that you got all het up about something."

"Maybe," I replied. "What's the story with Lynch anyway? There's something odd about him. What's he so scared about?"

Anne Reid looked down at her hands on the glass tabletop before she spoke. "I didn't think that I'd have to say this," she answered. "But there is something about Vincent that you need to know," she told me.

"Which is?" I replied.

"That he's dying of cancer," Anne Reid told me. "And is afraid of not being around to protect his family if you go after O'Sullivan."

I thought back on my two meetings with Lynch, about his pale pallor, the sheen from his skin, the smell of peppermint from his breath, and his warm clothes. I was disappointed that I hadn't spotted what Anne Reid had just told me.

"I'm sorry that Vincent Lynch has cancer," I admitted. "That makes a lot of sense. He was very philosophical when I met him earlier, told me that he doesn't trust me, and then declared that I was an amateur."

Anne Reid smiled. "Don't worry, Vincent doesn't trust many people," she said. "His wife died five years ago, so now Vincent's family only consists of his two sons and his only daughter. One of his sons, a guy called Ken, is a Garda detective, while Vincent's other son, Aidan, is an accountant. His daughter, Shona, lives in England, and rarely comes home to see him."

"Right," I said.

"Vincent doesn't get out much these days either," Anne Reid continued. "And spends most of his time in the pub that he owns and runs with his brother, Aidan."

"Lynch owns a pub?" I asked Anna Reid.

"Yes, he bought a place out in Givenstown a while back," she confirmed.

"Right," I said and then asked Anne Reid another question. "Lynch is really afraid of O'Sullivan?" I asked. "Does he know something about him that we don't?"

"Vincent knows a lot about Cormack O'Sullivan," Anne Reid said. "After Declan was fired, Cormack O'Sullivan went after Vincent," she revealed. "Cormack O'Sullivan kept assigning Vincent to cases where large volumes of information had to be analyzed in a short amount of time, gave him tasks that tied him to his desk, and treated Vincent really badly in order to get rid of him. And yet, Vincent didn't take the bait, never complained, and wouldn't let Cormack O'Sullivan break him. Then Vincent heard something. After that, O'Sullivan left him alone."

"Really?" I said. "So, Vincent Lynch found something out about O'Sullivan and they came to some sort of agreement. Is that why Lynch leaves O'Sullivan alone even though he knows that he's completely corrupt?"

Anne Reid nodded. "Vincent wouldn't even take action against Cormack O'Sullivan when he suspected that he might have been involved in Declan's death, and I told him what Cormack O'Sullivan had said about my dead husband."

"That's why you called me, isn't it, Mrs. Reid?" I asked. "Because you knew that I would go after O'Sullivan even though Vincent Lynch wouldn't and you want someone to revenge your husband's death."

Anne Reid nodded again in reply to my question. "Vincent knows Cormack O'Sullivan well, knows what he's capable of, and won't go after him," she said. "That's why, when Vincent told me that he had spotted on the TV news that your brother was killed deliberately, I phoned you. I knew that you'd go after O'Sullivan when you heard that he might have been involved in your brother's murder. The problem is that Vincent doesn't think much of you, doesn't want to start something that he won't be around to finish, and feels that I'm taking a big risk by helping you to get O'Sullivan for me."

"Yeah, well Vincent Lynch doesn't know much about me," I said. "I'm going to get O'Sullivan, especially since I heard that he's out to get me, that he's going to have me arrested and charged with organizing the murder of my brother. I'll disappear when O'Sullivan does that. That's why I need to get him first."

Anne Reid's face projected an expression of satisfaction. "I knew that you would get Cormack O'Sullivan for me," she said. "Although, I never thought that I'd be putting your life in danger by doing so," she said. "What do you need from me to make Cormack O'Sullivan go away?"

WEDNESDAY — FOURTEEN

I told Anne Reid that I needed information about anything that O'Sullivan would have difficulty answering questions about if he was grilled by a journalist.

"I don't know as much about Cormack O'Sullivan as Vincent does," Anne Reid answered. "And I can't go back too far either," she added. "But I'll tell you everything that I know if that will help."

"Go ahead," I said.

"Cormack O'Sullivan and Tony Maguire were once the best detective team in Ireland," Anne Reid began. "And then something happened between them. After that, Tony just did whatever O'Sullivan told him to do, and they became like a master and slave."

"Did your husband, Declan, know what had happened between them and why they had started to behave like that?" I asked.

"Maybe," Anne Reid replied. "But Declan never discussed that, even after he had figured out how corrupt Cormack O'Sullivan was."

"What do you mean by corrupt?" I enquired.

"According to Declan," Anne Reid replied to distance herself from what she was about to tell me. "Cormack O'Sullivan is in control of a bunch of criminals and keeps them out of prison as long as they work for him."

"He protects bad people and gets them to work for him?" I asked her.

Anne Reid nodded again. "Cormack O'Sullivan operates a crime-for-hire operation," she said. "That's why he's so dangerous."

"How did Declan find that out?" I asked Anne Reid.

"Declan first spotted that all wasn't what it seemed with Cormack O'Sullivan on a Christmas night out for the detectives that he worked with. All the detectives attending that event threw in some money and Cormack O'Sullivan collected it and booked a Chinese restaurant." she replied.

"And?" I asked.

Anne Reid sighed. "Declan's drinking had been noted by then, so he was off the booze that night and spotted that the money that Cormack O'Sullivan had collected from the detectives wouldn't go far in that restaurant," she said. "That the party looked like it had been subsidized."

"Subsidized?" I repeated.

Anne Reid nodded some more. "The Chinese guy who owned that restaurant knew Cormack O'Sullivan well and, during the night, Declan overheard him asking him if he wanted to sample one of their waitresses."

"Sample her," I repeated. "He actually said that?"

"They were the exact words that Declan heard the Chinese guy using," Anne Reid said. "Cormack O'Sullivan laughed off the offer but Declan did some digging the next day and discovered that some cases against the Chinese guy had been dropped, while some of the incidents that had been reported in rival restaurants had never been pursued."

"Did Declan assume that O'Sullivan had something to do with that?"

"Yes, he did," Anne Reid answered. "But nobody was brave enough to confront Cormack O'Sullivan, or even to talk to him about that, so Declan saw that he had to be very careful."

"Right," I said. "So, no one ever went public about O'Sullivan's crime-for-hire operation either. Did your husband ever tell you what O'Sullivan did with all the money he got from that?"

"Sort of," Anne Reid said, withdrew a tissue from a cardigan pocket and dabbed it beneath her nose. "One summer, Declan, Robbie, and I went to Benidorm in Spain on a package holiday," she said. "While we were there, Declan hired a car and we drove down to Alicante and located one of those traditional Spanish stone villas with an ornate black ironwork gate." Anne Reid said. "I can still see the purple blossoms that flowed down one of its walls and the view of the Mediterranean from its lawn. Declan got drunk that night and told me that Cormack O'Sullivan owned that villa. That it was his holiday home."

"Did Declan tell anyone else about that when you got back to Dublin?"

"Not really," Anne Reid said and sniffed. "Over a few drinks, Declan told some of the other detectives about the villa. After that, Cormack O'Sullivan claimed that Declan was always late, that he drank too much, and that he wasn't as good a detective as he used to be. Basically, Cormack O'Sullivan made life so difficult for Declan that he forced him to leave the police force."

"And yet your husband never exposed Cormack O'Sullivan?" I asked.

"No, because he couldn't," Anne Reid replied. "Declan was scared about what Cormack O'Sullivan or the bunch of scumbags that he controlled would do to Robbie and me if he talked about him."

"So, Declan just stayed quiet?" I enquired.

Anne Reid nodded. "Yes, except with his old partner, Vincent Lynch," she confirmed. "Declan talked to him a lot and might have told him some of the things that he had found out about Cormack O'Sullivan."

"But Lynch has never repeated those things to anyone," I said and then stayed quiet for a moment until I had thought of another question. "Do you remember the name of that Chinese restaurant?"

"No," Anne Reid replied. "All I remember is that it had an orchid in its name. It was the Paper Orchid, or something like that."

"Going back to Vincent Lynch," I asked. "How much do you think that he knows about O'Sullivan's operation?"

"I'm not sure," Anne Reid said. "Vincent has always been reluctant to talk about Cormack O'Sullivan. I think he does that to protect himself and his family."

"But you're not sure about that?" I asked.

"No, I'm not," Anne Reid replied.

"How about Frank Hennessy?" I asked Anne Reid. "Vincent Lynch told me today that Hennessy and O'Sullivan have remained friends. Do you think that Frank Hennessy knows what Cormack O'Sullivan is up to?"

"Yes, I do," Anne Reid replied. "When Frank Hennessy was Cormack O'Sullivan's boss, they became close friends, and then, when Frank Hennessy left the cops and became Jasper's head of security, their restaurants stopped getting robbed. How do you think that happened?"

"Are you saying that Frank Hennessy got Cormack O'Sullivan to make sure that the Jasper's Restaurants were off limits to the bad guys?" I ventured.

When Anne Reid nodded back to me, I looked away. What the elderly woman had just told me could explain my father-in-law's fast rise up through the ranks of Jasper's Restaurants, and also lent credence to Jill Maguire's claim that the two men had talked about her visit to my apartment on the night of Dave's death.

I leant across the kitchen table.

"I'm going to get O'Sullivan," I told Anne Reid. "But I'm going to need your help to do that. If I get a journalist to come here and ask you some questions, will you repeat to them what you've just told me?"

Wednesday — Fifteen

I spotted the rolled-up brown paper package at the base of my apartment's front door as soon as I had stepped out of the lift.

"Good man, Rory," I said aloud, carried the tubular parcel into what used to be my apartment's TV room, sat down on one of the room's leather couches and opened and unfurled the printout from The Sunday Globe on the coffee table in front of me.

The article took up two tabloid pages and detailed the awful deaths of Frank Hennessy's beautiful daughter and granddaughter during a violent kidnapping that had gone wrong. Written in The Sunday Globe's usual racy style, the article also included two other color photographs in addition to the large head and shoulders shot of my father-in-law. In one of them, a landscape image, Frank was captured in a restaurant setting after he had received an award for his work in promoting the integration of foreign communities into Irish society.

In that shot, Frank Hennessy was applauded by a mixture of Irish, Chinese, Asian, East European, and African representatives as he held up a framed certificate and beamed out at his adoring audience from behind a black-and-silver podium.

I leant in closer, examined that photograph in more detail and was able to make out the words engraved on the front of the podium.

They read 'The Pearl Orchid Chinese Restaurant'.

The other photograph was a holiday snap of Frank and his wife, my mother-in-law, Catherine, as they smiled into a strong breeze that blew their hair back. The caption beneath the photograph noted that the happy couple had been married for thirty-six years.

I let my eyes wander up from the photographs to the banner headline about the leading Irish businessman who had lost his daughter and granddaughter in a failed kidnap, and then spun my head around as a noise sounded behind me.

The second noise was a lot louder than the first one and I let the printout recoil on the surface of the coffee table as I stood up, turned around, and began moving towards the apartment's front door.

The third noise was a violent creak as something metallic was wedged into the gap between the apartment's front door and its frame.

Now, on my tiptoes, I crept quickly and silently across the lounge as the wooden door into my home groaned under pressure.

Despite the temptation to do so, I didn't shout out to try to scare off the person who was about to break into my apartment, something I had been told never to do by the overweight security expert who oversaw the installation of the advertising agency's new alarm system after our renovated building had been burgled for the fifth time.

"In my experience, that warning is usually the last thing that a victim ever says," the heavy man had emphasized. "Shout a warning and start the mourning," he recited. A rhyme that had stayed with me ever since.

Now certain that someone was about to break into my home, I lifted one of the dumbbells from the floor, continued towards the apartment's front door as quietly as possible, and had just taken another step when the door burst open in front of me, revealing a man clad in a black boiler suit, a matching ski mask, and holding a serrated hunter's knife instead of the sawn-off shotgun that he had used to kill my younger brother.

Glaring at me through the slits in his mask, the intruder in the black outfit took two steps inside my apartment, lowered himself into a bent knee stance, and then thrust the hunter's knife at me.

As I swiveled away from the knife's shiny blade, I swung the dumbbell towards the ski mask with my right hand.

My attacker saw the blow coming, was agile enough to duck beneath it, balanced on his left foot and then delivered a powerful kick to the side of my head with his right foot.

Stunned by the blow, I stumbled backwards, fell over the corner of a low table, sprawled back onto the floor, and then became disarmed as the dumbbell bounced out of my grip, and rolled away from me. Digging my heels in, as the man in black advanced towards me, I scrambled backwards across the floor until I collided with a sofa and was unable to retreat any further.

That was when I slapped my feet together, folded back my thighs, and kicked up at the man in the ski mask.

Once again, the assailant in black saw my blow coming, was agile enough to evade it, and then slashed out with his knife as my legs fell back to the floor.

I screamed out in pain as the knife's sharp blade sliced into my right calf and then twisted around and clambered forward on my hands and knees towards the sliding glass doors that led from the apartment's lounge to its balcony.

Walking coolly behind me as I made, what must have looked to him like a last futile bid to escape, the man in the black ski mask waited until I had almost reached the balcony doors and then dipped down to me.

"Sorry Pal, but you're not going anywhere," he sneered as he poked his knife into my right buttock.

Despite the sharp pain as the tip of his knife lanced into my flesh, I rolled over, grasped the second dumbbell from the floor and swung it at my attacker's knife-holding hand.

My blow resulted in a loud clash of metal, and the man in black swished his head around to follow his knife's trajectory as it flashed through the air and then clanged against the wall next to the door into the apartment's kitchen.

He looked back at me just in time to see the dumbbell arc back towards him again. This time, while the man in the black was fast enough to dodge the dumbbell aimed at his head, he wasn't fast enough to escape my blow entirely, and was knocked back onto the floor as the dumbbell thumped into his left shoulder.

Now hurt and disarmed, my brother's killer scrambled to his feet, yelped in fear when he saw me rise up and approach him with the dumbbell in my right hand, and then turned and raced out of my apartment through its violated front door.

I stood and watched his panicked departure, heard the emergency door at the rear of the building crash open as he accessed the concrete staircase behind it, and then limped out to the kitchen and snatched down a first-aid kit from a shelf over the sink.

Grimacing in pain, I then climbed the stairs to my bedroom, sat on the edge of my bed as I removed my blood-soaked shoes and socks and then hobbled into the bathroom to treat my injuries.

While more painful than my other wound, when I had lowered and then stepped out of my trousers and underpants, I saw in the mirror that the puncture to my right buttock from the tip of the attacker's knife, was a small but deep cut which, when pinched together, stopped bleeding long enough for me to apply a padded adhesive bandage.

When I had taped that bandage into place, I stepped into the bath-tub, washed away the curtain of blood from my right leg and saw that the knife's blade had penetrated deeper into my calf muscle than I had first assumed.

This time, I positioned an absorbent pad over my sliced skin, ran a length of gauze bandage around my lower leg a couple of times, and then taped it into place with self-adhesive strips.

Finally, to hold everything in place, I wrapped and tied another, wider dressing from the first aid kit around my leg, and then pressed another self-adhesive strip against the wound to my right buttock.

After dressing quickly in clean clothes, I leant heavily on the stair's brass banisters, descended to the apartment's lounge, returned to the old TV room, and folded up the printout from The Sunday Globe.

I called Anne Reid as I slid that folded printout carefully into the left back pocket of my grey cords. "I was just attacked by the guy who killed Dave," I told her and shuffled back across the battered lounge towards what was left of the apartment's front door. "He might have followed me from your house, so you need to get out of there now. Call Vincent Lynch. He'll know what to do," I advised her.

"Are you all right?" Anne Reid asked me as I stepped tenderly inside the lift and pushed the button for the building's underground car park.

"Yes, I'm fine," I replied. "But you need to get out of there now."

In the underground car park, I limped with as much speed as I could from the lift across the concrete floor to my black Audi, clambered in behind its steering wheel, and then drove off with a screech of car tires.

I knew that the journey to Greg Moore's home would be a sore one, and that, when I got close enough, I would have to abandoned my car and hobble the rest of the way there, and yet I needed to get my friend's advice about what I planned to do next.

WEDNESDAY — SIXTEEN

"That will never work," Greg stated as he pushed the printout of the two pages from The Sunday Globe away from him and then removed and placed his spectacles on the desk in his home office.

"Why not?" I asked my friend.

"Because you've got it all wrong," Greg explained to me. "No journalist will write anything about Cormack O'Sullivan until they have some hard facts. Otherwise, they'll get sued, or he'll come after them. That's why they won't touch your story."

"But Anne Reid agreed to confirm what she had told me to a journalist," I said. "Surely that's enough."

"No, it's not nearly enough," Greg said. "The only thing that Anne Reid can confirm is her belief that Cormack O'Sullivan had her husband killed. Everything else, apart from her claim that you lied to her when you gave her money three years ago, will either be deemed hearsay or conjecture, so it won't get published."

"But I know someone who will talk to Anne Reid," I said. "She's a journalist friend of mine and I've known her for years."

"Then don't call her," Greg said. "Because when your friend's editor gets the newspaper's solicitors to check out her story, she'll be in big trouble and might even get fired. Because there's no way that any newspaper would run a story without checking if it will stand up," he continued. "If they do that, then her newspaper's solicitors will determine that Anne Reid's story isn't based on facts and won't run it. Plus, there might be another reason why her newspaper won't publish anything bad about Cormack O'Sullivan."

"Which is?" I asked Greg.

"Some newspapers get a lot of their stories from the cops," he replied. "If your friend's newspaper is one of those, then the last thing that they'll want to do is to piss off the cops with a story about some corrupt detective that might, or might not, be true."

Despite the pain from the wound to my right buttock, I sidled back in my chair on the other side of the desk in the small room that Greg referred to as his man shed.

I had just told Greg everything. What Jill Maguire had told me about my life being under threat, what Anne Reid had said about O'Sullivan, and how I had escaped an attack by the man in black who I presumed had killed Dave.

I had even shown Greg the pages from The Sunday Globe that Rory Shields had obtained, and told him about my plan to talk to a journalist that I knew who would expose Cormack O'Sullivan. And yet, my friend didn't agree with my plan.

"What do you suggest that I do now?" I asked him.

"Get hard evidence against Cormack O'Sullivan," Greg said. "Some hard facts that a newspaper can print without being sued. Once you have those, talk to this journalist friend of yours."

"Right," I said. "And how do you propose that I get that evidence?"

"I answered that question this afternoon," Greg said. "I advised you to hire a private detective. Someone who will put the evidence together."

"Fine, but that will take time and I don't have much of that," I told Greg. "Jill Maguire told me that if I don't stop O'Sullivan soon, he's going to have me arrested and that I'll disappear."

Greg looked like he was about to say something but then closed his eyes and shook his head. I looked around his office when he did that and saw that its bookshelves displayed a mixture of biographies, legal texts, history tomes, a brightly colored paper house that his son had made in school years earlier and a selection of items that included a Rubik's Cube, a cracked ceramic phrenology head, some old toy cars, and a miniature brass bust of Michael Collins.

Amongst those items was a player of the year plaque that Greg had received from our old soccer club, a tarnished silver tennis trophy, and a framed and strutted photograph that showed a pair of young men with perspiration-dampened faces as they smiled out at a crowd in their local tennis club.

Each of the two young men in that photograph had an attractive woman at his side. Standing next to me was a tall blonde with straight hair and blue eyes called Claire, while Greg was flanked by a shorter brunette with thick, curly auburn hair, big brown eyes, and cherry red lips who was known as Nikki.

"Those were the days," Greg said when he opened his eyes and saw where I was looking. "Do you remember that time when a fast winger got passed me and you tripped him up and sent him flying?" he asked me.

"Yes, I do," I said and smiled. "Has he landed yet?"

"No, I don't think so," Greg said and laughed. "And he wasn't the only one who you fouled back then, was he?"

"No, he wasn't," I said and then fell silent as I thought about Greg's reminiscent of me as a tough defender. Was his comment another example of about how much I had changed and become nice since I had lost Claire and Sarah?

WEDNESDAY — SEVENTEEN

"**H**ow about your father-in-law?" Greg asked as he drew my attention back to the printout on his desk. "Frank used to be O'Sullivan's boss, so maybe he could tell him not to arrest you?"

"I'm not sure about that," I answered. "After what I heard about Frank today, I don't know if I can trust him anymore."

"Why, what did you hear?" Greg said and then leant forward, and focused on the words written on the podium in the Pearl Orchid Restaurant.

I was about to answer him when he asked me another question.

"Were you ever in that place?" he asked me.

"No," I replied. "Were you?"

"A few times," Greg admitted, as if confessing to a minor offense. "I have a client who likes to go there for lunch. He's an old guy, so he just likes to look, nothing else."

"Sorry Greg, what do you mean?" I asked. "What does your client look at."

Greg looked uncomfortable as his head rose up from the print out.

"Declan Reid obviously didn't tell his wife everything about that restaurant," he said. "And I'm surprised that I have to tell you this, Killian, but The Pearl Orchid Restaurant is better known for the girls who work there than for the food that it serves. In fact, some guys claim that the Chinese girls who work there are the best thing about the place."

Greg's comments about the waitresses in The Pearl Orchid Restaurant made a connection with a distant memory in my mind. I had heard about that Chinese restaurant before but years earlier.

"Wait a minute," I said. "Is that the place…"

"Where some diners tip the girls well?" Greg interjected. "Yes, it is."

"What do you know about the Chinese guy who owns that restaurant?" I asked my friend.

"His name is Freddy Chuang," Greg answered as he sat back. "He came to Dublin about thirty years ago from Hong Kong and is held up as a model immigrant. It's politically correct to be seen in his company but the rumor is that he's into lots of illicit things. Drugs, gambling, porn, human trafficking, that sort of stuff."

"Then how come he's not locked up?" I enquired.

"Because Freddy Chuang has friends in high places," Greg replied.

"Friends like O'Sullivan?" I guessed. "Maybe I should talk to Chuang."

"I don't think that would be a good idea," Greg said and shook his head in a warning to me.

"Why not?" I asked him. "According to you, I need to gather some evidence against O'Sullivan, if that's the case, then Chuang's restaurant sounds like the perfect place to start."

"Let's just say that Chuang has a certain reputation," Greg said, and then bolted forward. "Wait a minute! Does anyone else know that you're here now?" he asked me.

"No, I didn't tell anyone else that I was coming here," I replied.

"How about your car, where's that?" Greg pressed me.

"It's on the seafront, around the corner from the bus station, why?"

Greg ignored my question. "What about your mobile phone, where's that?"

"It's here," I said, took out my mobile phone and showed it to him.

With a swiftness that I hadn't anticipated, Greg swooped forward, snatched the mobile phone from my hand and opened its back cover to remove its battery and SIM card.

"I'm sorry, Killian, but I'm going to have to get rid of these," he told me as he spread the mobile phone's components across his desk. "Mobile phones can be traced, and I don't want anyone to show up here looking for you, okay?"

"Right," I replied, and then watched in horror as Greg snapped the phone's SIM card into two pieces, tore my new mobile phone apart, and discarded the various bits into a wastebasket that he kept beneath his desk.

"You know something that you haven't told me, don't you?" I asked Greg as he swept his hand across his desk to get rid of any remnants of my mobile phone.

Greg sat up straight and pushed his glasses back on his nose. "After I spoke with you this afternoon, I made some calls," he disclosed.

"And what did you learn?" I asked him.

Greg swallowed. "I learnt that Cormack O'Sullivan and his pals can make life very unpleasant for anyone who gets on their wrong side," he replied. "And, according to you, he wants you out of the way, right?"

"Right," I agreed.

"That's why I'm nervous about having you here," Greg said.

"Do you want me to leave now?" I asked my friend.

"No," Greg stated. "I invited you for dinner and to stay over, and that's what you're going to do. If anyone comes here looking for you, they better have a court order to get by me."

"Thanks, Greg," I said and then bolted upright and swung my head around as I heard the front door into Greg's house open.

"Don't worry, that's just Nikki and Steve coming home," Greg said, pushed back his chair, and went out to the hall to greet his wife and son.

Left alone in Greg's den, I tried to make out the muffled conversation in the hallway between my friend and his wife. Then the door into the small room was pushed open and Nikki stepped inside it.

"Hi, Killian," she said. "I can't tell you how sorry I was to hear about Dave."

"Thanks, Nikki," I said as Steve, her thirteen-year-old son, followed my friend's wife into the room and took my right hand in his.

"Hi, Killian," the teenager said and let his hurt face express his commiserations.

"Hi, Steve," I said and shook his hand.

Greg laid his hands on Nikki's shoulders, looked on approvingly at the interaction between his son and me, and then informed his wife about my knife injuries.

"Killian has a wounded leg," he told her. "You should take a look at it."

"No, that's all right," I said and waved Greg's proposal away before Nikki could respond. "I bandaged it up myself. It will be fine."

"Nikki should take a look at it anyway," Greg said. "She's a doctor and all that."

"Yes, I should, what happened to you?" Nikki asked and looked down at my legs.

"Nothing much. It's all right," I lied. "It's just a little cut, that's all."

"Someone broke into Killian's apartment and stabbed him," Greg told his wife. "He was limping when he got here. So, you should take a look at his leg."

"Come on, Killian," Nikki said. "I need to see that wound."

"No, really, I'm okay," I argued. "I bandaged the cuts myself. I'll be fine."

"The cuts!" Nikki exclaimed. "You have more than one wound?"

I displayed the back of two fingers. "Just two," I said. "Seriously, I'll be all right."

Greg ignored my comment. "Which room do you want to use?" he asked his wife.

"The upstairs bathroom," she replied. "I've got some medical things up there."

"There, Killian," Greg said as if the matter had been settled against my protests. "Go upstairs with Nikki while I start the dinner," he instructed me.

Wednesday — Eighteen

I tried to disguise my pain as I got to my feet and followed Nikki as she quickly ascended the house's staircase in front of me.

Halfway up those stairs, I inspected the framed color photographs that lined the wall next to them. Mostly holiday snaps, they featured a smiling Greg and Nikki, and a progressively older Steve, in a variety of foreign locations.

Nikki waited for me on the landing, shook her head at the one-foot-at-a-time manner with which I climbed the last few steps, and then opened a wide door on the other side of the landing.

Inside it, the Moore's family bathroom contained a deep oval bathtub, an enclosed semicircular glass shower cubicle, plus the original white porcelain hand basin and toilet bowl that had been installed in the detached redbrick house when it had been constructed seventy-two years earlier.

I noted that the bathroom's nautical theme was reflected in its blue-and-white wall tiles, in the replica lighthouse candle holder behind the bathtub, and in an old metal bucket that was painted in blue and white hoops and filled with sea shells.

"Where are your wounds?" Nikki asked as I shuffled to the bathtub.

"To my right calf and right buttock," I replied.

"Well then I'm sorry, Killian," Nikki answered. "But you're going to have to take down your trousers and underpants."

As I opened my grey cords and then gently lowered them and my underpants down to my ankles, I looked back over my shoulder and watched

Nikki for a few seconds as she pushed the bathroom door closed, locked it, and then busied herself lifting items from the glass shelves of a mirrored bathroom cabinet above the old sink.

"Ready," I told her when I had finished lowering my jeans and underpants and had looked away from her again.

A few seconds later, I heard Nikki snap on a pair of surgical gloves behind me, and pretended not to be too distressed as she prized away the bandage over the wound to my right buttock.

"Thank you," I whispered back as she attended to my wound. "Greg told me earlier that you confessed about our affair to him but that you refused to tell him who you had it with."

There was a pause before Nikki responded.

"Please don't thank me for that," she whispered back. "You and I both made a stupid mistake three years ago," she added. "Our selfishness could have messed up a lot of lives but luckily it didn't, so let's just leave things that way, okay?"

"Okay," I agreed and then sighed in pain as Nikki poked my calf injury.

My affair with Nikki had started one morning when I had paid an unnecessary visit to her surgery and had ended abruptly when Claire was murdered six months later.

In the three years since then, Nikki and I had met each other on numerous occasions in the tennis club, and in mutual friends' homes, and yet this was the first time we'd been alone together.

My recollections of that affair were suddenly terminated when Nikki's fingers pinched the skin around the wound to my right calf and I felt a severe sting of pain.

"What exactly happened to you?" Nikki queried as I squirmed.

"Some guy broke into my apartment with a knife," I told her, and then hissed as she dabbed my wounds with a stinging disinfectant. "He cut me twice before I fought him off."

"I see," an obviously unimpressed Nikki replied. "Both of these injuries need to be sutured," she stated. "How come the police didn't take you to a hospital?"

"Because I didn't call them," I disclosed. "I just patched myself up and came over here to meet Greg."

There was silence for a full two seconds before Nikki spoke again.

"I'll treat your injuries as best I can," she told me. "But they both really need to be stitched up and I don't have what's needed to do that here, okay?"

"Okay," I agreed. "I'll go to a hospital first thing in the morning."

"You had better," Nikki said. "In the meantime, I hope that your presence here isn't putting Greg, Steve, or me, in any kind of danger?"

"You know that I'd never do that," I replied and looked back over my shoulder as Nikki peeled the adhesive backing from a padded bandage then stooped down to adhere it to the back of my right calf.

"I'll leave here right now if you want me to," I added.

"No, you won't," Nikki replied. "Greg doesn't know about us, and I'd like to keep it that way. If you leave this house after being up here alone with me then he might ask some questions that I'd prefer not to have to answer."

"Okay then, I won't go," I promised her. "I'll just leave first thing in the morning."

"Good," Nikki said, covered the wound to my right buttock and then slapped my uninjured left buttock loudly. "Those bandages will last until tomorrow," she said. "But you will need to get them changed by then and your cuts stitched up, okay? You also need to get cleaned up for dinner," she added and then tossed a blue and white striped towel towards me.

"Thanks for everything," I said as Nikki removed the surgical gloves, deposited them in a wastebasket, and then left the bathroom.

Wednesday — Nineteen

Greg was in the kitchen when I got back downstairs and swung around to face me from the cooker's hob.

"You, okay?" he asked me.

"Yeah, I'm fine, Nikki looked after me," I replied. "What are you cooking?" I asked when I saw that two saucepans and a sizzling frying pan were vying for his attention.

"An amazing Italian eating experience," Greg answered. "Most people just make pasta, I cook it," he declared. "Do you want to have a beer before dinner?"

"Yes, please," I said and then examined an old black-and-white framed photograph on the wall above the pine kitchen table.

In the dated image, a young man with short black hair wore a white running singlet and was draped with a shiny medal at the end of a dark ribbon as he smiled self-consciously into the camera's lens.

I nodded towards the image as I accepted a bottled beer from Greg. "We had a similar shot of our dad in the house where I grew up," I told him. "He always claimed that it was only there to remind me and my brother that dreams don't come true unless you work at them."

"That was good advice," Greg said, and then turned back to the cooker and deftly used a spatula to lift trimmed strips of fried bacon from the frying pan into the smaller of the two saucepans. He then stirred the contents of the saucepan with a wooden spoon and bent forward to inhale its rich aroma.

When the meal was over, Nikki leant across the pine kitchen table, emptied what was left of a bottle of Chianti into my glass, and looked towards the doorway as her teenage son sauntered back into the kitchen to kiss her goodnight.

Having delivered a kiss to his mother's forehead, Steve then slapped open palms with his father and nodded a farewell to me before he left the room.

"He's off to spend a few hours on his iPad," Nikki commented when Steve had left us. "And in the morning, we'll have to drag him out of bed for school."

"It's always been like that," Greg stated. "When I was his age, I used to hide a miniature radio under the bed covers and listen to the latest pop music."

"Boys," Nikki commented and shook her head.

Greg took exception to his wife's comment. "At least we don't have a teenage daughter," he responded. "Then I would have gone from hero to zero as soon as she hit puberty. Apparently, that's how they behave towards their fathers," he said.

"That's lovely, Greg, exactly what Killian needed to hear," Nikki said as she got up from the table. "I'm sorry, Killian," she said. "But I've got an early start in the morning, so I'm going to have to leave you here all alone with Greg's wit and wisdom. Goodnight, and apologies for my husband's insensitivity."

"Goodnight, Nikki, and thanks again for patching me up," I said and turned my right cheek to receive her gentle peck. I then watched my former lover kiss her husband goodnight on the lips.

Greg followed Nikki's back with his eyes until she had left the kitchen and then turned to me.

"Now, let's have a real drink," he said and swung around to a cupboard, opened it, and lifted out a three-quarters-full bottle of Jameson.

An hour later, Greg reached out for the much-depleted whiskey bottle on the table to pour out our third drinks and then froze as a car screeched to a halt in the quiet cul-de-sac outside his house and was followed by the slamming of two car doors and a metallic squeak from the gate into his front garden.

"I think that you need to get out of here, Killian," Greg said as his head wobbled when two insistent knocks sounded on the house's front door.

"Shit," I exclaimed loudly but forgot my knife injuries as I leapt up from my chair. Unable to keep my balance as a searing pain shot up through my damaged right leg, I staggered backwards and then sat heavily on the edge of an antique sideboard.

"Sorry Greg, but I don't think that I'll get very far," I told my friend.

Greg ignored my self-pity. "Of course you will," he said. "I keep the gates along the side of the house locked," he said as he picked up my now empty whiskey tumbler from the table and placed it on the sideboard. "So, there's still plenty of time for you to get over the back wall before I answer the door to the callers," he said and then flung the kitchen's patio doors open to the back garden.

"What's going on?" I heard Nikki shout down the stairs as I thrust myself away from the sideboard, snatched my blazer from the back of my chair at the table, and stumbled towards the open patio doors into the house's back garden.

"There's someone at the front door. Don't worry, I'll look after it," Greg yelled, came out into the back garden and directed me towards the tall redbrick wall at its base.

"The tennis club is on the other side of that wall," he reminded me in a hushed but slurred tone. "I'm going to tell whoever's at the door that you left here hours ago. Good luck," he said and slapped my left shoulder as the front doorbell rang out a long blare.

"Thanks, Greg," I replied and then winced in pain as I hopped through the grass to the end of the back garden.

When I reached the redbrick wall, I leapt high, slapped my hands on its rounded top bricks, and hauled myself up until I was at its pinnacle.

Just before I let myself plunge down to the wall's other side, I threw a glance back up the garden towards Greg and Nikki's house and saw that two male figures had stepped out into the triangle of light that had spread from the kitchen's open terrace doors.

An instant later, I landed heavily on moist, well-trimmed grass, tumbled over a few times, and then righted myself and looked around the tennis club as my eyes adjusted to the dim moonlight.

Directly in front of me, I identified the flat-roofed outline of the tennis club's storeroom, hobbled forward, and leant a hand against one of its concrete walls as I checked its steel door.

When I saw that the door into the storeroom was locked, a smile came to my face and I rolled back the ribbed rubber mat on the ground in front of it to see a silver key glistening back up at me.

Years earlier, Greg and I were always the first two junior members to arrive at the tennis club on summer mornings. Back then, we would retrieve the key to the storeroom from under the mat, set up a net across what we considered to be the best of the tennis courts, and be on our third set by the time the club's caretaker arrived, shook his head when he saw us, and then used the equipment in the storeroom to set up the other courts.

When I had unlocked the storeroom door, I staggered inside, and then shut and locked it behind me. A moment later, I heard a car drive into the tennis club's car park and saw the light from its headlights seep into the storeroom beneath the door. When one of the car's doors had closed, I then heard a man's footsteps as he approached the storeroom and tried to open its door.

"It's locked," he shouted to his partner as I stepped further back into darkness.

"Then try the club house," his partner hollered back.

When, a few minutes later, I heard the car drive away, I sat down carefully on a folded tennis net in the darkened storeroom and thought back over my earlier conversation with Jill Maguire in the wet laneway and her prediction that O'Sullivan would have me arrested the next day.

What had I done that would have prompted her boss to come after me sooner that she had anticipated, I thought, and then shuddered with dread when I concluded that O'Sullivan might have been forced to take action against me when he had heard that the attempt on my life had failed.

THURSDAY — ONE

The foyer of the hotel was furnished like the main hall in a castle, which was probably why there wasn't a phone booth on display.

When I had crossed its unyielding flagstone floor, I asked the blond, middle-aged woman behind its reception desk if they obtained a public phone that I could use.

"Are you a guest here, sir?" she quizzed and appraised my unshaven face, ruffled hair, and disheveled clothes.

"No," I informed her, leant in closer to the reception desk, and saw that she was wearing a smart grey uniform and had her hair in a pageboy style. "I'm sorry, I didn't realize that you have to be staying here to use one of your telephones. Is that a new policy?"

The receptionist tilted her chin towards me, rotated a black telephone on the desk in front of her, and gave me a false smile. "You can use this one if you like," she said.

I looked down at the black telephone, shook my head, and lifted my eyes to her.

"I know that this might sound odd," I said. "But I'd prefer to use a phone booth, if that's possible."

The woman gestured to my left. "There's a public phone box just behind that staircase over there," she said. "You can use that one if you like."

"Thank you," I said, limped across the stone floor again, rounded the mock stone stairwell, and then stepped inside an antiquated wooden phone booth with an arched window of mottled glass inset into its front door.

I had gotten little sleep in the tennis club storeroom during the night and now found it hard to focus as I flicked through the pages of a well-thumbed telephone directory in search of a specific number.

"Garda Headquarters," a man answered when I had dialed that number.

"Hi, I'm looking for Detective Ken Lynch," I said in a mock country accent.

"Please hold on," the man told me. "I'm going to transfer you to our Stolen Motor Vehicles Investigation Unit," he said.

My call rang three more times before a woman came on the line and confirmed that I was through to the Stolen Motor Vehicles Investigation Unit.

"Grand, would Ken Lynch be there?" I asked.

"Detective Ken Lynch?" she responded.

"That's right," I confirmed and, after another short delay, was put through to Vincent Lynch's son. That was when I dropped the mock accent.

"This is Killian Doyle," I stated bluntly. "Get your father to call me on this number within the next minute."

"The number on my display?" the younger Lynch asked.

"One minute," I stated and hung up.

Fifty-three seconds later, the wooden telephone booth vibrated to an incoming call.

"What do you want?" Vincent Lynch asked when I answered his call.

"I did a lot of thinking last night and reached a conclusion," I replied.

"Yeah?" Lynch said.

"Yeah, I realized that you're a liar," I stated. "You didn't work out that my brother was murdered just by watching that news report on TV on Monday night, did you?"

"I don't know what you're talking about," Lynch replied.

"You know why my brother was killed and who did it, don't you, Lynch?"

"I still don't know what you're talking about," the retired detective said.

"Yes, you do," I stated. "And you know a lot more about O'Sullivan than you've told Anne Reid too," I said. "So why don't you start telling the truth?"

"I'm going to hang up now," Lynch said. "Goodbye, Mr. Doyle."

"Fine, you do that, Lynch," I said. "And my next call will be to Frank Hennessy to tell him that your little boy knows why Dave was murdered."

Lynch took a long breath. "Where are you?" he asked.

"Why, do you trust me now?" I teased.

"I asked you where are you?" Lynch replied.

"I'm in the Kincora Castle Hotel," I replied.

"I'll be there in twenty minutes," Lynch stated. "Where will I find you?"

"In the overflow car park," I said and hung up.

The call with Lynch over, I exited the antique telephone booth, stepped back out into the hotel's foyer, and then jarred to a standstill when I noted that the blond woman at the hotel's reception desk had been joined by one of her male colleagues as they looked down at a screen beneath the reception desk that cast a blue light up onto their faces.

When they lifted their heads in unison to stare at me, I realized that what Vincent Lynch had said to me in the park the previous day was true, that I was an amateur.

Maybe, I should have paid more attention to his advice?

Turning away from the reception desk as fast as my wounds would allow me to, I hobbled out of the hotel knowing that my presence there had been noted, and that my image had been captured on video.

Thursday — Two

Thirty-seven anxious minutes later, I watched as a slate-colored Ford Focus entered the hotel's overflow car park, circled it slowly twice, and then came to a stop.

When I saw Lynch behind the steering wheel of that Ford Focus, I stepped out of the bushes that I had been hiding in, and limped towards his car.

"You're late," I chastised the retired detective, dropped painfully into his car's passenger seat, and then fanned my face as I was enveloped by heat.

The older man didn't seem upset or surprised by my reaction to the high temperature in his car. "There are times when my body needs all its energy just to fight my illness, so I get cold," he told me. "I presume Anne told you that I'm sick?"

"Yes, she said that you have cancer and are going to die soon," I said. "Apparently, that's why you're such an asshole."

"Anne would never say that about me," Lynch replied.

"Maybe not in the past," I conceded. "But I bet that she would say that about you now. You thought that I would never get O'Sullivan for her and expected him to kill me before I got any evidence against him, didn't you?"

Lynch thought about what I'd said and then shook his head. "No, I didn't," he lied.

"O'Sullivan sent someone to kill me last night, the same guy who he got to kill Dave, but I fought him off," I continued. "Later, he sent two of his goons to get me, but I escaped them too. That's why I'm still here, and why you're going to tell me the truth."

"Hold on a minute and I'll tell you everything that I know," Lynch said, scanned the nearly empty car park and then drove his car into a secluded corner where the white lines were tainted green by some moss that had spread from the lawn.

"Okay, now tell me what you know," I said as Lynch stopped his car and killed its engine. "Or will I call Frank Hennessy and tell him that your son knows everything?"

The retired detective ignored me and held up a photograph that he took out of his jacket instead. "Do you know this guy?" he asked me.

I studied the image in Lynch's hand. It was a mug shot of a clean shaven but balding young man. "He looks familiar," I replied. "Who is he?"

"His name is Barry Galvin," Lynch said. "He's a small-time criminal who rats out his pals to Cormack O'Sullivan from time to time. On Monday, he made a Garda statement that you crashed your car into his and then drove off at speed."

"Now I remember him!" I yelled and grabbed the photograph from Lynch's hand. Galvin had grown a beard and had a cap on when I'd met him, and yet there was no doubt in my mind about the identity of the man in the photograph. "He's the creep who crashed into me when I was driving to The O'Malley Centre to meet Dave. Where did you get this?"

For the first time since I had met him in Anne Reid's house, Lynch smiled.

"So, I was right," he said. "Cormack O'Sullivan got Barry Galvin to slow you down on your way to The O'Malley Centre. That way, you never got to talk to your brother."

"I don't get it," I said. "How would anyone have known that I was going to drive out to that particular Jasper's Restaurant on Monday morning?"

Lynch shook his head. "Because Cormack O'Sullivan knew that your brother wanted to tell you something, and worked out that there were only two ways he could do that. Over the phone, or in person. All he had to do was monitor the phone calls between you and your brother to know if you spoke, and to cover the road between your advertising agency and The O'Malley Centre to see if you met up."

"Sorry, you've lost me," I told Lynch.

"It's simple," the retired detective said. "Cormack O'Sullivan knew that there were only two ways that your brother could talk to you on Monday morning, so he covered both of them until he was dead."

"But why would O'Sullivan do that?" I asked.

"Because he was covering something up," Lynch said. "Ken told me that Cormack O'Sullivan called his unit on Monday morning and wanted an update on a hit-and-run that happened out in Sutton on Sunday evening."

"Remind me?" I asked Lynch.

"Some kid chased a football out onto Quinn Road in Sutton on Sunday night and got killed," Lynch replied. "The car that hit him stopped for a moment and then drove off."

"And O'Sullivan was interested in that?" I asked him.

"Yes," Lynch affirmed. "Ken said that Cormack O'Sullivan claimed that he wanted something to share with the dead boy's family as he knew them."

"And did he get something?" I asked.

Lynch shook his head. "No, he didn't," he replied. "The only witnesses to the hit-and-run were kids and Ken told Cormack O'Sullivan that the forensics guys hadn't found anything either."

I dropped my eyes to the car's floor. The hit-and-run had been one of the news items on the media list that Jimmy Nixon from the advertising agency's media department had supplied, but I had discounted its relevance when I saw that the incident took place in the northeast of Dublin a full twenty-eight minutes before Dave had telephoned Louise.

My younger brother would have still been on his way back from Wexford and on the other side of town at that time.

I turned back to Vincent Lynch.

"Do you have a map of Dublin here?" I asked him.

"Yes, I do," the retired detective replied, bent forward and took a folded map from the car's glove compartment. "Why, what are you looking for?"

THURSDAY — THREE

I located Sutton on the map of Dublin that Lynch had taken out of his car's glove compartment, ran a finger along the beige line that represented Quinn Road, reached back for the safety belt that was hanging next to one of the car's door pillars, pulled it tight across my lap, and clicked it into place on the other side of the passenger seat.

"What are you doing now?" Lynch asked me.

"I'm putting on my safety belt before you drive us out to Sutton to see where that kid was killed," I replied. "After that, we're going to visit the Royal Griffith Golf Club, which is also on Quinn Road in Sutton. Frank Hennessy is a member of that club, so we're going to see if he was playing there on Sunday."

"We are?" Lynch said.

"Yes, we are," I replied. "And on the way there, you're going to tell me what you really know about my brother's murder and O'Sullivan. Now, let's get going."

After shaking his head and exhaling loudly, Lynch started his car, steered it out of the hotel and took the left exit at the next roundabout.

"I presume that you've heard about the taxi that picked up your brother's killer when he got back into town on Monday?" he asked me as we accessed the coastal road that would take us to Sutton.

"Yes, I did," I answered. "Why?"

"Because Ken has a theory about that taxi," Lynch replied. "His team have been keeping an eye on a scumbag called Pierce McDermott for the past few months. McDermott learnt how to fix cars when he was behind bars for stealing them. These days, he and his son tart up crashed cars and then sell them to some Nigerian gang that rents them out as taxis. Ken reckons that the taxi that picked up your brother's killer was one of the cars that McDermott and his son had fixed up. Apparently, it was sprayed a shade of brown that they use a lot because they bought that color in bulk."

"Who else has your son shared his theory with?" I asked.

"No one," Lynch told me as we stopped at traffic lights.

"And yet this McDermott guy and his son might know who killed my brother?" I asked.

"Yes, they might," Lynch conceded as the traffic lights turned to green. "But there's a problem," he added. "McDermott and his son know Cormack O'Sullivan well and will call him if anyone talks to them. If we speak to them and they do that, Cormack O'Sullivan might spot that it was Ken who leaked information to me, and go after him."

"Do you know where to find this McDermott guy and his son?" I asked.

"Yes, I do, why?" Lynch answered.

"Because we need to check them out as soon as we're finished in Sutton," I said.

Lynch shook his head again. "I just told you why that wouldn't be a good idea," he said. "McDermott and his son know me and might work out where I got my information about them and the taxi. Plus, they'll call Cormack O'Sullivan as soon as we leave them. So, it might be better if you talked to the McDermott father and son alone."

I turned to Lynch. "I get it now," I began. "Anne Reid had already told you about me before Monday, so when you spotted that O'Sullivan might have had my brother killed, you got her to call me. You knew that I would go after O'Sullivan when you told me your theory about Dave's death being a crime within a crime, didn't you?"

"Sometimes, you think too much," Lynch said.

"Yes, I do," I said. "But now I know why you told me to back off yesterday, because you knew that I'd never do that, and would try even harder to find out who had killed my brother just to prove you wrong."

"Yeah, right," Vincent Lynch said.

"You knew that I would eventually hone in on O'Sullivan if you drip-fed me just enough information about him," I added. "That way, you would get me to risk my life while you and your son stayed safe," I said. "That's it, isn't it, Lynch, you're using me to get O'Sullivan?"

When Lynch didn't deny my accusation, I continued. "I'll get O'Sullivan," I said. "But you're going to have to help me to do that by telling the truth."

"The truth?" Lynch asked.

"Yes, the truth," I stated. "I need to hear everything that you know."

Lynch checked the car's rear-view mirror, signaled left, and then pulled the Ford Focus over to the side of the road. When he had switched off its engine, he turned to me.

"Look, Doyle, let's settle this," he said. "I'll tell you everything that I know about Cormack O'Sullivan but only if you agree to keep my son out of this. I don't want to die with Ken's life in danger, do you understand that?"

"Yes, I understand that," I replied. "And I'll agree to keep your son out of this. But only on one condition, Lynch, that you tell the truth and don't keep anything from me again, okay?"

"Okay," Lynch replied, checked the car's rear-view mirror again, and then steered his Ford Focus back out onto the coast road to Sutton.

We didn't speak to each other for a mile and then I broke the silence.

"Anne Reid told me last night that her husband spotted something between O'Sullivan and the owner of a Chinese restaurant," I said. "What do you know about that?"

"The Chinese guy that she was talking about is called Freddy Chuang," Lynch replied. "He's into various criminal stuff but has never been charged with anything."

"Why not?" I asked and then stirred in the passenger seat to relieve the pain from my right buttock, which I felt was bleeding again.

Lynch paused before he spoke again, "Because Chuang has got a lot of friends in high places and no one has ever been able to pin anything on him," he said and then took his right hand away from the steering wheel long enough to tip a finger against the bridge of his glasses. "Why, what were you thinking?"

"That Chuang might tell us something about O'Sullivan," I said.

From the grimace on Lynch's face, I knew that he didn't agree with my suggestion.

"I'm not sure about that," he said. "Chuang is a hard nut to crack, so I don't think that he'd say anything to us about Cormack O'Sullivan."

Lynch's response concerned me. "Do you think that it would be a waste of time visiting Chuang?" I asked him.

"Yes, lots of people have questioned Chuang but didn't get anywhere," he said. "And I don't think that he'd say much to us this time either."

I let a moment go by and then asked Lynch another question. "What's this Chuang guy into?" I asked him.

"Whores, drugs, gambling, protection, that sort of stuff," Lynch replied.

"And yet he's still free," I said and then changed the subject. "Anne Reid told me something else last night that I'd like to hear more about too."

"Yeah, what was that?" Lynch queried as he turned his car right at a junction.

"She told me that the relationship between Tony Maguire and O'Sullivan changed significantly at some point," I said. "Afterwards, Tony Maguire acted like a slave to O'Sullivan. What do you know about that?"

Lynch shook his head. "Nothing," he said. "Anne asked me about that ages ago. I told her back then that I didn't know what she was talking about."

"So, you're not aware of anything that happened between Tony Maguire and O'Sullivan that changed the way that they worked together?" I asked him.

Lynch shook his head again. "No," he answered.

"You didn't like that question, did you?" I asked as Lynch dropped the car into a lower gear and applied more pressure to the accelerator as we climbed a hill. "Remember, that you promised to be honest with me to protect your son," I reminded him.

"I don't know the answer to that question, okay?" Lynch replied as we reached the turn onto Quinn Road and I saw a lamppost with a floral tribute attached to it.

THURSDAY — FOUR

"**D**o you reckon this is the place?" I asked Lynch as he stopped his car and I saw that the bunch of flowers was adhered to the lamppost with once-clear tape that had bubbled and browned in the summer sunshine.

"It looks like it," he replied, applied the handbrake, and then left his car to take a closer look at the wilted flowers that were cloaked in crinkled cellophane.

I climbed painfully out of Lynch's car, stood next to him on the pavement as he made a clumsy attempt to see if there was a note attached to the flowers, and then looked across the road at a rectangular green area that was hemmed in on three sides by semi-detached houses with short front gardens.

The patch of grass that I was looking at measured about eighty-yards by forty, and from the oval patches of dried earth at either end of it, was where I assumed that the local kids gathered to play football.

When I turned back to Lynch, I noted that another shadow had joined his on the pavement, raised my right hand to shield my eyes from the sun, and saw that it belonged to a large elderly woman in a light raincoat with a shovel-shaped face, horn-rimmed glasses, and curly hair that had recently been blue-rinsed.

I cleared my throat to get Lynch's attention as some petals from the abused bouquet of flowers fell to the dusty ground.

"What?" he barked and then jolted when he spotted the woman.

"Do you want to know something about those flowers?" she asked.

"I was just checking to see if someone had left a note," Lynch replied. "This is where the little boy was killed on Sunday night, right?"

"Maybe," the woman said. "Who are you?"

"Two men who are interested in what happened here," Lynch stated.

"Then I suggest that the two of you take your interest someplace else," the woman advised. "Because we don't have much time for people like you around here."

"People like us?" I queried and limped towards her. "We're trying to find out who killed the little boy here," I said. "And could do without your attitude."

The woman glared back at me for a moment and then nodded across the road to one of the houses located around the green. A dormer bungalow with a red front door.

"I live just over there and was one of the first adults on the scene when little Sean died here on Sunday night," she said. "Since then, lots of people have stopped by to have a gawk at where he died and to ask stupid questions. I thought that you were more of them. Obviously, you're not."

"No, we're not," I told her. "We have a reason for being here."

"Then I'm sorry. What do you want to know?" she asked.

"Not much," Lynch said as he entered the conversation. "Just if anyone around here saw anything."

"None of the adults, if that's what you mean," the woman replied to him. "In fact, apart from the other kids that Sean was playing with, there were no witnesses."

"What did the kids say happened here?" Lynch asked her.

"They said that the car that hit Sean stopped just down the road and two men got out of it," The woman said. "They looked back up here," she added and then pointed to the road just in front of the lamppost. "Saw that little Sean was lying there, and then just got back into their car and drove off. The kids said that they were big guys. But then kids always say that about grown-ups, don't they?"

"I suppose so," Lynch agreed. "Did they say anything about the car?"

The woman nodded. "They said that it had two doors and looked expensive. Some of the kids said that it was a BMW, others that it was a

Mercedes. They also found the car's color a bit hard to make out," she added. "Some of them said it was dark blue, others that it was black. It must have been the twilight or something."

"Thanks," Lynch said as the woman moved away from us and continued her journey across the road to her home.

When she was gone, I gazed down at the surface of the road where the little boy had died and then followed the road as I looked up the hill and saw that the entrance to the Royal Griffith Golf Club was just three hundred yards away.

"That's where we're going next, isn't it?" Lynch asked me.

"Yes, it is," I said and then cautiously got back into his Ford Focus.

"What type of car does Frank Hennessy drive?" Lynch asked me as he started his car's engine again.

"A navy-blue Mercedes coupe," I responded. "Frank usually parks it outside the entrance to Jasper's Head Office. Only it wasn't there on Tuesday morning," I added and clicked my safety belt closed again.

"You need to get answers to three questions when you go into that golf club," Lynch said as he steered his car back out onto the road and we headed up the hill again.

"I need to get answers to three questions?" I queried.

"Yes, you'll be fine in there on your own," Lynch said. "If I went in with you, it might look odd, so I'll wait out in the car," he stated as he drove his Ford Focus through the open gates into the golf club's grounds and we ascended the curving driveway that led up to its clubhouse.

"What three questions?" I asked Lynch as he pulled his car into a parking space that offered a view of a well-tended lawn that was bordered by a natural stone wall, beyond which Dublin Bay sparkled in the late summer sunshine.

"It's nice here," Lynch commented as he shut off his car's engine again and engaged its handbrake. "The questions are if Hennessy and O'Sullivan were there on Sunday? If so, what time did they leave at? And if they were drinking?"

"Right, so I'll just go in there and ask those three questions?" I queried Lynch who looked back at me as if I was an idiot.

"No," he replied. "When you go in there, you pretend that you already know the answers to those three questions," he told me. "That way, people will open up and tell you things that they wouldn't otherwise. I thought that you'd know all that?"

"Of course I do," I replied, got out of Lynch's car, and made my way into the Royal Griffith's clubhouse, the interior of which had been repainted in a matte cream finish since my last visit there with my father-in-law.

Frank Hennessy regularly played golf at the exclusive club, and his image smiled out at me from a poster promoting a senior members' competition as I passed the club's notice board and climbed the double flight of carpeted stairs that led up to the golf club's scenic lounge.

Thursday — Five

The thin man on duty behind the counter in the club's lounge bar wore a white shirt, a black dickey-bow, and a wine-colored waistcoat with a fake brass nametag pinned to it that identified him as Billy. He also had pock marks that shadowed his cheeks and a pair of green eyes that opened wide in surprise as I limped towards him.

"Hi, Billy, how are you?" I asked on reaching the bar counter.

"Fine," Billy replied and lowered a recently washed beer glass and a white bar towel to the counter top. "Are you here alone, Killian?" he asked me.

"Yes, I had to meet someone nearby, so Frank asked me to pick up something for him," I lied. "He told me that he left one of his credit cards here on Sunday."

Billy furrowed his brow and turned back to the rear bar counter where a neat row of spirit bottles was lined up on either side of the cash till, their labels facing outwards.

"If anyone leaves anything here, I usually put it over there next to the till," Billy said. "But I don't remember Frank using a credit card here on Sunday," he added. "In fact, I'm pretty sure that he paid for his drinks with cash."

"Wow, that's some memory," I complimented Billy. "You can probably even remember what Frank had to drink."

Billy nodded. "Frank had his usual two gin and tonics, and Cormack had two pints of Heineken," he told me.

"That's amazing," I said and shook my head. "You can remember all that, and yet Frank mistakenly recalled leaving his credit card here. I presume that you were the only one on duty here on Sunday night?"

Billy nodded again. "When Frank and Cormack were here, yes," he said. "They left at about seven and I was alone behind the bar until eight," he replied. "I can check back through the credit card receipts if you like, but I'm fairly certain that Frank paid for his drinks with cash."

"No, that's okay, Frank must be mistaken," I said and turned to leave.

"Sorry, Killian, please hold on a minute," Billy called out after me and then extended his right hand when I turned back to him. "I was terribly sorry to hear about Dave," he said and shook my hand. "I always enjoyed his company."

"Thanks, Billy," I said and patted the back of his hand.

Back outside the clubhouse, I crossed over to Lynch's car, slid into its passenger seat carefully, bent forward, closed my eyes, and moaned loudly.

"What is it?" Lynch asked me.

"The answers to the three questions were that Frank Hennessy and O'Sullivan were there on Sunday, that they left just before the boy was knocked down, and that they were both drinking," I said without opening my eyes.

"Which means?" Lynch asked.

I opened my eyes and stared across at Lynch. "Which means that everything adds up," I said. "If Frank was driving the car that killed that little boy, and O'Sullivan was with him, then they could have driven back to Jasper's Head Office on Sunday night and met Dave there just as he got back from Wexford."

"I still don't get you?" Lynch said.

"If Dave was at Jasper's Head Office on Sunday evening when Frank and O'Sullivan got back there, he would have seen that Frank's car was damaged," I said. "And then he could have heard about the death of that kid in the hit-and-run near the golf club that Frank is a member of."

"Do you think that's why your brother arrived home in such an odd mood, ignored his wife, and then called you?" Lynch asked me.

"Yes, I do," I said. "If I had taken his calls, Dave was probably going to tell me about what he had seen. That could explain why he gave me that look on Monday. Because he thought that I knew what was going on."

"We don't have any proof that's what happened yet," Lynch said. "Until we do, there is no evidence against O'Sullivan, and no way of knowing what your brother was thinking either. So don't even go there."

"Don't even go there," I repeated. "Maybe if you weren't such a coward, then O'Sullivan would be locked up by now instead of being free to harm my brother. Give me your mobile phone," I said and reached out an open hand towards Lynch.

"What do you want my phone for?" Lynch asked as he took out his mobile phone, handed it over to me, and then reversed his Ford Focus out of the parking space and aimed it back down the golf club's driveway.

"We need evidence against Frank and O'Sullivan and I know where to get it," I said, dialed the phone number for the advertising agency and asked to be put through to Jimmy Nixon in its media department.

"Jimmy isn't here, he's in a meeting," his assistant, Christine, told me.

"A meeting in the advertising agency?" I asked.

"Yes," Christine replied. "In the conference room on the second floor."

"Then get him," I instructed her. "This is urgent."

Jimmy's droll voice came on the line about twenty-seconds later.

"Hi, Killian, what's up?" he asked me.

I dispensed with a response. "On the list that you compiled on Tuesday, one of the radio items that Dave could have heard on Sunday evening was a news story about a hit-and-run accident that a little boy died in."

"So," Jimmy replied.

"I need to know exactly what that report said," I told Jimmy. "How quickly can you get a transcript of it for me?" I asked him.

"I'm not sure?" he replied.

"Yeah, well I need that transcript as soon as possible," I said. "So, I'll call you again in about ten minutes. Have it by then, okay?"

When the call to Jimmy had ended, I handed the phone back to Lynch.

"That transcript will prove nothing," he told me.

"Yes, it will," I countered. "It will prove that Dave could have heard about the hit-and-run on his way home on Sunday night."

"Yeah, right," Lynch said. "Like everything else that we have now, that transcript is circumstantial. It won't prove that Hennessy knocked down that kid on Sunday evening, won't prove that Cormack O'Sullivan and him went back to Jasper's Head Office afterwards, won't prove why your brother phoned you, and won't prove that your brother was listening to the radio that evening either."

"Then what do we need to do?" I asked him.

"Get some hard evidence," Lynch replied. "If we suspect that Cormack O'Sullivan got Pierce McDermott involved in your brother's death, based on what we heard from my son, Ken, then that's who we need to talk to next. I know where McDermott and his son hang out. However, there's a problem talking to them there."

"Which is?" I asked.

"That McDermott and his son know me and will call Cormack O'Sullivan if I go near them or their place," Lynch said.

"Great," I said. "You know where this McDermott guy and his son hang out, and yet we can't go there to get the evidence that we need."

"No, we can't," Lynch said. "But maybe you can."

"What!" I shouted. "Go there alone?"

"Yes," Lynch said. "You did really well in that golf club earlier, so maybe you could talk to McDermott and his son alone too."

I thought about what Lynch said, and our need to get evidence against O'Sullivan. "Okay, I'll do it," I said. "But you're going to have to tell me what to say and drive me there."

"I can't do that," Lynch said. "I can tell you where to go, and what to say, but if I drive you there either of the McDermotts might spot me and know what we're up to. If that happened, they'd call O'Sullivan and I'd be putting Ken's life at risk, and I can't do that."

"You can't even go near the place?" I asked him.

Lynch shook his head. "No, it's too risky," he said.

I stayed quiet, saw from the rigid expression on the dying man's sweating face that he was unlikely to be swayed, and then thought of something.

"Okay, I'll borrow a car and go there and talk to them myself," I said. "But only if you do something for me first."

"Do something for you?" Lynch asked me.

"Yes," I said. "I want you to get someone's mobile number from that son of yours. Do that and I'll take it from here."

Lynch called his son, Ken, waited for him to call back, and then wrote down the number that was given to him and handed it and his mobile phone across to me.

"You want to borrow my car?" Nikki howled when I phoned her mobile phone number and advised her of what I needed.

"Yes, but just for an hour," I promised.

"Have you gone completely mad?" Nikki asked me as I looked across at Lynch. "Why the hell would I lend my car to you?"

"Because I need it to do something," I said. "Please, Nikki."

"After last night, I'm not sure about this," Nikki said. "You promised that you wouldn't involve Greg, Steve, or me in whatever little drama you have going on right now, and yet, a while later, two detectives called to our house to arrest you. Things could have been a lot worse if Greg hadn't known what to do."

"I'm sorry about that, Nikki," I said. "But please lend me your car for an hour."

"Those detectives told us that you are dangerous," Nikki continued. "They warned us to contact them if you got in touch with us again. And now you want to borrow my car!?"

"Please, Nikki," I said. "You know that I'm not dangerous. I just need your car for a while, that's all, do this for me and I'll stay out of your life for a long time, Greg's too."

Nikki didn't reply to me but I could hear her labored breathing. If I was a doctor and she was my patient, I'd have a word with Nikki about that breathing.

"Okay, here's what I'm going to do," she eventually stated, "I'm going to lend you my car for an hour but afterwards you don't phone Greg or me for a long, long time. Is that understood, Killian?"

"Yes, that's perfectly understood," I replied.

"Okay, where will we meet?" she asked and exhaled loudly.

THURSDAY — SIX

"**Y**ou're getting a loan of a car?" Lynch asked when I had hung up the call to Nikki and handed him back his mobile phone.

"Yes," I said, and tried to get more comfortable in the car's passenger seat. "Now all you have to do is drive me back to where we met earlier, tell me how to get to McDermott's place, and then advise me what to say when I get there."

"McDermott has a unit in an industrial estate called Dolphin's Dock," a relieved Lynch replied as he drove us back to the hotel. "It's off the Long Mile Road, near the junction with Keane Road. Heading out of town, Dolphin's Dock is on your left-hand side. You turn off at a pub called Wright's, and then take the next right. The industrial estate is straight ahead about a half-mile down that road."

"Thanks for that," I said. "Now, what will I say when I get there?"

Lynch told me how to deal with McDermott and his son as we drove back to the hotel car park and then pulled his car up.

"Thanks," I said as I exited his Ford Focus. "I'll call Anne Reid after I've talked to McDermott and get her to call you."

"I'd prefer if you didn't do that," Lynch replied.

"Of course you would," I said. "That way, you'll be able to pretend to Anne Reid that you weren't involved today."

"Do you have a problem with that?" Lynch enquired from his car.

"Yes, I do," I replied. "What happens if I can't find McDermott's place, or if him and his son aren't responsive to those questions when I get there," I asked him.

"If those things happen, then you won't have any evidence against O'Sullivan," Lynch answered. "If that's the case, then you'll need to confront your father-in-law, Frank Hennessy. Start by telling him that you know all about the hit-and-run in Sutton on Sunday night and see how quickly he turns on Cormack O'Sullivan to save himself."

"See how quickly Frank turns on O'Sullivan?" I asked. "Do you really think he'd do that?"

"Yes, I do," Lynch said. "Scumbags like him do that all the time. When Hennessy knows that the game is up, he'll blame Cormack O'Sullivan for everything. It will be Cormack O'Sullivan who encouraged him to drive away when he ran over that little boy, it will be Cormack O'Sullivan who got him to get rid of his car, and it will be Cormack O'Sullivan who decided to murder your little brother. You'll see."

"You'd like that, wouldn't you, Lynch?" I said. "Because then O'Sullivan will become the fall guy and that's why you manipulated me, wasn't it, to get him?"

Lynch shook his head. "Manipulate is a very strong word," he said. "Yes, like you, I want to get rid of Cormack O'Sullivan, but I never manipulated you. I just pointed you in the right direction."

"Of course," I said and looked back into Lynch's car. "You just pointed me in the right direction and then sat back and watched me while you stayed safe."

"Don't try that, Doyle," Lynch retorted. "You didn't have to respond when Anne Reid called you on Tuesday, but you did. That's why you nearly lost your life last night, and why we're here now."

"And now that O'Sullivan is after me, I can't let this go," I said. "You spotted that he would come after me, didn't you, Lynch? And yet you still haven't told me what you know about O'Sullivan and Tony Maguire's relationship."

"What I know about their relationship?" Lynch asked me.

"Yes, and there you go again, Lynch," I said. "Dodging my question with one of your own. Until the next time," I stated and started to walk away from his car.

"The next time?" Lynch shouted after me.

"Yes, until the next time," I called back and then limped across the hotel's spillover car park and exited its grounds to meet Nikki.

I didn't trust Lynch, and didn't believe his negative reaction when I had suggested visiting Freddy Chuang's restaurant either. What was he afraid that I would discover there?

I was also weary that Lynch had only agreed to meet me after I had threatened to tell Frank about his son.

THURSDAY — SEVEN

"**Y**ou didn't get those cuts looked at, did you?" Nikki asked as I sat gingerly into her racing green Mini Cooper around the corner from the hotel in Clontarf.

"No, not yet," I admitted. "I was planning to do that later."

A disappointed Nikki shook her head of auburn curls and then pointed down at a circular display on her car's dashboard.

"It says that there's half a tank of fuel," she said. "You'll have to replace any petrol that you use and get my car back here undamaged in one hour, agreed?"

"Yes, that's agreed," I confirmed. "I'll contact you as soon as I'm back here."

"You better, and I mean that Killian. And don't call my office when you get back here either, use my mobile number again. It's on this," Nikki said as she handed me a business card. She then leant across her car and kissed the side of my face. "Take care," she said and left.

I waited until Nikki had walked away, groaned loudly as I moved across to the driver's side of her car, and then settled in behind the steering wheel and adjusted the rear-view mirrors.

Then, as Nikki looked back at me, I put her Mini Cooper into gear and attempted to advance forward slowly.

Unfortunately, I pressed my injured leg down too firmly on the accelerator as I released the clutch pedal and Nikki's car howled loudly as it darted forward.

I had soon gained full control of Nikki's car and, apart from the brief appearance of a Garda helicopter overhead, the rest of my drive across town to Dolphin's Dock was uneventful, easier, and quicker than I had envisaged.

On spotting a battered phone box in front of a row of shops, I stopped Nikki's car and called Jimmy at the advertising agency.

"Did you get the transcript?" I asked when I was put through to him.

"Yes, I'll read it to you," Jimmy said. "A ten-year-old boy was knocked down and killed by a hit-and-run driver on Quinn Road in Sutton shortly after 7:00 p.m. this evening. The Garda are looking for two men in a dark, coupe-type car, and have asked anyone with information to contact them at Howth, or their local Garda Station."

"That was it?" I asked.

"In its entirety," Jimmy confirmed. "Anything else?"

"No, just read it to me again," I answered him.

When Jimmy had finished reading the transcript for a second time, I thanked him, hung up, got back into Nikki's car, and completed the journey into the industrial estate.

Although what that Jimmy had read to me was brief, if Dave had heard it on his car's radio after he had seen Frank Hennessy's damaged Mercedes, then it might have contained enough detail for him to work out who the driver was that the cops were looking for.

That would explain Dave's change of mood on Sunday night and clarify why he had tried to contact me instead of talking to Louise.

I slowed Nikki's Mini Cooper down at the security hut into Dolphin's Dock Industrial Estate and saw that, while the security hut itself was a burnt-out shell, the sign above it that mapped out the location of the businesses within the estate was still legible.

A moment later, after negotiating some of the looped and corrugated concrete roads within the industrial estate, I spotted a front-facing yard that was home to two gigantic mounds.

One those mounds consisted of rusting motor parts while the other was a collection of wrecked cars. Behind the two mounds was a blue two-story building. The name McDermott didn't appear anywhere on that building, and yet, I assumed that I had arrived at the right destination, parked on the side of the road, entered the cluttered yard on foot and began limping along the rust-stained driveway that led to the front of the building.

I had almost arrived there when I became aware of the frenzied wheeze and heavy footfall of a charging animal behind me and turned to see that a black Doberman was racing towards me.

"Shit, no!" I cried as the dog leapt up at me with a nasty snarl.

I then heard a sharp metallic snap as the Doberman froze in midair with its sharp teeth just inches away from my face.

Puzzled, I took a step back as the Doberman fell to the ground and saw what had restrained him. A metal chain that was attached to a pole next to a timber dog's hut

"There's a good boy." I said, showed my palms as the dog clawed at the dusty concrete and then breathed a sigh of relief as the Doberman's head dropped and it wandered away to return to its home.

When the dog had abandoned me, I turned and continued my journey towards the blue office building on shaky legs.

Up close, I noticed that the blue building had once been a much deeper blue color before a lot of its paint had either faded or flaked away, and that a steel security door used to cover its entrance was tied back in an open position, revealing what used to be a white wooden door.

Convinced that anyone inside the building would have heard the commotion in the yard, I was surprised that no one was looking out of a window as I knocked on that door, stood back, and then saw that a rectangular patch of lighter-colored concrete covered the ground next to the blue building.

The absence of any vehicle in what was so obviously a parking space, it even had a circular oil stain, and the fact that no one seemed to have heard my yell as the Doberman rushed towards me, led me to believe that the blue building was unoccupied.

After glancing back into the yard, I reached forward, turned the once white wooden door's round handle and pushed it open. Inside the door was a small, square hallway that offered me two more choices.

A slightly ajar and grease-stained plywood door that lay directly in front of me, or a flight of steep steps that rose to my left.

I chose the plywood door but tried to make out the noise on its other side before I opened it. The sound that I heard consisted of an occasional mechanical splutter that evolved into a severe hiss and was followed by a smoother whipping sound.

That noise sounded power-driven, and yet possessed a rhythm suggestive of human involvement. I waited for five seconds and then stretched out my right hand and pushed the plywood door open a few more inches.

When I bent forward to look through the enlarged gap that I had made between the plywood door and its frame, I saw that an untidy workshop was occupied by a man with his back to me who was operating a spray gun.

Dressed in paint-stained tan overalls, the elasticated strip from a respirator mask ran across the back of the man's fair-haired head as he compressed the spray-gun's trigger again, and, as the noise increased, I realized why he had failed to hear me in the yard.

With the noise from the spray-gun assailing my ears, and the workshop's hazy air filling my nostrils, I stepped-back, gripped the edge of the plywood door with my fingertips and pulled it back into its original position until I had closed it as far as it would go.

I then turned painfully in the small square hallway, gripped the rickety wooden banisters on either side of the narrow staircase, and stealthily landed one foot at a time on the varnish-free semicircle at the front of each step until I arrived on the narrow landing above and had three more doors to choose from.

Inset with a frosted glass window, the first of those three doors opened into a constricted cubicle that contained a soiled and a seatless toilet bowl, some newspapers, and a bad smell.

The second door opened into a storage room where steel shelves bulged downwards as they bore the weight of salvaged electronic car parts.

The third door on the upper floor of the blue building gave me access to a small rectangular office furnished with two damaged veneer desks and two brown plastic stacking chairs.

Affixed with masking tape to the wall above one of those chairs was a color photograph of two booze-happy men behind a lot of empty-glasses that had piled up on a pub table.

Dressed in replica Manchester United jerseys, both men had large square noses, wide foreheads, and short, fair hair.

The age difference between them indicated that they were a father and son and that I had indeed found McDermott's place.

That was when I heard the heavy sigh of air brakes, rushed across that room to its dirt encrusted window, and saw that a yellow tow-truck had pulled into the yard.

As that yellow truck progressed between the rusted mounds towards the patch of cleared concrete on the ground next to the blue building, I decided to get out of there as fast as I could.

Thursday — Eight

If I really hurried, I calculated that there was still just enough time for me to make it downstairs before the driver of the yellow tow-truck entered the building.

I had made it halfway down the flight of wooden stairs when a flash of pain shot through my right leg and I lost balance.

"What the fuck?" the man from the tow-truck shouted as he opened the white door into the small hallway and then had to dodge back outside to avoid me as I tumbled forward down the remaining steps of the stairs into the tight entrance hallway.

On getting back to my feet, I reached out for its internal handle, slammed the white door shut to keep the man from the yellow tow-truck in the yard, and then spun back around to the plywood door to find myself standing eye-to-eye with the man inside the respiration mask.

From the startled but widening eyes staring back at me from inside the mask, I realized that he was the same man who had been wearing a black ski-mask when he had tried to kill me the previous night, rammed the heel of my right hand into his masked face, shoved him back into the workshop, and then snatched up a steel wrench from a battered metal bench as he fell back to the floor.

"Tell me who paid you to kill my brother or I'm going to hit you?" I yelled as I advanced towards him holding up the steel wrench.

Before the masked man answered me, I was forced to dive beneath a metal workbench after a bullet sped past my head, ricocheted off a naked car frame, and smashed into one of the glass-fronted storage cases bolted to one of the workshop's walls.

"My son isn't going to tell you anything," I heard Pierce McDermott shout as I rolled over and a second bullet clanged off the surface of the metal workbench.

"Okay, okay, I give up," I said from beneath the workbench as a pair of men's legs came towards me from the entrance into the workshop.

"Good," the older man with the gun said as I kicked both my feet up against the base of the metal workbench and then scrambled towards the building's small hallway where I froze when a gunshot thudded into the plywood door.

"Nice try, Doyle," Pierce McDermott said, and then instructed me to turn around as I held my hands up in a gesture of surrender.

Behind him, his son rose from the floor, yanked the mask free from his face, and then inhaled some air.

"Thanks, Dad, he nearly had me there," he told his father.

"It's over now," his father in the oil-stained navy-blue overalls said.

"Why, what are you going to do, kill me?" I asked.

"No," the older McDermott said. "We're not going to do anything to you if you tell us the truth."

"Tell you the truth?" I repeated.

"That's right, do that, and we're not going to kill you," Pierce McDermott said. "Start by telling us how you found us here?"

"You know that I'm not going to answer that question, McDermott," I stated. "Someone is with me and will raise the alarm if I'm not out of here soon."

Pierce McDermott shook his head. "Tough shit, Doyle, but we both know that isn't true," he said, lowered his gun and pointed it at my groin. "Now, I'm not going to ask you again. How did you find us here?"

"Frank Hennessy told me all about you," I replied while keeping my hands up. "He told me that you repaired his car after he killed that kid in Sutton on Sunday, and then had your son murder Dave the next morning. He told me that he's going to rat you out."

Surprised by my answer, McDermott Senior maintained his silence until his son spoke up from behind him.

"He's lying, Dad, just shoot the fucker," he said.

"I'm warning you, Doyle, don't lie again," his father said. "Now, who told you about us?"

I considered telling McDermott about Lynch and his son, Ken, but realized that I would probably be killed as soon as I said that, so changed what I was about to say.

"I'm not going to give you their name," I said. "But the person who told me about you and your son knows that I'm here, knows all about Frank Hennessy and Cormack O'Sullivan, and knows about that hit-and-run in Sutton too. So, you pull that trigger or just surrender," I replied.

The older McDermott smiled as a shrill whistle sounded behind him. When he turned to see where that noise was coming from, I followed his vision and spotted a dark spiral of smoke that was twirling out of a hole in one of the glass fronted-storage cases that had been hit when the first bullet that he had fired at me had ricocheted off the car frame.

"That doesn't look too good," his son said when he too spotted where the noise was coming from. "Maybe we should get out of here."

"Don't worry," Pierce McDermott said, and then turned back to me just as the storage case behind him blew asunder and a geyser of yellow flames rippled across the workshop's ceiling.

I didn't see much of Pierce McDermott or his son after that, just their silhouettes against the flames as I plunged to the ground and covered my head as a thundering fireball rolled out of the workshop, seared the air above me as it left the blue building, and tore up into the summer sky.

I turned, clambered back to my feet, register the pain from my wounds as I did so, and then stumbled out into the yard and was limping towards the yards' exit when I heard the Doberman charging towards me again and shuddered to a halt.

This time, just as the Doberman leapt at my head, it was blown away from me by a massive explosion from the building behind me.

Thrown to the ground and momentarily deafened by that blast, as the Doberman righted itself, shook its head, and then wandered back towards the safety of its timber hut, I looked back and saw that the explosion had splintered the blue building's tiled roof and spewed a cloud of debris into the air. I then got up again and began the journey back to Nikki's car on the road outside.

On the way there, I evaded the smoldering shards from the building's roof that rained down into the yard by bending forward and shielding my head as the broken glass crunched beneath my feet.

When I had reached and gotten into Nikki's Mini Cooper, I drove off, stopped at the row of shops at the entrance to the industrial estate and shouted out in anger.

While I was happy to have escaped, the fire had destroyed any evidence that linked O'Sullivan to my brother's death, and had left me with nothing that connected him to the hit-and-run.

I now had only one option left. As Vincent Lynch had advised, I was going to confront Frank Hennessy about the hit-and-run and what I knew about Dave's death, and see if that would make him turn on O'Sullivan.

Then, I recalled something, that Lynch had wanted me to stay away from the Chinese guy who owned the Pearl Orchid Restaurant.

THURSDAY — NINE

B ack in the city, I parked Nikki's Mini Cooper on the fourth floor of a multi-story car park, slid its keys under the driver's front wheel, and then ran a hand along the lumpy paintwork on the car's badly blistered roof.

When my visit to the Chinese restaurant was over, I planned to call Nikki and promise to compensate her for the parking fee, the petrol that I had used, and the repairs needed to the car's paintwork as a result of the embers that had landed on it.

Nikki's response to my call was likely to be unpleasant and prompted me to check the back of my right leg. I saw that a wine-colored stain had spread up the back of my trouser leg but decided to ignore it as I limped the short distance to the Pearl Orchid Restaurant.

Apart from the fact that it was populated almost exclusively by male diners, I didn't initially spot anything that differentiated the Pearl Orchid Restaurant from other upmarket Chinese outlets.

Its walls were adorned with the usual oriental fabric paintings, its tables were illuminated with recessed lighting embedded into the low ceiling, and the background music consisted of the usual twang of traditional Chinese music played on old stringed instruments.

I stopped in front of the restaurant's lacquered cherry wood reception desk behind which a thin Chinese man in a light brown suit smiled back at me.

"Hello, sir, you like table for lunch?" he asked me.

"No, thanks," I told him. "I'm just here to have a quick word with Freddy Chuang."

The man behind the reception desk blinked twice.

"Mr. Chuang expect you?" He asked me.

"Not exactly," I replied. "My name is Pat Daly and I'm a friend of Cormack O'Sullivan," I lied. "He suggested that I talk to Freddy."

"Cormack O'Sullivan," the Chinese man repeated. "Maybe you like to wait here," he said, bowed slightly, and then motioned for me to walk ahead of him across the front of the restaurant to a table in the restaurant's cocktail lounge that doubled as a waiting area.

"You please to wait here," he said when we got there, gestured for me to sit on one of the four low stools positioned around a small circular black glass table that was embedded with a silver graphic of an orchid, and then ambled back to the restaurant's reception desk and lifted up the telephone's receiver.

While I waited for Freddy Chuang to arrive, I flicked through one of the menus that had been left on the table, and then glanced over at the reception desk to see that the Chinese man in the brown suit was staring directly back at me as he talked into the telephone.

He broke his stare as he lowered the telephone's receiver and then smiled broadly as he greeted three comfortably proportioned businessmen, who struggled to contain their grins as the Chinese man drew a line through an entry in the restaurant's reservations book, and then led them to their table.

Once the businessmen were seated, a trio of young Chinese waitresses steeped forward and it became instantly obvious to me why Greg had hesitated before he told me about his client's preference for dining at the Pearl Orchid Restaurant.

What I saw, was that in place of the usual demure costumes that reflected their culture and hid their shape, the three bubbly young Chinese waitresses wore high heels and were dressed in revealing uniforms that were more suited to a nightclub and that displayed their curvaceous bodies.

When he got back to the reception desk, I caught the attention of the man in the brown suit and tapped a finger against my left wrist. He nodded back to me, picked up the telephone receiver again, and then lowered it when he spotted a short, trim, and older Chinese man descend the last few steps of the staircase that was positioned on the left-hand side of the restaurant's entrance.

Immaculately attired in a tan suit, crisp white shirt, and dark brown silk necktie embroidered with a pattern of small swans, the man who I took to be Freddy Chuang was a well-maintained sixty-something and gave me a toothy smile as he walked directly towards my table in the cocktail area.

"Hi, I'm Freddy Chuang," he announced, shot out his right hand with a rattle of jewelry, and then sat down across the small table from me. "Johnny, say you want to talk to me," he said and nodded his head of dyed black hair towards the reception desk.

"Johnny?" I repeated. While I was aware that some Chinese business-people adopt first names that are easy for Westerner businesspeople to pro-nounce, I still had difficulty linking the man behind the reception desk to the name Johnny.

"I hear Cormack O'Sullivan send you," Freddy Chuang said.

"Yes," I lied. "I work with Cormack, so he suggested that we talk."

"You work with Cormack?" Chuang stated as the smile on his face turned to puzzlement and he directed his eyes to my stained clothing.

"Yes," I repeated. "Cormack told me that he comes here a lot."

On hearing my latest words, the smile abandoned Chuang's face entirely, and he sat up straight. "That right, Cormack come here for dinner sometime and bring wife," he said. "She nice lady. You know her?"

I stared back into Chuang's eyes for a moment.

"No, I don't know Cormack O'Sullivan's wife," I answered. "And I never met Tony Maguire's wife either," I added. "But I heard that she worked here, is that true?"

Chuang didn't like my question. "You know nothing, do you, Mr. Daly?" he said, relaxed back on his short, padded stool, and cracked his mouth open to reveal his unnaturally white teeth.

Deflated, I broke eye contact with Chuang, scanned the restaurant, and saw that Johnny had left the reception desk again to show some more male diners to their table, leaving Chuang as the only person between me and the restaurant's exit. I considered making a run for it, but then remembered my sore leg, and realized that even if I did manage to escape, I would leave the restaurant empty-handed, and without any of the evidence that I was there to collect against O'Sullivan.

When I turned back to Chuang, I smiled weakly across at him. "I'm sorry," I admitted. "Obviously, I made a big mistake coming here. But before I leave, can I ask you a quick question about your menu?" I asked and lifted a mock-leather-bound tome from the table's glass surface.

"Sure," Chuang said, and seemed to relax as I scanned the menu's embossed pages.

THURSDAY — TEN

"**W**hat I was just wondering," I asked Freddy Chuang and paused to smile over the Chinese Restaurant's menu at him. "Is why anyone in their right mind would pay good money to eat the overpriced shit that you sell in here."

Chuang's head jerked backwards. "We no overprice," he barked. "This one of best restaurants in Dublin."

"It is?" I replied and looked at the menu again. "But you offer exactly the same food that's sold in every other Chinese restaurant in Dublin but charge twice the price for it. Like a lot of other restaurants, I bet that your food gets delivered to your back door from a refrigerated truck with a British registration. Right?"

"No, you wrong, you very wrong," Chuang shouted. "We make all own food here," he proclaimed as his nostrils flared. "We make good food."

"Yeah, and judging by your clothes, you make good money too," I said.

"My clothes none of you business," Chuang stated.

"I saw a black Porsche Cayenne parked outside," I asked. "Is that yours too?"

Chuang jumped up from his stool. "We finish here!" he said.

"No, we're not, so why don't you just sit back down and shut the fuck up," I countered. "I haven't even asked you about the girls here yet. Where do you get them from anyway? Do you traffic them in from some piss-poor village in China?"

Chuang's face darkened. "You get out now or you get hurt," he threatened and then looked nervously over at the restaurant's abandoned reception desk.

I shook away what Chuang had said, lunged forward, grabbed a handful of his hair with my left hand, delivered a punch to his groin with my right and then, as he folded over, propelled his head downwards until the glass-topped table shattered as his face slammed into it.

"Now Chung," I whispered and lifted his bloodied head a few inches up from the fractured surface of the table. "I've got a few more questions that you're going to answer honestly. Understood?"

Despite my grip on his dyed hair, Chuang nodded.

"Firstly," I asked. "Did you call Cormack O'Sullivan before you came down here?"

"No, I no phone him," Chuang squealed.

"I warned you not to lie to me." I rammed Chuang's face back down onto the shattered tabletop and grated his left cheek back and forward across the splintered glass a few times.

"Now, you've one last chance," I said when I stopped doing that and lifted his shredded face from the table. "Did you phone Cormack O'Sullivan and tell him that I was here. Yes, or no?"

"Yes, I call him," Chuang cried. "I tell him you here."

I kept holding Chuang's bloodied head just above the table. "You see, sometimes the truth doesn't hurt," I told him and then looked up and around the restaurant.

I saw that the attention of its open-mouthed customers had been drawn to the cocktail area by the sound of breaking glass and watched as Johnny rushed back to the reception desk, picked up and dropped the telephone receiver, and then ran through the double doors that swung into the restaurant's kitchen.

I smiled back at the restaurant's customers and then addressed the elderly Chinese restaurateur again. "Okay, Chung, I only have a few more questions," I said.

"Thank you," the restaurant's owner replied in a childlike voice as blood from his torn left cheek dripped down onto the wrecked cocktail table.

"One, what does Cormack O'Sullivan give you when you let him fuck the girls here?" I asked in a voice that was loud enough for everyone in the restaurant to hear.

When Chuang took too much time answering my question, I bounced his head off the surface of the broken glass table a couple of times.

"I'm not going to ask you that question again, Chuang, and don't have all day here," I told him. "My question was what O'Sullivan gives you in return when you let him fuck the girls here?"

"He keep bad people away," Chuang answered. "He help me."

"How about Tony Maguire," I asked Chuang. "Did you let him fuck the girls here too?"

"No, he different," the bleeding Chinaman said. "He no like that."

"He no like what?" I asked Chuang, and then snapped my head around as the kitchen doors burst open and two stocky Chinese men in stained kitchen overalls rushed out into the dining area holding shiny silver meat cleavers and looked over at me.

As they advanced towards me, I jumped to my feet, tugged Chuang into an upright position in front of me and then lifted a triangular shard of broken glass from the table top.

"Stop right there or I'm going to slash your boss," I said and punctured the wrinkled skin on Chuang's throat with the piece of broken glass.

"Do what he say!" Chuang commanded the two kitchen workers as a bead of blood ran down his neck and disappeared beneath the collar of his white shirt.

The first of the two men halted in response to his boss's order. "Let him go or we kill you," he instructed and pointed his shiny meat cleaver at me.

"Yes, you leave him alone," the second man shouted over his colleague's right shoulder.

"Sorry, guys," I replied and gripped Chuang tightly again as I stepped back towards the restaurant's entrance. "When you drop the meat cleavers and take three steps backwards, I'll let him go," I said. "Otherwise, I'm going to slit his throat."

The compromise that I suggested was greeted with a murmur of relief from the restaurant's diners and a loud endorsement from Chuang.

"Do what he say!" he pleaded and issued instructions in a language that I didn't understand.

For a second, nobody moved, and then the first of the two kitchen workers bent forward, dropped his meat cleaver to the restaurant's carpeted floor, and took three paces backwards. The second kitchen worker followed his colleague's example and then nodded for me to hold up my end of the bargain.

I knew that as soon as I released Chuang, the two Chinese men would snatch back up their meat cleavers and jump forward to harm me, so I feigned that I was about to lower the sharp triangular glass shard and then ran it lightly across their boss's throat, shoved the shocked Chung to the ground in front of them, and then hobbled out of the restaurant after grabbing the reservations book off the reception desk.

When I reached the bright sunlight outside, I knew that it was only a matter of seconds before the two kitchen workers with the meat cleavers would dash out of the restaurant after me, darted right and then stumbled to a painful stop as a Garda patrol car mounted the pavement just inches in front of me and screeched to a halt.

Pushing myself away from that cop car as its passenger door opened and a uniformed Garda began to exit, I spotted the entrance into an archway across the street and limped as fast as I could between the traffic to reach it.

I didn't get far and had just ducked to my left and entered the laneway under that archway when I heard scuffed footsteps on the cobblestones behind me

"Stop!" the chasing policeman shouted at my back as he came after me.

Although relieved that I was being chased by a uniformed cop instead of the two Chinese kitchen workers with the meat cleavers, I wasn't about to give myself up, so continued limping forward at speed until I had reached the end of the laneway. That was where I backed into a doorway and waited for the policeman who I couldn't outrun to arrive.

A second later, that policeman didn't slow down when he got to the end of the laneway. I presume that's why he flew so high when I tripped him up.

Thursday — Eleven

The youth facing me had a turned-up nose and possessed a square of tightly trimmed hair on top of his almost bald head. That patch of hair measured about four inches square, had been dyed bright red, and looked like a small carpet sample.

Arranged at intervals underneath that hair were four black symbols that had been shaped from the stubble that grew from his pale skin.

I could only see two of them, but guessed, based on the diamond and heart shapes that I could see, that the club and spade symbols would be found on the other side of his head.

"Twenty for my hoodie and the use of my mobile?" he repeated and then glanced nervously at the friend standing next to him.

That other, taller, youth had a full head of forward-combed ginger hair, a fat and freckled face, and a bulging stomach that stretched the green-and-white hoops of a Glasgow Celtic football jersey.

"That's what I said," I confirmed and then checked behind me again to make sure that neither the cops, nor the kitchen workers from the Chinese restaurant, had seen me enter the corporation estate that comprised of six blocks of four-story flats.

"Let's make it fifty," the youth with the strange hairstyle said.

"Forty," I bargained as a cop siren troubled the air in the distance.

"Deal," the youth agreed, pointed a finger tattooed with the letter H at a redbrick tower next to a block of flats, and then took off towards it.

I hopped after the youth and then noticed, as we got nearer to it, that the redbrick tower housed a curving concrete stairwell. I knew that the two young men could rob me when we reached the interior of the dim tower, but, if I was to evade arrest, then it was vital that I changed my clothes and gained access to a mobile phone.

"Here, what happened to your fucking leg?" the overweight Celtic fan asked me when he spotted the blood stain on the back of my trousers as I lumbered into the tower and began to climb the stairwell that served the block of flats behind it.

"I got stabbed and the bandage came loose," I replied honestly.

The Celtic fan nodded as though familiar with the situation that I had just described and then pointed a finger at the bloodstains on my shirt.

"Is that your blood too?" he asked.

I examined the rust-colored and round stains on the front of my shirt and shook my head.

"No," I replied. "I got those from a Chinese guy when I slashed his throat."

"Right," the fat youth responded and looked unmoved.

"We need to go upstairs to the landing," the other youth announced, rapidly turned away from us and ascended the curving flight of concrete steps to his right in a few strides.

When Celtic jersey and I eventually got to the circular landing on the first floor of the staircase tower, we found that the youth with the patch of red hair was waiting for us.

"Now, give me the money," he said and held out a hand towards me while his friend in the Celtic jersey huffed past us, crossed a short concrete bridge with metal railings that was connected to the stairwell tower, and then ducked low as he ran along a walled-in balcony that ran in front of the row of doors that led into flats on that level of the block.

As I got my breath back, and painfully removed the wallet in my back pocket, I saw that the overweight youth in the Celtic jersey had ducked down behind the end of the balcony wall and had raised his head just high enough to scan the courtyard below.

Reassured that he had taken up a sentry position, I thumbed out two twenties, and passed them over to red patch's outstretched hand.

"This is for your hoodie and the use of your mobile phone, right?" I asked him.

"Right," the youth agreed, grabbed the two banknotes from my hand, extracted a mobile phone from a back pocket of his shorts, and began to remove his mostly green camouflage patterned hoodie.

"One call," he instructed me, swiped the mobile phone's screen open, and then handed over his hoodie.

I nodded, took the two items from him, swiped the little green telephone icon on the mobile phone, and then dialed in a number that I knew off by heart into its keypad.

"Hi, Eva," I said. "Please don't act surprised by my call or use my name," I instructed the advertising agency's receptionist when she answered me.

"Killian is on the phone!" Eva shouted in reply.

"Jesus!" I said and held the mobile phone away from my ear.

"I'm sorry, Killian," Eva replied. "But everyone here has been worried sick about you. Are you okay?"

"Yes, I'm fine," I replied. "I just need to talk to Kate for a minute."

"She's not here," Eva told me. "She left just after the cops."

"What cops?" I asked.

Eva dropped her voice. "The cops who told me to contact them if you got in touch with us here."

"Oh right, those cops," I said. "I was just talking to them, so you don't have to contact them," I advised Eva and then asked her to give me the number for Kate's mobile phone.

The call with Eva over, I held up a finger to the youth with the red patch of hair.

"I just have to make one more call," I told him as he shook his head.

"Yes, hello," Kate answered in her plumy accent.

"Hi, Kate, it's me," I told her. "Can you talk there?"

"Not really, I'm at the rehearsals for Jasper's Telethon," Kate told me, asked me to hold on for a minute and then treated me to the sound of a live orchestra and her hurried footsteps on a wooden floor as she left the area that she was in.

"Hi, where are you calling from?" she asked when she came back on the line from a quieter part of the telethon venue.

"A block of flats off Dunphy Street," I told her, unable to provide more precise details. "Can you collect me here?" I asked her.

"Yes, of course I can," Kate pledged. "But you're going to have to tell me where are you exactly?"

"One second," I replied and then covered the lower half of the mobile phone with my left palm. "What's the best way to get here by car?" I asked red patch and noted that beads of sweat had formed on the sides of his shaved skull.

"This is Cunningham Buildings," he said. "Tell them to hang a left before Irwin Bridge on their way down Dunphy Street."

I nodded my understanding, relayed the directions to Kate, and then enquired how long it would take her to reach me.

"Ten minutes," she replied. "Maybe a little longer."

"Great," I declared, and then lowered my voice. "I'm sorry, Kate, and I know that this is going to sound odd," I said. "But there's something that I need you to do."

"Go on," an intrigued Kate whispered back.

"I need you to leave your mobile phone there," I said.

"That is odd," Kate replied. "Why do you want me to do that?"

"Because mobile phones are easy to trace," I said.

"I'm not too sure what you mean by that," Kate said. "But I'll leave my phone here anyway."

"Thanks, Kate." I said, ended the call, and then handed the mobile phone back to its owner, who wiped it free of my fingerprints before returning it to his shorts.

"Someone will be here soon to collect me," I told him, and was then startled as the overweight Celtic fan cursed loudly, ducked behind the balcony wall, and rushed back across the concrete bridge towards us.

THURSDAY — TWELVE

"**A** fucking cop car just pulled into the yard," the Celtic fan reported to his friend. "They must be after him," he said and nodded his big head towards me.

"Are they after you?" the youth with the odd hairstyle asked me.

"Probably," I admitted. "Is there somewhere that I can hide out around here until my friend arrives?"

"Yes, but it's going to cost you," the youth with the red patch of hair replied, turned away from me, dashed up to the next flight of the dank concrete stairs, and then waited for me on the landing above.

"Really," I said after I had hobbled up after him. "I'm going to hide here?"

"Yes," he said. "But you have to stay on the left as we cross the bridge and then dip beneath the balcony wall until we have reached the yellow door," he commanded. "My gran lives in that flat so you can hide in there for a while."

I nodded my understanding of his instructions, kept left as we crossed the short concrete bridge, and then stooped low as we scurried beneath the balcony wall on the second-floor level until we reached the flat with the yellow front door.

When we had both sunk to our knees outside that door, the youth searched in the front pockets of his shorts until he found a bronze latchkey, stretched up, unlocked the yellow door and then motioned for me to enter his grandmother's flat.

"Is your grandmother home?" I asked and crept onto its floral carpet.

"No, she's in hospital," The youth behind me replied as he closed the yellow door behind us. "That's why you can stay in her gaff for a while."

"Thanks," I said.

"My name's Ace, what's yours?" he asked as I put on his green camouflage hoodie.

"Killian Doyle," I answered and inspected my new top. "How much extra is hiding here going to cost me?"

"Another twenty," Ace replied. "And don't worry about the cops," he said. "Eammo and me will get rid of them for you."

"Thanks," I said, and handed over another banknote to him.

After Ace had dropped back to his knees and crawled out to the walled balcony again, I closed the yellow door after him, disregarded the hallway's peach blossom wallpaper and time-faded St. Bridget's Cross, and pushed the door open into the flat's front room.

After a quick scan of the room, I saw that its window only provided a limited view of the courtyard below, dragged a plush red armchair over to it, and perched up on one of its padded armrests as I edged the flimsy net curtains apart.

The police patrol car had parked in front of the entrance to the stairwell tower and the Celtic fan had engaged its occupants in conversation through one of its windows.

I continued to look down at the cop car, as the youth that I now knew was named Ace, sauntered out of the stairwell tower, leant both his arms on the car's roof, and joined his friend in the conversation.

Although unable to hear the words exchanged, I could tell by the way that Ace and Eamonn looked at each other, shook their heads, and then shrugged their shoulders that they had informed the cops that they hadn't seen anyone in the flats complex who resembled my appearance.

After they had spoken to the cops, the two young men stepped back to let the patrol car move forward and I spotted Ace's mobile phone on its roof. Initially puzzled as I stepped down from the red armchair, I smiled on realizing that Ace had used the police patrol car to remove his mobile phone from the flats complex and distance it from his possession.

When I had lugged the armchair back to its original location, I noticed that a number of framed photographs of an elderly woman were arrayed on top of a sideboard in the front room.

Those images captured her as she stood next to a newly married couple, as she held a baby at a christening, and as she was surrounded by family and friends at what looked like a special birthday party.

In a smaller photograph, the woman was seated on the red armchair, that I had just used, and was flanked by a blond woman, about half her age, and on the other side by a young boy in an Ireland soccer shirt.

Back when that photograph had been taken, Ace had worn his hair in a different style. In those days, his black mane was cropped short all around his head except for his fringe, which sagged down over his forehead and was cut in a zigzag fashion.

A stack of women's magazines also rested on the top of that sideboard. The front cover of the first magazine announced, in a vivid headline and photographic image, that a young female star's battle with booze had resulted in her going into rehab.

I picked up and flicked open that magazine, located the cover story, and saw that while it was spread over six pages, that article consisted mainly of headlines, subheadings, and large quotations that had been reproduced in a variety of colors

Interspersed amongst the written commentary were slanted photographs of the young woman on a childhood holiday with her parents, of her in a delivery room shortly after she had become a mother for the first time, plus a number of snaps of her in the company of men, some of whom were famous for just being famous.

I quickly read that entire magazine article even though I had little interest in the famous female star.

I saw that, aside from her agent's admission that she had recently attended a posh rehab clinic for alcoholics, there was no evidence that the young woman had a problem with booze.

That magazine article made me look at the whole evidence thing from a new angle. Had I risked my life getting factual material against O'Sullivan when I could have just made a public accusation against him?

When I had returned the magazine to the sideboard, I went into the flat's kitchen, and lifted a blue enamel mug from the stainless-steel draining board next to the sink.

As I filled and drained that mug's cool contents, I considered how different the young woman's reputation management requirements were from those of a global brand.

For celebrities, negative media exposure can sometimes be beneficial, and might even attract more online clicks and sales, while for brands with performances that are dependent upon a positive reputation, such as Jasper's Chicken Restaurants, a good image always needs to be maintained or a sudden dip in sales can ensue.

When I had finished drinking the refreshing water, and had washed the mug and returned it to the stainless-steel draining board, I was shocked to hear my first name being shouted out in the courtyard below.

THURSDAY — THIRTEEN

Despite the pain from the wound to my right leg, I raced back down the flat's carpeted hallway towards its yellow front door, pulled it open, and crossed over to the balcony just as Kate wrapped her hands around her mouth to call out my first name again in her distinctly upper-class accent.

"Hi, I'm up here," I roared down to Kate, pulled the yellow door shut, hopped along the walkway to the stairwell tower, and descended the concrete steps as fast as I could.

"Thanks," I said on reaching the bottom of the stairwell tower and encountering the two youths. "My friend got here sooner than I expected," I told them and then limped out into the sunshine towards Kate's cream and brown Volkswagen Beetle.

"Jesus, you look like shit," Kate observed as I approached and got into her car.

"I'll be fine," I told her as she sat in behind the steering wheel. "And thanks for getting here so quickly. For a while there, I was afraid that they'd come back before you got here."

"You were afraid that who would come back?" A puzzled Kate asked.

"The cops," I told her. "Those two guys helped me out the last time."

"Those two guys?" Kate quizzed and looked over at Ace and Eamonn in the stairwell tower as if she had just registered a bad smell.

"Yes," I confirmed. "The cops want to arrest me for killing Dave but they helped me to avoid that."

"The cops want to arrest you for killing Dave?" Kate asked me.

"Yes," I repeated and nodded. "Apparently, I paid Dave to murder Claire and Sarah, and then had him killed when he came back looking for more money from me," I said.

"That's insane," Kate said. "Why don't you just tell the truth?"

"Because if I give myself up there's a good chance that nobody will believe anything that I say," I replied. "Plus, there's something else."

"What?" an anxious Kate asked as we drove out of Cunningham Buildings.

"To escape earlier, I had to trip up a cop," I told her.

Kate turned to me as we stopped at a set of traffic lights. "I heard about that on the car's radio," she said. "The report said that a policeman was assaulted by a man who had just tried to behead a foreign immigrant. Please tell me that wasn't you, Killian?"

"Of course that wasn't me," I replied. "All I did was slash the Chinese fucker's throat with a piece of broken glass. I never even tried to behead him, even though I heard that he traffics sex slaves into Ireland."

"Jesus, Killian, this is bad, isn't it?" Kate said.

"Yes, it is," I agreed and slid my right hand inside the front waistband of my grey cords, gripped the reservations book from the Pearl Orchid Restaurant, and extracted it. "But this changes everything."

"Why, what's that?" Kate asked and peered across at the reservations book in my hands as if it was about to explode.

"It lists all the people who go to the Chinese guy's restaurant," I said. "There's a guy in in Givenstown who's going to look after it for me."

"A guy in Givenstown?" Kate queried as the traffic moved forward.

"Yes, can you please drive me there now?" I asked her.

"Yes, of course I can," Kate replied.

"Great," I said. "Because I've got some good news to share with you along the way."

"Good news?" Kate asked without looking at me.

"Yes," I said. "I now know that your affair with Dave had nothing to do with his murder," I told her. "Plus, I now know who was behind what happened to Dave, and why he was killed."

"What! Who was it?" Kate asked as she slammed on the Volkswagen Beetle's brakes and pulled it over to the side of the road.

"Okay, I'll tell you," I said. "But before I do that, you have to answer one question about the telethon tonight."

"What?" Kate asked.

"I need to know the time when Frank Hennessy will go on stage tonight to present his tribute to Dave," I said.

"Frank is due on at ten-fifteen," Kate answered. "Now tell me who killed Dave?"

"Frank is due on at ten-fifteen," I repeated and then asked Kate another question instead of answering her. "Can you arrange to get me on stage with a microphone at that time too?"

"Yes, of course I can," Kate replied. "Now, who killed Dave?"

THURSDAY — FOURTEEN

"**F**rank Hennessy and a corrupt cop called Cormack O'Sullivan had Dave killed to hide a hit-and-run that a kid died in and that he might have found out about," I told Kate. "That's why I want to go onto the stage at the telethon tonight. To ask Frank some questions about Dave's murder."

"Frank Hennessy and a corrupt cop called Cormack O'Sullivan," Kate repeated, swallowed hard, blinked a few times, and then spoke again. "I'm sorry, Killian, but if you believe that Frank and this cop were responsible for Dave's murder then instead of confronting him at the telethon why don't you talk to some other cops?" she queried and looked across at me.

"Because, this way, I'll get to make accusations against Frank that will make him suffer when everyone hears what he has done," I replied. "Plus, I can't go to some other cops. Because they might lock me up."

"So, your plan is to expose Frank Hennessy in front of everyone watching the telethon tonight," Kate said. "Do you think that's wise?"

"Yes, I do," I confirmed. "Frank was involved in Dave's murder so I want him to suffer too," I stated. "Now, please take me out to Givenstown so that I can get rid of this reservations book. I don't want to have it near me in case I get arrested."

"Right," Kate said as she started her car again. "But I need to get back to the telethon rehearsals soon," she added. "Otherwise, someone from Jesper's might spot that I'm missing, ask some questions, and prevent me from helping you tonight."

"Don't worry, Kate, I won't spend much time in Givenstown," I told her.

Kate stayed silent during most of our journey and then asked me another question as I flipped through the reservations book from the Pearl Orchid Restaurant, tore out some of its pages, and slipped them uncomfortably inside the front of my grey cords.

"I'm sorry, Killian," she asked as we neared the roundabout where Lynch's Bar and Lounge was located. "But if you have already concluded that Frank and this corrupt cop were responsible for Dave's murder then why are we doing this?"

I turned to Kate. "Because I want to get rid of this and get some more information," I said. "Anyway, I thought that you'd want to be involved in all of this," I said. "Is that not the case?"

"Not really," Kate said. "I loved your brother but because of that, you seem to have decided that I should help you, even if I go to prison."

"Don't worry, Kate," I said. "You'll never go to prison because I'll insist that I ordered you to follow my instructions. Plus, things are nearly over, Frank and his corrupt cop friend will be finished tonight, and the scumbag who they paid to kill Dave is already dead."

"The scumbag who they paid to kill Dave?" Kate repeated.

"Yes, they got a scumbag called McDermott to kill Dave," I said. "He died in a fire earlier."

Kate turned to me. "He died in a fire," she repeated. "Please don't tell me that that was in Dolphin's Dock," she said.

"Maybe it was," I replied. "Did you hear about that on the news too?"

"Yes," Kate said and shook her head. "I should have listened to what Dave said about you," she added. "He warned me that you like to manipulate people. That's what you've done to me, isn't it, Killian, you've manipulated me and got me to do what you want?"

"No, I haven't," I replied. "And manipulate is a very strong word," I contested and then directed Kate to pull into the car park at Lynch's.

Typical of the large pubs that opened in Dublin's suburbs during the 1960s, Lynch's Bar and Lounge was a wide, two-story building, that was supposed to blend in with the new housing around it.

Vincent Lynch was standing behind the bar counter halfway down the lounge and was wearing a navy woolen sweater, a white apron that was wrapped tightly around his midriff, and a look of astonishment when he saw me advancing towards him.

"Surprised to see me, aren't you, Lynch?" I declared loudly and slammed the reservations book from the Pearl Orchid Restaurant down onto the mahogany bar counter in front of him, an action that attracted the attention of some of the lounge's customers.

"What's that?" Lynch said and looked down at the book.

"It's the reservations book from the Pearl Orchid Restaurant," I told him. "It lists all the people who go there. At least it did, until I removed and kept some of its juicier pages."

"I don't want anything to do with that," Lynch said and looked at me. "Why did you bring it here?"

"So that you could call your friend Freddy Chuang and tell him that you have it," I answered. "When you make that call, tell Chuang that I have kept some of its pages," I said. "Tell him that if he doesn't want to see those pages in tomorrow's newspapers, then there are two things that he has to do. One, Chuang has to drop any charges against me for knocking the shite out of him, and two, he has to get out of Ireland and stay out of here forever. Do that, Lynch, and I mightn't tell O'Sullivan about the information that your son, Ken, supplied about that hit-and-run near the golf club in Sutton."

Lynch's right hand trembled as he rotated the reservations book on the countertop and then slipped it inside the wide pocket on the front of his apron as another barman, a short, fat, and bald man, arrived next to him.

"Is this guy hassling you, Vinny?" that barman asked and glared across the counter at me.

"No, Aidan," Lynch replied to his brother. "But I need you to look after things here while I have a quick word with him."

I looked around the well-appointed lounge. "Nice place you have here," I commented. "It must cost a lot of money."

Lynch pointed over my left shoulder towards the lounge's smoking area. "We can talk in there," he told me.

I followed Lynch into the lounge's weather-proofed smoking area which consisted of a roofless rectangular room with brown lattice-work walls, two picnic tables, and three gas-fueled heaters.

The place was empty apart from a grey-faced old man who sat hunched on one of the benches and sucked the smoke from a cigarette into his lungs.

"Don't mind him, he's almost deaf," Lynch told me.

Despite that comment, I lowered my voice. "You didn't expect me to show up here, did you, Lynch?" I asked. "Or expect me to talk to Freddy Chuang either, did you?"

"No, I didn't," Lynch admitted. "Even after Ken phoned to tell me that your visit to McDermott's place hadn't gone too well."

"What do you mean my visit to McDermott's Place didn't go too well?" I said and pulled a startled expression. "Pierce McDermott and his son are dead. Were they supposed to kill me, or something? Is that why you made up an excuse to send me there alone, Lynch? Because you thought that I'd get killed and then you and your precious little boy could stay safe?" I asked him, and noted that the perspiration on Lynch's forehead was heavier than usual.

Lynch shook his head. "No, that wasn't it at all," he said but was shakier than usual. "I was delighted when I heard that they were both dead."

"Really?" I snapped. "Because you stayed out of the Golf Club this morning too, Lynch. That way you weren't seen with me. Was that your intention?"

When the retired detective didn't deny my accusation, I continued.

"Now, give me a truthful answer to the question that I asked you earlier," I instructed Lynch. "You know what happened between Tony Maguire and O'Sullivan that changed their relationship, don't you?"

Once again, Lynch failed to mask his dislike of my question and touched the bridge of his glasses before answering me.

"Maguire and O'Sullivan were the perfect detective team," he told me. "Tony was the brains and Cormack was the brawn. But then Cormack realized something about his partner."

"Which was?" I asked Lynch and stepped closer to him.

"Cormack saw that Tony was into other men," Lynch replied.

I stared back into Lynch's eyes, thought about Tony Maguire, and recalled that Anne Reid had mentioned the dead detective's strained relationship with his Chinese wife, the comments that Jill Maguire had made about him really listening to girly stuff, and about Freddy Chuang's assertion that Tony Maguire wasn't like that.

Everything that I had heard about Tony Maguire should have led me to question his sexuality, and yet, despite my various meetings with him, I had never even considered that possibility.

Before I could respond to him, Lynch spoke again. "Without Tony's smarts, Cormack knew that he would be just another overly physical cop, so he made Tony hide his sexuality."

"And Tony Maguire agreed to that?" I asked Lynch.

Lynch nodded. "You have to remember that this was back when being gay wasn't as accepted as it is today, particularly for a cop," he said. "Plus, there was something else too. Tony liked Cormack, liked him a lot."

"Really?" I asked. "Because Tony Maguire didn't seem to like his partner much when they worked together on the investigation into my daughter's kidnapping," I said. "In fact, Tony Maguire gave me the distinct impression that he didn't trust O'Sullivan much back then. Was there some reason for that, some issue between them?"

The expression on Lynch's face indicated that he liked my latest question even less than he had liked my earlier one about the change in the relationship between O'Sullivan and Tony Maguire.

"Yes, they had fallen out by then," he replied.

"Over what?" I asked.

For a moment, Lynch didn't look like he was going to answer my question. "Over money," he then said. "Tony's wife had cancer, but, even though he had lots of money, Cormack wouldn't fund his partner's wife's treatments or lend him any money."

"Why did O'Sullivan take that stance?" I queried.

"Because Cormack wanted Tony's wife out of way," Lynch replied.

"What!?" I asked. "Why would O'Sullivan want that to happen?"

Lynch released an uncomfortable sigh. "Because Cormack got Jill Maguire's mother pregnant with her," he said.

"What!?" I repeated.

Lynch nodded. "After he got Jill Maguire's mother pregnant, Cormack arranged for her to marry Tony," he said. "That way, Jill's mother could start a new life and Tony would become a married man with a daughter, and look straight."

"Does Jill Maguire know about this?" I asked Lynch.

"No," Lynch replied. "And Cormack made sure that she never heard the truth about her father."

For a moment, we stood in silence, and then I thought of something else to ask Lynch. "As O'Sullivan was so secretive about Tony Maguire's sexuality, how did you find out about him?" I asked Lynch.

"I don't remember," the retired detective replied.

I looked around the pub's smoking room and then turned back to Lynch.

"Anne Reid told me that O'Sullivan put you under a lot of pressure after he had fired her husband, but then suddenly left you alone. Was that because you found out about Tony Maguire?" I asked Lynch.

"Sometimes you think too much, don't you, Doyle?" Lynch said.

"Yes, I do," I replied. "And here's some more of my thinking. I've a feeling that O'Sullivan paid you to keep your mouth shut about Tony Maguire. That's how you could afford to buy this place, isn't it?" I asked Lynch who shook his head again. "You also didn't want me to talk to Freddy Chuang today in case I found out that you used to fuck the girls there too, and that he was the one who told you about Tony Maguire," I said.

Once again, Lynch shook his head.

"Or how about this one, Lynch," I added. "I think that you feel guilty about Declan Reid's death. Is that why you're so loyal to his widow? Do you know who killed Declan Reid when he was on his way to tell me who had arranged to kidnap my daughter?"

When Lynch didn't say anything. I stepped towards the exit.

"I have to go now," I told him. "But I'll be back soon. In the meantime, I suggest that you call Freddy Chuang and tell him to get out of Ireland."

"I'll call him now," Lynch said.

"Good, see you soon," I replied and left Lynch's pub.

Thursday — Fifteen

Apart from asking me the same question over and over again, Kate didn't speak much as she drove us back into town and then parked her car in front of a narrow grey stone building that was located in a laneway behind a terraced row of Georgian houses.

"Are you sure you're all right?" Kate asked me when she had parked her Volkswagen Beetle in that laneway.

"Yes, I'm fine," I answered her again. "There are just a lot of things on my mind right now."

"What kind of things?" Kate asked.

"Things that I don't want to talk about," I said.

"Are you still going ahead with what you plan to do tonight?" Kate asked.

"Yes, I am, that's when this all ends," I said. "That hasn't changed."

"But something else has changed," Kate concluded. "What?"

"Nothing," I answered and then looked towards the narrow two-story building that we had parked outside. "What is this place?" I asked Kate.

"It's where I live," she replied and removed the key from the car's ignition. "It's an old mews building that used to be where the big Georgian house's horses and carriage were kept. My sister and her husband live in that house now, and this place was derelict until my sister had it renovated a few years back and I moved into it."

"It's where you live?" I queried.

"Yes," Kate replied. "My sister and her hubby are away on holiday at the moment, so you can hang out here for a while," she added and then stepped out of her Volkswagen.

When we had reached its red door, and Kate had unlocked it, I saw that the main interior of the mews building was an open living space with rough, whitewashed stone walls, a beige Berber carpet, and a battered brown leather sofa with stout wooden legs that faced a large flat-screen TV.

"It's very homely," I commented, conscious that my dead brother had probably been in Kate's home on numerous occasions.

"Thanks," Kate replied and dropped her front door key in a green glass bowl. "There's a kitchen and a small dining room down here," she added as we advanced through the living room into a small hallway.

In the short hallway that led to the kitchen, Kate pointed up a laddered wooden staircase to the mew's next level. "My bedroom is up there," she told me. "There's a bathroom up there too, and a nook that I keep my computer in."

"Sounds good," I said and then looked through the windowed top half of the door at the end of the short hallway and saw that a paved pathway from the mews climbed some steps and then ran through a long, narrow garden up to the big Georgian house. "You're sure that no one's there?" I queried.

"Absolutely," Kate replied. "I'll get you some fresh clothes and some black hair dye from there in a minute," she said and then opened the door into the kitchen. "You can wait for those things in here, then I better get back to the rehearsals."

Left alone in the mews, I used the bathroom upstairs, looked into Kate's bedroom, inspected her laptop computer and the printer on the desk crammed into the nook on the landing, and was back in the kitchen when Kate returned from her sister's house with a bulging canvas bag.

"These are my brother-in-law's clothes but should fit you," Kate said as she removed a white short-sleeved polo shirt, a dark grey cotton V-neck sweater, and a pair of blue denim jeans from the shopping bag.

"They're perfect, thanks Kate," I said and gathered up my change of clothes.

Kate then took a pair of chrome scissors and a blue plastic bottle of hair dye from the bottom of the canvas bag.

"I can't stay here and help you with these," she said. "They're for your hair."

"That's no problem, thank you for everything," I said.

"And thank you, too," Kate said as she folded the canvas shopping bag. "Without you, I'm not sure how I would have handled Dave's death. I'll see you later, okay?"

"Yes, you will, at the theatre at ten past ten," I said.

"Ten-ten, see you then," Kate rhymed as she backed out of her kitchen and I remembered something that I had meant to ask her.

"Sorry, Kate," I said and hobbled after her. "I'll have to make a couple of phone calls later. Is there a public payphone near here?"

"Yes, there's a phone box outside the library down the road," Kate answered. "It only takes phone cards but you can get them in the convenience store across the road," she said and then faltered when she realized that she had exposed how much she knew about the phone box. "I've used that phone box a few times," she explained. "The mobile signal around here is crap sometimes."

It was obvious to me that Kate had used the phone box to disguise her calls to my dead brother Dave, but I thanked her again anyway and then expressed another farewell.

"See you later," Kate said as she left the mews.

When I heard Kate's Volkswagen Beetle pull away, I gathered up the clothes, the hair dye, and the scissors that she had given me and made my way up the steep steps to Kate's bathroom again.

Once there, I showered, trimmed my hair, dyed it black, restyled it, and then put on Kate's brother-in-law's clothes, which she had been right about, they fitted me perfectly.

After I had filled a black plastic bag from her kitchen with my old clothes, the hair trimmings, and the now-empty bottle of black hair dye, I went into Kate's bedroom and checked out my change of appearance in the full-length mirror that adorned the front of her wardrobe.

Satisfied with my new image, I then stepped out onto the nook on the landing, removed two sheets of paper from the tray at the base of Kate's photo-printer, and found a blue pen and a manila envelope in the desk's drawers.

Back downstairs in the small kitchen, I leant on the aluminum table as I wrote out a set of instructions for Ted O'Shea on the two sheets of paper.

If I wasn't around anymore, I advised Ted to get in touch with certain people in the media, and to speak with Peter to ensure that the advertising agency ran well without me.

When the letter to Ted was complete, I sealed it in the envelope, wrote his name, title, and Institute of Communications address on the front of it, returned the pen to the desk, and then sat on the old leather couch in the living room until the time came for me to leave Kate's home.

Thursday — Sixteen

Once I had deposited the black plastic bag in a public waste-bin, I located the phone box that Kate had told me about and crossed the road to the convenience store to get a phone card.

One of the sales assistants inside the convenience store was a thin young woman dressed in a branded blue polo shirt with short sleeves.

"Can I help you?" she asked, and then gave my recently dyed black hair a curious look.

"Hi, yes, I need to buy a stamp and a phone card," I said, unsure if my hair had given me away and I should make a run for the shop's entrance.

"What value do you want the stamp and phone card in?" she asked me.

"I'm not sure," I answered. "What prices do they come in?"

"Lots of prices. It depends on what you want them for?" The pierced and tattooed young sales assistant replied as if she was talking to someone with a learning disability.

"I need to post a letter to an address in Dublin, and to make a phone call to someone in Dublin too," I explained. "How much will that be?"

Without replying, the young woman turned to a shelf behind her, tore a single stamp from a sheet that was kept inside a folder and then slipped a phone call card from a pile held together with a rubber band.

"There, this is for your letter," she said and handed me the stamp. "And this is for the phone," she added and handed me the phone card. "That will be two-fifty. There's a post box around the corner and a payphone in that box right across the street," she added.

I paid the young woman, avoided eye contact with the two customers standing in line behind me, and then left the convenience store.

When I had posted the letter to Ted O'Shea in the green mailbox around the corner, I limped back across the road to the phone box and found that it was occupied by a plump, brown-haired, young woman who turned and raised a finger to me that indicated that she wouldn't be much longer.

"Nice night, isn't it?" she commented a moment later when she held the door into the phone box open for me.

"Yes, it is," I agreed. "Very mild."

There was nothing mild about O'Sullivan's voice when he answered my call. "I knew that you'd call," he sneered. "People like you usually do."

"People like me?" I queried.

"Yeah, the ones who think that they're smarter than me," he stated.

"And I'm like that, am I?" I asked him.

"Yeah, you're just like that," O'Sullivan replied. "I suppose that you want to meet up with me?"

"Maybe," I fudged, surprised that O'Sullivan had predicted the reason for my call. "But, before we go any further, there's something that you should know."

"Yeah, and what's that?" the detective replied.

"That I won't be here for long," I said. "So don't even bother trying to have this call traced."

"Jesus," O'Sullivan asked. "Where did you get that one from, some old movie that you were watching?"

I ignored O'Sullivan's question.

"I want to meet you and Jill Maguire and no one else," I said. "If you bring anyone else with you, then I won't show, understood?"

"Yeah, yeah," O'Sullivan replied. "Where and when?"

"Do you know where the Bird Bath is?" I replied.

"Yeah, I know where the Bird Bath is," O'Sullivan replied.

"Then be there at ten-thirty tonight," I told him. "And don't try anything, because I've got someone lined up to talk to the media if you do that."

"To talk to the media about what?" O'Sullivan asked me.

"To talk to them about a hit-and-run in Sutton last Sunday, and the reservations book that went missing from a Chinese Restaurant today," I replied.

"Please don't try to catch me out like that, Doyle," O'Sullivan said. "And don't try anything yourself tonight either, unless you want me to release some video footage to the media of the advertising man who tripped up a uniformed Garda who was trying to make an arrest for the attempted murder of a well-respected migrant. Or the forensic evidence that links that same man to a blaze in a motor repair shop in which two men died."

"Ten-thirty tonight," I stated over the detective's words, and was about to hang up when O'Sullivan spoke again.

"Hold on, Doyle, there's something else," O'Sullivan told me.

"Go on," I told him and peered through a window of the phone box.

"You're going to need a new solicitor," the detective said.

"Why is that?" I responded in a more curious tone that I wanted to use with O'Sullivan.

"Because Greg Moore knows that you fucked his wife," he replied. "You know, Doyle," O'Sullivan continued. "I always had you down as a smart guy and never thought that you'd be stupid enough to use a car park where all the number plates are digitally registered at its entrance. And yet, that's exactly what you did when you abandoned Doctor Nikki Moore's wrecked car near the Pearl Orchid Restaurant today. That led to her getting mad and telling her husband the truth about you. Tony Maguire always reckoned that you were having an affair when your wife and daughter were bumped off," O'Sullivan added. "I bet that he never suspected that you'd be low enough to shag your best friend's wife. Anyway, I'll see you later," he said and hung up.

When O'Sullivan was gone, I slammed down the telephone receiver and searched frantically in the pockets of my jeans until I had found Nikki's business card.

"Yes," my former lover answered when she took my call on her mobile phone.

"Hi Nikki, it's Killian," I stated. "O'Sullivan just told me that Greg found out about us. Is that true?"

When Nikki didn't respond to me and had hung up my call, I lowered the payphone's receiver to its cradle, closed my eyes, shook my head, and took three deep breaths.

Nikki had described the affair that I had started between us as a stupid mistake. I now fully appreciated what she had meant by that, was aware of the pain that I had caused Greg and her, and was more determined than ever to get O'Sullivan.

After exiting the phone box, I went around the corner, found the nearest bus stop, and then waited for the bus that would take me to the suburban theatre where Jasper's Telethon was being staged.

Directly across the road from that theatre was the hillside public park where a large manmade pond that most Dubliners referred to as the Bird Bath was located.

Thursday — Seventeen

Kate had brought a change of clothes to the telethon venue that morning and was dressed in a long black evening dress, stood four inches taller in a pair of gold satin high-heeled pumps, and had her long neck and slender ears enhanced by sparkling jewels.

"That's incredible," she said when I met her at the theatre's stage door and she ruffled my short black hair.

"Thanks," I said, patted down the hair that Kate had tossed, and then asked her if everything was ready.

"Yes, everything is in place," she told me. "How about you, are you okay?" Kate asked as she checked to see if any of the black dye from my hair had rubbed off on her hands.

"Yes, I'm fine," I said, and then smiled at the burly man in the dark uniform at the theatre's backstage security desk.

"Hi, Marek, this is the guy from work that I told you about earlier," Kate told him. "Is it okay if he comes inside with me now?"

"Yes, that's no problem," Marek replied in a heavy industry voice.

Inside the theatre's backstage area, Kate walked ahead of me, led me halfway down a narrow corridor, and then used one of her bare arms to open a door into a small dressing room where a stocky man in his twenties was waiting for us.

"Killian, this is Ronan," Kate informed me and then closed the door behind us. "He's the sound technician who's going to hook you up with a microphone for your appearance on the show," she said.

Ronan introduced himself and then invited me to sit down at a make-up table where he clipped a slim power pack to the rear waistband of my jeans and connected it to a capsule microphone that he taped to my right cheek with a flesh-colored plaster.

"Be careful with the wires from the power pack to your mic," Ronan, who was wearing a black polo-neck sweater and a pair of tan combat trousers advised me. "And remember to switch everything on before you go on stage," he added, and then nodded at Kate as she opened the door for him.

"Are we still on time?" I asked Kate when Ronan was gone.

"Yes, but we need to get moving," she advised.

Seconds later, we left the dressing room, turned right, and walked further down the corridor.

"The show is on a commercial break at the moment," Kate told me. "When that ends, Frank Hennessy will present the tribute to Dave."

At the end of the corridor, we passed through a thick, soundproofed door into the main backstage area, where, even in the dim light, I recognized the reverse of the massive curved structure in front of me as the back of the telethon's semicircular set.

On reaching its left wing, I blinked twice before my eyes adjusted to the bright floodlights and I saw that the identical twin sisters, Jacinta and Teresa O'Brien, were standing behind a clear glass podium at the front of the stage.

The MCs for Jasper's Telethon, The O'Brien Twins were clad in matching silver minidresses, and wore their blond hair in dense plaits that rose a foot above their heads.

The two sisters maintained their nervous smiles and bobbed from foot to foot as they looked down from the front of the stage at a long-haired young man with glasses and large earphones who would alert them before the conclusion of the commercial break.

In response to a nudge from Kate, I then panned further left along the stage in front of me until I spotted my father-in-law as he stood waiting for his cue to be called forward.

Like the twins in front of him, Frank Hennessy was also watching the long-haired young man with the big earphones who now held up his right hand, counted down from five, and then pointed his right index finger at

The O'Brien Twins as the commercial break ended and the live televised show recommenced.

Back-on-air, the twins wiggled their shoulders in tune to the lively music, smiled at each other, and then resumed their seemingly spontaneous patter, which was displayed on an autocue screen at the front of the stage.

"And now," Teresa O'Brien announced as Frank Hennessy stepped forward.

"It's the big man himself, Mr. Frank Hennessy!" her sister, Jacinta, shouted as the two young women jumped into the air, spun around, and beckoned Frank Hennessy to join them at the podium.

"Ladies and Gentlemen, Jasper's Chief Executive in Ireland, Mr. Frank Hennessy!" a hidden narrator declared as the orchestra belted out the opening bars of the Jasper's Chicken Restaurants anthem, 'Kids of the World Dream Together.'

Embraced and kissed on each of his bearded cheeks by the two young women, Frank Hennessy raised his huge arms, waved a salute to the crowd, and then swapped places at the podium with The O'Brien Twins as the music faded and they backed away from him.

"Ladies and gentlemen. Tonight fills me with both a strong sense of pride and one of great sadness," Frank began. "As most of you know, Dave Doyle lost his life as he performed a JimiJix show in one of our restaurants this week," he added and shook his head to convey the massive effort that it was taking to keep his emotions in check. "That's why my heartfelt condolences go out to his wife, Louise, and their wonderful young son, Philip, who is just four years old," he said, and was interrupted by a spontaneous round of applause from the audience.

Incensed by his pretension, I took a series of deep breaths and controlled my anger as I watched Frank Hennessy's pathetic performance from the left wing of the stage.

"Thank you, ladies and gentlemen," Frank Hennessy said as the amplified sound from the crowd receded. "Tonight, instead of simply mourning Dave's passing, I felt that we should celebrate his life too. Dave was passionate about making sure that this telethon was successful and that it benefited as many children as possible," my father-in-law said.

"That's why I'd now like to share with you a short video about Dave," he said and stood aside as a massive video screen at the back of the stage pulsed into life.

Two and a half minutes long, the video displayed was edited to a recording of 'Kids of the World Dream Together' and featured Dave in his JimiJix outfit as he deftly performed magic tricks, encouraged others to join him in song, gyrated in dance, played football awkwardly in his big jester's slippers, united firemen, ambulance workers, and hospitalized children in laughter, and presented outsized charity cheques.

At its conclusion, the video footage froze and the music reached a crescendo as a still image of Dave was displayed on screen in which he held a money-filled Jasper's Telethon Trophy high above his head at the climax of a previous telethon.

The titles that appeared at the base of that image listed the date when Dave had been born, and the horrible day, just thirty-one years later, when my brother had died.

When the crowd had risen to their feet to give Dave's memory a rapturous standing ovation, I nodded to Kate, waited as she flicked on my power pack, and then proceeded out onto the brightly lit stage.

Obviously puzzled by the dark-haired man who was limping across the stage towards him, Frank Hennessy didn't recognize me until I was just six feet away from him.

"Is that you, Killian?" he then asked.

"Yes, it's me, Frank," I replied and stopped. "Is it true that you had Dave murdered when he found out about the little boy that you ran over in Sutton last Sunday?"

While shocked by what I had asked him, Frank recovered quickly and displayed a hurt expression. "I'm sorry, Killian, but I've no idea what you're talking about," he said and glanced behind him at the two well-built security men in the grey suits who had proceeded out onto the brightly lit stage, stopped, and were now eyeing me suspiciously. "Please let me get you some help."

"No, that's okay, Frank," I said. "All I need to know is if you killed that little boy and then had Dave murdered. Did you do that, Frank?"

Before he answered my question, I turned away from Frank, shook my head, and made my way back across the stage, leaving my father-in-law to make another announcement behind me.

"Ladies and gentlemen, that was Dave's brother, Killian," Frank said and began to clap his hands together.

This time there was no applause from the audience, just a rising hum of confused conversation as they discussed what they had just seen and heard.

Kate wiped some tears from her eyes as I approached her and we embraced.

"Well done, but you need to get out of here now," she said as she stooped down and flicked off my power pack.

"Thanks for everything," I told Kate and then limped as fast as I could towards the stage door.

Despite the shouts from the security men, Marek, didn't try to stop me as I lopsidedly rushed past his desk, exited the stage door, and then slalomed between parked cars until I had reached the side of the road that ran in front of the theatre.

The timing was tight, but I knew that if I hurried, I could reach the public park across the road and arrive at my scheduled rendezvous with O'Sullivan and Jill Maguire at the man-made pond known as the Bird Bath by ten-thirty.

THURSDAY — EIGHTEEN

With only seconds left, I entered the public park's moonlit darkness, let the gradient increase my speed as I painfully raced down the grass embankment that led to the Bird Bath, and then groaned loudly on spotting the glow from Jill Maguire's mobile phone.

"Don't listen to that!" I shouted at her as O'Sullivan stood up from a bench that faced the lake and stepped forward when I reached the pavement that ran around the man-made lake.

"Ah, Mr. Doyle, bang on time," he declared as Jill Maguire aimed her shocked face at us and a ring tone sounded from the mobile phone inside O'Sullivan's jacket.

"Quick, you need to listen to that," Jill Maguire yelled at O'Sullivan. "It's someone telling you what Doyle just did at the telethon."

"Nobody needs to answer any calls about me," I countered. "I'll tell you what I just did across the road."

O'Sullivan nodded, reached inside his jacket, took out a handgun, and pointed it at me. "Okay, now tell us what you just did, Doyle" he said.

Prompted by her boss's action, Jill Maguire put away her mobile phone, took a step back from the edge of the pond, extracted her handgun, and pointed it at me too.

"Before I say anything, I want to make it clear that I'm not armed, so you don't need to do anything rash," I said, put up my hands, and then told the two detectives what I had just done at Jasper's Telethon.

"Why did you do that?" O'Sullivan asked as his expression turned from one of disbelief to one of anger. "Why did you ask Frank Hennessy if he killed a kid and had your brother killed when you have no evidence that he did either of those things?"

"Because I don't need any evidence," I replied to O'Sullivan. "Right now, people all around the world are watching Frank Hennessy, the Chief Executive of Jasper's in Ireland, being asked whether he killed a kid and then organized a hit-man to murder a JimiJix. A lot of those people are Jasper's customers and don't give a shit about me having any evidence. Frank is finished, has probably been fired by now, and will bring you down with him. Do you not get that O'Sullivan?"

"Yes, of course I get it," O'Sullivan said. "But you've no evidence to back up your questions, so you'll get into big trouble, and there will be lots of consequences for your actions."

"Really?" I said. "So Frank Hennessy isn't finished and won't bring you down with him."

"Bring me down!" an enraged O'Sullivan retorted. "Your trial by media might get rid of Frank but nothing will happen to me," he asserted. "Because you have no proof that I did anything wrong."

"Trial by media," I repeated. "Wake up, O'Sullivan, to save himself, Frank Hennessy will tell everyone that you were with him on Sunday. He'll say that it was you who convinced him to drive away after he had hit and killed that kid, and will state that you were the one who arranged to have Dave killed."

"What's he talking about, Cormack?" Jill Maguire asked her boss.

I turned and answered Jill Maguire's question. "On Sunday, Frank Hennessy and your boss played some golf in Sutton," I told her. "They had a few drinks afterwards, and then Frank Hennessy knocked down and killed a little boy as they drove away from the golf club. So they went back to Jasper's Head Office. The car park there is usually empty at night, but last Sunday it wasn't. My brother arrived there on his way back from Wexford," I told her. "Later, as Dave was driving home, he was listening to the radio, heard a description of the car that had killed the little boy in Sutton, and realized that it sounded like Frank Hennessy's damaged car. That's why Dave was in such a strange mood when he got home on Sunday night, why he wouldn't talk to his wife about what had upset him, and why he tried to reach me."

"Don't mind him, Jill," O'Sullivan interjected. "That's all made up."

I ignored her boss's comment. "The next morning, I drove to The O'Malley Shopping Centre to talk to Dave, but was too late getting there because someone crashed into me and The JimiJix Show had started by the time I got there. Dave was murdered before it ended, so I never got to talk to him. But now I know why my brother gave me a strange look during the robbery. Dave knew that he was about to die, and thought that I was in on his murder. That's what he died believing."

"Yeah, yeah," O'Sullivan ridiculed. "Only you can't prove any of that, can you, Doyle?"

"No, as I've already said, I can't prove anything," I replied. "In fact, all I know is that it was Pierce McDermott's son who killed my brother and Barry Galvin who crashed his car into mine."

"Pierce McDermott, Barry Galvin," Jill Maguire repeated. "You know both those men, don't you, Cormack?"

O'Sullivan didn't respond to Jill Maguire's question as he raised the barrel of his gun towards me. "I think that we've heard enough of your bullshit now, Doyle," he said and advanced towards me.

"But I haven't even told Jill the big secret about her father yet," I blurted.

"Wait a minute," Jill Maguire instructed O'Sullivan as she stepped forward and blocked his aim. "I want to hear what he has to say."

"What big secret?" she asked as she turned back to me.

THURSDAY — NINETEEN

"The big secret about Tony Maguire, the man who you thought was your father" I replied. "That one."

O'Sullivan cut in. "Don't listen to him, Jill. Just step back out of my way and I'll get rid of him."

"What are you saying?" Jill Maguire asked as she took another step closer to me.

I remained silent as the pond's water lapped against its concrete banks, then answered the question that Jill had put to me.

"Tony Maguire was gay and wasn't your real father," I stated and then nodded in O'Sullivan's direction. "He's your real dad."

"What are you talking about?" Jill Maguire asked me and scrunched up her face.

"Your mother used to work in a Chinese restaurant called the Pearl Orchid," I said. "In return for protection, its owner allowed O'Sullivan to screw the waitresses there. Your mother worked there and when he got her pregnant with you, O'Sullivan got Tony Maguire to marry her and move into a house near his. That way, O'Sullivan saw lots of you, and got his daughters to befriend a little Chinese girl who was an only child."

"Don't mind him, Jill, he's just trying to save himself," O'Sullivan said as the sound of sirens signaled that the police had arrived at the theatre.

"Get O'Sullivan to take a paternity test," I told Jill Maguire.

The Chinese-Irish detective swept her hair back from her forehead and spoke again. "Are you saying that Tony Maguire wasn't my real father," she asked.

"Yes, I'm sorry, but that's exactly what I'm saying," I replied. "Tony Maguire probably loved you a lot, but he was gay and would have lost his job if he was ever outed. O'Sullivan knew that but wanted Tony Maguire to remain as his partner because he was so smart. That's why he got him to marry your mother and pretend to be your natural dad. That made Tony Maguire appear respectable, but then O'Sullivan and him fell out over money when your mother got ill."

"Don't listen to him, Jill," O'Sullivan interrupted again. "He's talking a load of nonsense."

"Please hear me out, Jill," I pleaded. "When your mother got cancer, O'Sullivan refused to help pay for her treatment, or even to lend any money to Tony Maguire."

"See what I mean," O'Sullivan said. "He's talking crap."

"Wait a second, Cormack, I need to hear what he has to say," Jill Maguire responded and then nodded for me to continue.

"When O'Sullivan wouldn't provide any money, your dad was forced to find it elsewhere," I continued. "That's why he had Frank Hennessy's granddaughter kidnapped and why Claire and Sarah lost their lives."

"Jesus!" O'Sullivan shouted. "That's complete shite."

"No, it's not, and you know it's not," I shouted at O'Sullivan. "Three years ago, you had Tony Maguire murdered to avenge Frank Hennessy's daughter and granddaughter being killed in the kidnap that he had arranged. Didn't you, O'Sullivan?"

"Yeah, right," O'Sullivan answered. "Get out of my way, Jill."

Jill Maguire didn't budge. "Go on," she instructed me.

"When things went wrong and Claire and Sarah died, Tony Maguire tried to blame the kidnapping on O'Sullivan," I said. "That was why he got me to hire Declan Reid. Your dad knew that Declan Reid hated O'Sullivan and was sure that his old colleague would go after him, but that's not how things turned out. Declan Reid worked out that Tony Maguire was the real culprit behind the kidnap, and was on his way to my apartment to tell me that when he drowned in the Liffey. I didn't spot anything about that back then because your dad told me that he hadn't listened to the telephone message that I left for him telling him that Declan Reid was coming to my home to tell me who was behind the kidnap."

"I'm sorry, Jill," O'Sullivan said. "But how much of this crap do you need to hear? Doyle has just told you that your dad was a gay murderer who killed his wife, his daughter, and Declan Reid. Do you believe that?"

"Yes, she does." I replied to O'Sullivan. "Because it's the truth."

"Go on," Jill Maguire told me.

"On the morning that he drowned; Declan Reid called me," I said. "He told me that he was coming to my apartment at four that afternoon to tell me who had killed the Gilroy brothers. They were hired to kidnap Sarah, so it was assumed that whoever had killed them was behind the kidnapping. After Declan Reid's call, I phoned Tony Maguire but didn't get him and left a message. That was why your dad wrote my phone number, Declan Reid's name, and 4:00 p.m. on that newspaper cutting that you found the other night."

"I'm sorry, Killian, but I don't believe all that," Maguire said as she lowered her gun and stepped back from me to clear a path for O'Sullivan.

"Wait a minute!" I shouted as O'Sullivan stomped forward, shoved me back towards the pond and lifted his gun as I threw my left hand up to cover my face.

Slammed backwards as the first shot from his gun tore two of the fingers off my left hand and was deflected into my left shoulder, I was then punched into the air as the second bullet from his gun rammed into my stomach.

The third bullet from O'Sullivan's gun whipped open the flesh over my left hip as I crashed through the surface of the pond and swallowed the fetid water that gushed into my open mouth.

Beneath the fractured surface of the water, I spun around, landed on the pond's concrete base on my hands and knees, scrambled forward until I collided with the pond's bank and then sprang up and gulped a mouthful of the night air.

As the pond's water drained from my eyelids, I saw that O'Sullivan had advanced to the edge of the pond and was now aiming his handgun directly at my forehead.

"Goodbye, Doyle," he said and then compressed his gun's trigger.

I once read that a bullet travels faster than the speed of sound, so you never even hear the shot that kills you. And yet, I clearly heard a gun blast and watched as warm brain matter pulsed from the exit wound just below O'Sullivan's right eye and left a wisp of steam as it plopped into the pond's cool water next to me.

When O'Sullivan's lifeless body crumbled to the side of the pond, Jill Maguire returned her smoking handgun to the holster at the back of her waistband, stepped forward, sank to her knees at the edge of the pond, and stretched out her arms towards me.

Friday — One

The next morning, when the television mounted on the wall opposite to my hospital bed came into focus, I saw from the little red X across its loudspeaker symbol that it had been muted.

The silenced TV program was one of those morning talk shows where an audience of women cheer on the show's host as they berate some man for his failings.

As one of the TV cameras from that talk show panned across its baying but silenced audience, I listened to the sounds around me.

In addition to the steady blips of the machines that monitored my vital signs, the labored breathing of someone asleep could also be heard.

That was when I turned painfully and saw that Jill Maguire was slumped next to my bed in a green, easy-wipe armchair, her shiny black quivering with each breath that she took.

In front of Jill, a news magazine rested on an over-the-bed table, while I saw that an ajar door adjacent to the room's window, opened into a white-tiled bathroom.

Looking down, I saw that my bandaged left hand had been swaddled in a medical dressing and was adhered to what looked like a white plastic canoe paddle, and then recalled the other gunshot injuries that O'Sullivan had inflicted on my body at the Bird Bath.

I was about to wake Jill Maguire and get a full analysis of my condition from her when another series of sounds emanated from the open door into my hospital room. That was when I heard the rustle of a newspaper, a restrained male yawn, and the creak of a plastic chair.

In the absence of any visual confirmation, I assumed from those noises, that a cop had been posted on sentry duty in the corridor outside my hospital bedroom and worried that I might be under arrest.

Uncertain about my status, I lowered my head back to the pillows, turned towards Jill Maguire as quietly as I could, and then jolted when I saw that she was fully alert.

Without issuing a word to me, the detective jumped to her feet and raced over to the open door into my hospital room.

"Quick, get a doctor, he's awake," she told whoever was on duty there.

This time, there was the noise of a newspaper being discarded in haste, the sound of rubber-tipped chair legs as they squeaked on a tiled floor, and the terse acknowledgement of a male voice.

When the cop outside of my hospital room had gone off to fetch a doctor, Jill Maguire rushed back inside of the hospital room, crouched down over my bed, and lowered her face close to mine.

FRIDAY — TWO

"**C**an you hear me, Killian?" she asked.

"Yes, I can hear you," I croaked through dried lips.

"Then please listen closely," Jill Maguire said. "When you're asked about what happened at the pond last night, say that Cormack O'Sullivan and I were outside when you left the theatre and dashed after you, okay?"

"Yes, okay," I said.

Jill Maguire nodded and then spoke again. "Tell anyone who asks you that we challenged you at the pond, and that Cormack thought that you had a gun when you spun back around to him, okay?"

"Okay," I agreed.

"Then say that Cormack fired his gun at you and that you fell back into the pond, okay?" she asked.

I again acknowledged what Jill Maguire had just instructed me to say.

"And finally," Jill Maguire continued. "Tell anyone who asks that I shot Cormack by mistake when you popped back up out of the water."

"Right," I said and tried a nod.

"Did you get all that?" Jill Maguire asked me anxiously.

"Yes, I got all that," I confirmed. "And I fully understand why you came up with that little story, but that's all it is, isn't it, Jill, a little story? In reality, you shot O'Sullivan deliberately. You murdered him in cold blood. Maybe, that's what I will say happened last night."

Jill Maguire straightened up, took a step back from my bed, brushed the hair from her forehead, and blinked her shocked green eyes at me.

"I don't believe it!" she said. "You planned what happened last night. You predicted that I'd shoot Cormack when you told me about him and my father. Didn't you?"

"How could I possibly have known that you'd react like that?" I said and then shuddered as a tremor of pain ran through my left arm.

Jill Maguire threw a glance towards the door into my room as an exchange of distant voices sounded along the hospital corridor.

"Tell me the truth," she asked and glared at me. "Did you predict that I'd shoot Cormack last night?"

"Sort of," I admitted. "Although you had me worried there for a while, especially when you stepped back. What took you so long to kill O'Sullivan anyway?"

Jill Maguire took another step back from my hospital bed.

"Cormack told me to stay away from you," she said. "He said that you manipulate people. That's what you did to me last night, wasn't it?" she queried. "You manipulated me, didn't you?"

"Manipulate is a very strong word," I said. "Let's just say that I motivated you and then pointed you in the right direction," I replied and then heard a posse of approaching feet in the corridor outside my room.

"You used me to murder Cormack," Jill Maguire said. "And now, I might go to prison for the rest of my life."

"Don't worry, Jill, you won't go to prison," I said. "Because I'm going to confirm that your little story is true. However, in return, you have to arrange something for me."

"Arrange something for you?" Jill Maguire asked.

"Yes, I want you to make sure that any charges against me for tripping that uniformed cop are dropped," I said. "If they aren't, then I might go to prison, and neither of us want that. Now do we, Jill?"

"No, we don't," the detective agreed. "But what about Frank Hennessy?" she asked. "He might come after me for killing his friend."

From the noise in the corridor, the approaching medical team were just doors away from my room as I shook my head.

"Don't worry about Frank," I told Jill. "O'Sullivan would have been a witness against him, so he's probably delighted that you killed him. Anyway, Jasper's have probably paid Frank to shut up and go away by now," I added.

Jill Maguire looked like she was about to say something else to me when a doctor, a nurse, and a uniformed male cop entered the hospital room and surrounded my bed.

"Killian Doyle is awake," she said. "But be very careful with him. He's not a nice man."

About The Author

Tom Dots Doherty is married to Aileen, and has two adult daughters, Megan and Ella.

He lives in Dublin, worked in advertising for more than thirty-years, was the managing director of a leading Irish advertising agency, is a Fellow of the Institute of Advertising Practitioners in Ireland, chaired the Irish Advertising Effectiveness Awards, and has lent money to more than two-hundred Irish firms and invested in a range of Irish start-ups. His hobbies include reading, writing, and supporting soccer and GAA.

www.ingramcontent.com/pod-product-compliance
Lightning Source LLC
Chambersburg PA
CBHW060304260626
47160CB00007B/2499